T0086490

THE
MOON
OVER
KYOTO

Nedra Bolden

THE MOON OVER KYOTO

Copyright © 2021 Nedra Bolden.

All rights reserved. No part of this book may be used or reproduced by any means, graphic, electronic, or mechanical, including photocopying, recording, taping or by any information storage retrieval system without the written permission of the author except in the case of brief quotations embodied in critical articles and reviews.

Cover Art Credit:
Steven Arthur Allen is the artist for my book cover and he is my cousin. I am so happy that he is a part of The Moon Over Kyoto. Thanks Steve.

iUniverse books may be ordered through booksellers or by contacting:

iUniverse
1663 Liberty Drive
Bloomington, IN 47403
www.iuniverse.com
844-349-9409

Because of the dynamic nature of the Internet, any web addresses or links contained in this book may have changed since publication and may no longer be valid. The views expressed in this work are solely those of the author and do not necessarily reflect the views of the publisher, and the publisher hereby disclaims any responsibility for them.

Any people depicted in stock imagery provided by Getty Images are models, and such images are being used for illustrative purposes only. Certain stock imagery © Getty Images.

ISBN: 978-1-6632-1745-5 (sc)
ISBN: 978-1-6632-1746-2 (e)

Library of Congress Control Number: 2021901728

Print information available on the last page.

iUniverse rev. date: 03/12/2021

ACKNOWLEDGMENT

The first person I would like to thank I do not know her name. She was a classmate in my Algebra class at West Los Angeles Community College. She is the person who said to me, "You should write a book." So, classmate thank you because I did.

The next person is my ex co-worker, Valerie Ward. I never kept contact with her, and she is a big part of me completing this task. I would type my pages on my lunch hour. She asked, "What are you typing?" I said, "I'm writing a book." She said, "Let me read it." Every day when I arrived, she would say, "Girl are you going to type the next page today because I need to see what happened." She gave me encouragement to keep writing. I do not know where she is. I said I would never forget her and would mention her in my book.

I would like to thank my parents and my family for giving me a life worth writing about. I would like to thank myself for writing a book and completing it. So many people laughed when I said, "I am going to write a book." I could have easily given up. Proud of me because I did not.

I am no writer. I had a story to tell. I would like David Bruskin, who helped me with the editing.

CONTENTS

CHAPTER 1

THE FAMILY AND THE BUSINESS

Over thirty years ago, a woman said to me, "You should write a book because your life is interesting and encouraging." I never thought so because I was always embarrassed about it and thought people would resent me if I told my story. When I was a kid my friends were told to stay away from me when they found out I was lying about what kind of work my parents did. Who me tell the world? Oh no. At the age of sixty-seven and after overcoming some of my fears, I hope I can encourage someone to pursue their dreams and no matter what make them come true.

It was three o'clock in the morning and very cold in Chicago. My sister Ava and I were cuddled under the warm covers when a loud violent crashing noise woke us up. We sat up in the bed and started crying and screaming. "Mommy! daddy!" Ava shouted. "I hear a noise, Arden What is it?" "I don't know, but Ava, I'm scared." Ava grabbed my hand and said, "Come on, Arden, Let's go and get Mommy and Daddy." As we were getting out of the bed, two white men busted into our bedroom with their guns out.

I was five years old, and my sister was six. Six FBI Agents bashed in our front door with a sledgehammer. We lived in the true ghetto; the nasty, filthy, roach, mice-and-rats-the-size-of-cats-infested projects on the south side at Thirty-Ninth Street off Cottage Grove.

When the men came into our bedroom, I started crying and screaming, "I want my mommy." Ava started hitting and kicking the other man and said, "Take us to our mom right now." He then pointed his big gun in Ava's face and said, "We're FBI Agents. Go downstairs with your mother and father." The man then pushed Ava out of the room, and we met our mother at the bottom of the steps. My mom was holding my younger brother and sister in her arms. "Oh, my babies, did they hurt y'all?" as she was inspecting us to make sure we were OK. I could have sworn she had grown another arm because she hugged me so tight, she was the one who was hurting me.

We sat in our living room while the FBI tore our house apart. They were desperately looking for something. Every drawer in our house were turned upside-down; everything was pulled out of our closets. Dirty clothes were out of the hamper and tossed across the floor.

The agents knew my daddy by name. "Hey Clayton, we need to see you upstairs." Four of the officers took my father upstairs and two stayed downstairs with my mother, Georgette, (Geo for short,) my sisters Ava and Gia, and my brother Little Clayton and me; I am Arden. My mom was crying and asking us if we were all right. Ava said, "Mommy, what happened to daddy? Where is my daddy?" We were all crying while my mom was trying to console us. She kept saying, "Don't worry babies, everything is going to be OK."

One of the officers took Ava and me by our hands and took us towards the kitchen. My mom was screaming, "Leave my girls alone, and bring them back, you bastard." In a nice tone, he asked Ava and me, "Have you girls seen your mom and dad sniff white powder in their noses or give themselves shots?" My mom stood up out of her seat and started cussing the officer and shouted to Ava and me, "Don't answer." My mother charged towards the officer as if she was going to beat him up and he spoke very mean to her and cussed and said, "Shut your mouth" and he then took my mom and swung her by her arm towards the chair and she fell into it.

The officer then took Ava and me into the kitchen and as he looked at me, he said, "Do you know where your mommy and daddy keep the white power wrapped in foil, little girl?" While sucking my thumb and playing with my hair, I hunched my shoulders and said in a slow and whining voice and as tears were running down my cheeks, "I don't know." The officer looked at Ava and asked her the same. She folded her arms and pouted her cheeks out and would not say a word. They could not get any information out of us. We were taught to never tell anyone about what went on in our home.

When it turned daylight, the police came down the steps and said to the other officers, "Okay, let's go, we found something." They put handcuffs on my father, and he left with them. My father and his friend were arrested. Between my dad and G-Man, the police found a large quantity of heroin and cocaine. My dad shouted to my mother, "Call Smitty, my lawyer." My mom got on the telephone right away and was crying so hard she could hardly talk.

The next day, my Aunt Doreen, my mom's sister, came by our house with a newspaper. (The Chicago Defender.) She was so excited. "Geo girl look at Clayton and his friend G-Man! Their pictures are in this newspaper!" The article talked about the dope raid at our house.

My mother took us to the courthouse for my father's court appearance. My Aunt Doreen and her son Erick went with us. When Doreen and Erick were around, which was all the time, it was so much fun. As we were walking towards the courthouse, I said, "Hey Erick, I bet you can't beat Ava and me to the water fountain over there." "Yes, I can." "No, you can't." We all took off running as fast as we could and did not look back. Our mothers shouted, "Stop running, y'all come back here right now." Our rough play ended with a big bruise on Ava's knee and a couple of switches from our mothers across the back of our hands.

Sitting in the courtroom, I got so bored. I was sitting next to my mother. I turned and asked, "Mommy, where is daddy?" She put her finger up to her mouth and shushed me. Soon I saw them bring my dad and G-Man out from a side door and they stood before the judge. While my dad was standing there, I got out of my seat and I ran to stand by his side and grabbed his hand. He looked at me and clinched my hand. I will never forget the way he looked at me and how tight he squeezed my hand. It made me feel special.

The judge dismissed my father's case. There were a lot of reasons as I remember my mommy and Aunt Doreen talking to each other. "Girl, it's a good thing those police didn't follow the correct procedures and Clayton was able to beat the case." "I know, Geo. I cannot believe those agents put the gun in Ava's face, and girl, they had the nerves to have an improper search warrant. And those stupid police officers thought we were stupid -- ha ha ha ha ha." Since the police botched the bust, my dad was free.

As a railroad worker, my father was a waiter on the train. He made a little salary but big tips. For extra money, he also gambled on the train. Once I saw my dad with a small box which had paintbrushes and blue and red ink spilled from the little jars. He also had one blue and one red deck of cards. He was sitting at our table with a bright light shining on what he was doing. He even had a doctor's smock on, and he was working hard putting paint on the cards. I said, "Daddy what are you doing?" He said, "Baby this is how your dad makes extra money on the train. I mark the cards, and my partner and I win all the money against the other cats we play because they don't know we know all the cards."

While working, my dad would be gone for a couple of days at a time. He would always return with all kinds of gifts for us. After he had been gone for a few days, he woke Ava and me early. "Ava, Arden, wake up, I have a surprise for you downstairs in the kitchen." My eyes got so big when I saw our Raggedy Ann dolls. I said, "Hey daddy, our dolls are bigger than us." He said, "Are you happy?" He also would bring us whistles, fruit, and all kinds of cute things. When the railroad found out about the heroin bust through the newspaper, they fired my dad. In 1959, it was hard for a black man to find a decent paying job, so my dad started making enough money to live on by buying and selling heroin and cocaine.

Born a country boy from a small town called Houma,

Louisiana, my dad, according to my mother's cousin Celeste, who she grew up with, was a square and had no street sense. He was five-feet-eight and had a dark complexion. Celeste said, "Girl, your father wore a process in his hair making it black and wavy. I called him Mr. Nat King Cole because he looked like him. Y'all's daddy was fine as hell." My dad told me his parents died when he was young. His sisters raised him until he was old enough to go into the military where he fought in World War II. When he got out of the Army, he came to Chicago to work for the railroad, and met my mother.

Unlike my dad, my mother was street smart and from the ghetto in Chicago. She had five sisters and one brother. Celeste, said, "Girl, y'all's mother's family was all stoned-out-of-their-minds crazy. There was always fighting and trouble going on at their house. I hated to go around them because they embarrassed me. Neighbors would sit on their front porches near y'all's granny house, eating popcorn as if they were watching an exciting movie full of all kinds of violent fights and action." Celeste told me while growing up, my mother was exposed to drugs and used them herself. If we wanted to know anything negative about my mom, Celeste would tell. She said they was raised on Forty-Seventh Street near the El train station.

One of my father's friends told Ava and me, "I was with about twenty people waiting for the bus on Forty-Seventh Street when a man walked past me and stabbed a man standing next to me." Ava said, "Was he dead?" "I don't know if he was dead, but he laid there on the ground with blood gushing out of his chest. When the bus came, I got on and went on about my business as if nothing had happened."

Another one of my dad's friends said, "My daughter was raped on Forty-Seventh Street while waiting for the bus. People watched and would not help or call the police." My mom always said to us, "Stay away from all the bums, drunks, drug addicts, prostitutes, pimps and just plain crazy people on Forty-Seventh Street." Forty-Seventh Street has always been the place to buy drugs, and because my mother was raised in the environment, she knew about drugs and was part of the scene.

Clementine, my mother's mother, was half white. Her mother was Irish, and her father was a Native American. However, one day we met Fannie, my grandmother's youngest sister who was visiting from Flint, Michigan. Sitting in her wheelchair, she said, "Clementine is a white woman. She ain't my real sister. Her mother and her father are white." She said, "You figure it out; she's the oldest child in our family and the only one who looks all white. Hell, she worked at Marshall Fields. None of us darkies could get a job there."

My grandmother never knew her mother. Aunt Fannie told us their mother was brutally killed when they were no older than three years old. She said, "They killed my mother because of her involvement with colored people. After our mother was killed, our father raised your granny and me in a whorehouse he ran as a pimp in Terre Haute, Indiana."

George Gurley Reed was my grandfather, my mother's father. He was tall, over six feet and handsome, with wavy hair and a sexy mustache. His complexion was like caramel. I was told women went crazy over him because he was such a good-looking gentleman. He liked half-white women who were prostitutes.

As my grandmother grew up, she made a living as a hooker. She had three marriages. Her first marriage did not work out, but she had a daughter. Then my grandmother met my grandfather when he was a customer in the whorehouse her father ran. Of course, they fell in love and got married. My grandmother no longer worked as a prostitute because my grandfather took good care of her, financially. My mother was born in 1927 and named after her father.

My grandparents got divorced when my mother was eleven years old. My grandmother remarried and had five other children by Butch Evans. When I was born, Mr. Evans and my grandmother were divorced, yet he was always at her house. When my grandmother was drinking wine with a group of her loud card-playing friends, I heard her say, "Whoo-whee, honey child, George Gurley Reed was the finest man I ever laid my eyes on. I loved him so much. Even Butch knew I could never love him as much as I loved George. I never even changed my last name to Evans when I married Butch. It stayed, and will always be Reed, and I will never stop loving George."

Mr. Evans was a funny man and joked with us all the time. He would say to Erick, "Come here, Hammer Head." He called Ava "Devil Eyes" and he called me "Monkey Face." He made his living selling produce to the neighborhood from the back of his truck. He would come to pick up Erick, Ava, and me, and we would ride on the back of his truck and laugh, shout, and sing, "Watermellllooon, fresh strawberrrries, bannnnnannas, get your greens, your 'tatoes' and 'matoes." People would run out of their houses shouting, "Stop, please stop!" and "Wait a minute." We would stop and take the money for whatever they wanted.

My mother told me, "Mr. Evans is not such a nice man. When I was seventeen years old, he told me to sit in his lap. When I did, he touched me down there," pointing between her legs. She said, "I picked up an iron skillet and I whacked him on his head about three times. Then I took a knife and stabbed him in his chest and in his arm. I tried to kill the dirty bastard. He had to be rushed to the hospital and it was a miracle he survived. So be careful when you are around him, and don't ever sit on his lap." My mother left home then. My mother was a hair model when she was a teenager. Her complexion was fair, and her hair was light brown and long. She was five-feet-ten and slim, with a nice shape--a very fashionable, sexy, gorgeous woman.

My mom had me laughing so hard when she told me this story: "When I worked as a cashier in a drug store, I could never get to work on time. My boss, Mr. Kaplan, told me, 'Geo If you are late one more time, I will fire you.' I kept being late and finally he changed my work time so I would not be late. Mr. Kaplan was a little old Jewish man, and every time he passed me, I wanted to slap the top of his head; I was much taller than he was. One day, I couldn't hold myself back, and as he passed me, I slapped his head." "Mommy!" I shouted, cracking up laughing, "What did he do?" He said, "Geo, you're crazy, and you're fired."

My mother took after her father. When my grandfather was a young man, he worked for Al Capone, helping to make bootleg alcohol. He considered himself a gangster, too, and did not take any mess from anyone. He told my mother, "Geo, if you have to fight someone because there's no way around it, fight dirty by picking up something heavy or sharp and hit them hard enough to kill them. If you have a gun, shoot them six times because you never want to leave an enemy alive."

After prohibition was lifted, my grandfather took all the illegal money he had made working for Capone and bought 80 acres of land in a small town called Climax, Michigan. He became a construction worker and learned how to do architectural engineering and design. He met and married Grandma Ruby, our step-grandmother, who had been working as a prostitute in Detroit. They designed and built a home for themselves from the ground up, with their own hands and materials. My grandfather was famous for his steel which made Moonshine in his basement. He would sell or give jugs to his friends.

My dad was thirty years old when he moved to Chicago in 1950. Bertha, my mother's oldest sister, had eyes for my dad and knew he would fall in love with her, but when he laid eyes on my mother, it was love at first sight. My mother said she took one look at my dad and said, "That's one black-ass man I have got to have." She had been dating an older man and was living with him at the time, but it did not take my parents long to realize they were meant for each other. They got married and moved into a small apartment. Celeste said, my mother then introduced my father to drugs. Ava was born on December 10, 1952; I was born on February 10, 1954. Little Clayton was born on November 7, 1956 and Gia was born on July 13, 1959. One big happy family, or so it seemed.

CHAPTER 2

SOME POWERFUL STUFF

When I turned five years old, I started going to school. My parents made enough money to send us to a private Catholic school. My teacher was a nun, and I respected her so much, I stared at her in awe. "Sister Ashley, If I'm good in your class, could you please give God a good report about me?" She said, "I will tell God if you are bad too."

Our school was named Holy Angels. (It is famous for being the church of Father Clements, whose life story became a TV movie, *The Father Clements Story*. He adopted an orphan to keep him out of street gangs, even though Cardinal Cody did not want him to.) I loved the statues in the church. I would stare and talk to them and beg them to speak to me. "Please God, please let the statues talk to me and guide me and let me know everything I do is right." I wanted so much to be a good girl. I was hoping to have the same experience as the young lead character in the movie *The Song of Bernadette*. She talked to the Virgin Mary and the statue came alive and would talk to her and performed miracles at her request in the town where Bernadette lived.

I loved my school, and I loved going to church. I would say, "Mommy, wakeup, it's Sunday morning. Can we go to church?" As she could hardly wake up, she would say, "No baby, not today," and she would fall back to sleep. I would cry and whimper for hours. "I want to go to church. I want to go to church." Eventually, my mother let me go alone to keep from hearing me whine on Sunday. I was the only person from my family who went to church.

The projects we lived in were little rows of red brick houses. About eight two-story family houses made up a row. All around us were several identical rows of houses, and we all lived there jumbled together. I remember the walls had little pricks sticking out of them, and many times running from room to room, I would scrape the skin from my arm, hand or leg until it would bleed.

The new Robert Taylor Home Projects were being built. When they were ready, we were going to be moving into them. These buildings were going to be sixteen stories high with twenty apartments on each floor. In each apartment there will be at least six people, so it will be about one hundred twenty people living on the same floor. In one building, there will be over seventeen hundred people. There are ten separate buildings. It will be about seventeen thousand black underprivileged and poverty-stricken people living all crowded together.

When Ava was in the first grade, one of the nuns hit her with a yardstick and left some marks on her legs. When my mother picked us up, she was surprised to see the marks and asked Ava, "What happened to your legs?" Crying, Ava said, "Sister Gregory hit me with a yardstick." "Why did she hit you?" "Because I couldn't open the door, but it was locked, Mommy." Before Ava could say another word, my mother took off for Sister Gregory's classroom, and we ran after her. When my mom walked into the classroom, Sister Gregory was standing there talking to another nun. My mother walked over to Sister Gregory, cussed her, and grabbed her by her collar and said, "I will kill you if you ever hurt my child again." Then my mom pushed her, grabbed us by our hands, and proudly walked out, leaving the sisters speechless. When the administrator found out about the incident, we were told we could not return to the school after the summer. We started attending public school. (Even so, I still went to the church every Sunday.)

The housing project we lived in was called the Ida B. Wells. I can recall my grandmother saying to my mother, "Ida B. Wells was a strong affluent black woman in our American history, so why would the housing authority name these nasty dwellings with all these trifling people after such a great person?"

Although we lived in the projects where a lot of people seemed miserable and unhappy, it was always a party going on and we had lots of fun. My mother taught Ava and me how to jump double Dutch jump rope. She could do all kinds of tricks while jumping rope. We also had fun playing other games, like hopscotch and hide-and-go-seek.

The teenagers in the neighborhood would get in a line and dance and sing to the latest songs. They did the Twist, the Mashed Potato, the Roach (with the lyric "Squish O' Squash, Kill that Roach,") the Madison, and the Watusi. They danced to Bebop and did Swing Dancing too. While the teenagers were listening to music and dancing, we little kids would play together. For one game, we would make a big train by holding onto the kid in front of us and go through the neighborhood, singing, "I am blind, I can't see, if I knock you down don't you blame it on me." Or we would play London Bridge.

Ava and I had two friends who were sisters, Dana, and Kris. They lived behind us. As we stepped out our back door, their house was in a row adjacent to ours. Dana said, "Hey, Ava and Arden, do you want to be blood sisters with us?" I said, "How?" Dana got a razor blade. "We have to cut our fingers and rub our blood together; then we'll be blood sisters." We did it, and the four of us became inseparable.

We would go throughout the neighborhood and sing at people's doors -- whether they wanted to hear it or not. Some of the people we sang for loved it. We would sing songs like "Meet Me in St. Louis" and "You Must Have Been a Beautiful Baby." At Christmas time, the ones who liked us would request Christmas Carols. The people would say, "Oh, you girls sing so nice." Sometimes, we got rewarded with candy or money – like a quarter. "Y'all be sure and come back now and sing for me again," is what most would say.

One time a mean old woman shouted, "Get away from my

door!" We kept singing because we were sure we could make her like us. A few minutes later, a police officer came. "OK, you girls go home now, and when someone tells you to get away from his or her door, don't stay there." Kris said, "I can't believe that old woman called the police on us. Let's not sing for her anymore," and we left.

About twice a year, my grandparents from Michigan would visit us. We were so excited. They would go deer or bear-hunting in Colorado and would stop in Chicago on their way home. The deer they killed would be strapped to the top of their car with blood dripping down the sides. Ava and I gathered all our friends and said, "You should see our grandfather. He is the richest, strongest and tallest man in the whole wide world." They said in amazement, "You're kidding." "I don't believe you." "Take us to see him." Ava and I soon had our skeptical friends trailing behind us, wanting to see our grandfather for themselves.

Ava said, "Granddaddy, stand up and touch the ceiling." He stood up and touched the ceiling. He was drinking a can of Budweiser Beer, so I said, "Granddaddy, bend this beer can in half." He bent the beer can in half. "Show our friends how much money you have in your wallet." He pulled out several $100 bills. "See, we told you: the tallest, strongest and richest man in the world." Our friends went away, convinced. Dana, Kris, Ava and I would put on talent shows for my grandparents. They enjoyed us singing and dancing for them. They would film us with their movie camera.

On a regular basis, there were a lot of people in and out of our house all hours of the day and night. They were my father's friends/customers. They came to buy drugs; referred to as a 'fix.' As far as the price of the drugs, I overheard one of my dad's customers asking him about the prices and how he sold his bags of dope. My dad responded, "I sell two kinds, pure and cut. If you want it pure," 'The P-Funk Uncut' so some call it,' "the price is $250 for a quarter of a spoonful. If you want it mixed, the price is $25 for the same quantity. I will sell two mixed quarters for $45 and two pure bags for $450." The more they bought the bigger the discount.

My dad would mix pure heroin and baking soda through a sifter to cut it. My parents did it in front of us all the time. Most of my dad's friends bought pure heroin and would spend up to $1000 a day or more. My parents were always upstairs in their bedroom with the door closed. My siblings and I would be downstairs in our living room or in our kitchen watching TV or playing games like Sorry or Monopoly. Gia, who could barely walk because she was less than a year old would be strapped in the baby highchair with wheels and we would swing her across the room.

We would then jump on the back of it and ride across the floor. We had a subscription to Dr. Seuss books, and we read them to each other. We always played school and I can recall being able to read at three years old. We liked music and we always played our favorite songs on our record player. We would dance and sing, and we would also put on talent shows.

While we were playing around the house, one of my dad's customers would knock on the door. He had about twenty-five different customers who would come by all day long many times in the day. They were each different and had their own individual character. Snuggie, my dad's longtime friend and customer, comes to my mind. One of us would yell upstairs to our parents, "Someone's knocking on the door." One of my parents would shout out, "Find out who it is but don't open the door." "It's Snuggie, daddy." "OK, let him in and tell him I'll be right with him." Snuggie would say, "Is your daddy home?"

When the customers came around, they would be sick and in desperate need of a fix. When they walked through the door, they would not speak or anything. I could look at them in their eyes and tell when they were sick and needed the drug. They had a blank stare with a wild look in their eyes and they would sniffle all the time. I would say, "Yeah Snuggie, come on in and sit down. My daddy will be right with you." Snuggie would sit there like a zombie as we played around him and he never said a word to any of us. He would wait until my dad summoned him to come upstairs.

We saw our parents prepare and shoot drugs in the veins of their arms or other parts of their bodies many times. While upstairs with my dad, the customers would buy the kind and quantity of drugs, which was powdered, and they would mix it with water and cook it in a soda-pop bottle top by lighting a match to the bottom of it. They would take a needle and a syringe, as the doctor would use when giving a shot, and squeeze the dope into the syringe. They would then tie a strip of rubber or a stocking around their arm to pop out the biggest vein and tap the needle into it.

The customers who shot pure heroin would feel the effect of the drug as soon as the needle hit their vein. Blood would be running out of the needle head as it was still sticking in their arm, and they would look helpless as they nodded out with their head bobbing and weaving back and forth. When they did it in front of us, my siblings or I would take the needle out of their arm and put a towel over the arm to keep the blood from dripping onto the floor.

When Snuggie would come back downstairs after shooting heroin, it was as if he was a different person. He was so animated. He would dance around the house. He would swing his arms from side to side and all around. His mouth would move from side to side in a funny way and he would be joking with us. He would say, "Hey Arden, my girlfriend quit me because I threw her mother in Lake Michigan." I would respond, "She's crazy for quitting you." I would then say, "Snuggie I got in trouble in school because I tore all my books up in front of the teacher." He responded, "How could your teacher be so silly for getting mad at you?" We each told silly little stories until he would leave.

The customers also talked to us about school. Most of them had children themselves and sometimes they would bring their children. My dad's customers were like family to us. We entertained them as they were waiting for their fixes. I remember my dad's friend G-Man coming over banging on our door late one-night. I went to the door and there he was standing with a bandage around his head and I could see blood gushing out from the bandages. I said, "G-Man, what happened to you?" He said, "Arden is your father here?" I ran upstairs and got my dad from the bedroom and said, "Daddy, G-Man is here, and he's got bandages on his head." My dad ran down and they sat to talk. "Man, they caught me down at the pool hall with the marked cards. I barely escaped. Man, we cannot go to Sixty-Third Street anymore. You got a fix?"

My dad had another customer. Her name was Gia. She had the same name as my youngest sister. When Big Gia, (what we called her) came around she was so funny. After she shot her drugs, she would start to take her clothes off, and she would talk nonstop. The next thing we knew; she was naked walking around our house. She was an old ugly looking woman. She talked and walked back and forth with no clothes on. Once, my mother's brother, Butch, Jr., came by, and he and Big Gia did the nasty in front of us on our couch.

Most of the time my dad was home. However, if he was not home and his customers came to the door, we were not allowed to let them in. I can recall his customer Billy coming to the door one day. I said as he stood there with his sick and wild look, "Oh hi Billy." "Hey, Arden is, your dad home?" "No Billy sorry my dad is not here." His voice got excited and his eyes got big and he said, "Is your mother here?" "No Billy she's not here either." "Where did they go?" "Billy, I don't know." "Do you know when they will be back?" "No Billy."

Billy looked at me and started crying like a baby and said, "Oh lord, I'm sick as a dog." He then said, "OK baby, I'll be back." He came back every fifteen minutes. Finally, three hours later, he was standing at the door asking if my dad was back when they pulled up in the car. Billy started crying again and looked at me and said, "Baby these are tears of happiness now." He got on his knees, praised my dad, and said, "Jesus is here. Thank you, God."

CHAPTER 3

CHAOS, FIGHTS AND
A LITTLE FUN

The first time I saw my parents fight I was four years old. They fought all the time. I heard my mom in the bedroom as Ava and I were standing outside the door, "Clayton, don't go see her. She is a whore and if you do, when you go to sleep tonight, I'm going to throw hot boiling water on your black ass." We heard something fall and it sounded like they were getting violent. Ava and I busted open the bedroom door and my dad and mom were on the bed fighting. My mother never backed down to my father, "I will kill you; you black ugly MF." She cussed my father out using the worst word ever heard. Even though she was not afraid of my father, he always got the best of her because he was much stronger. She was crying aloud. I could tell she was hurt. Ava and I were fighting my dad. "Stop hitting our mother!"

Finally, my dad stopped hitting my mom and he left. Ava and I were fighting each other, trying to comfort our mother at the same time. I kept pushing Ava and telling her, "Move out the way." She kept pushing me and telling me to move. My mom was kneeling and hysterically crying in the chair as she watched our father as he was walking down the street. I later heard my mother talking to Doreen and she said, "He's with her. I'm going to kill them."

To get even with my father, my mother went out with one of his customers, Woody, who was also my dad's friend. It was about three o'clock in the morning and I woke up and saw my mother and Woody kissing as they were standing outside my bedroom door. I was hurt. I slept on the upper bunk bed. I remember wanting to throw myself off the bunk to get them to stop kissing. Instead, I turned my back and pretended I did not see it. We woke up later to: "Geo, how you going to go out with my friend?" And they were fighting.

Another occasion, they were fighting outside in our front yard. People were crowded around watching them. My mom had a knife and threatened to stab my dad but somehow, she stabbed herself in the hand. All I saw was blood. I was so afraid. My siblings and I were screaming and begging, "Please stop fighting."

Finally, one of my dad's customers who was at our house at the time stopped them from fighting. "Clayton, Geo, stop this fighting. Someone will call the police and you know what's in your place." The mere mention of the police frightened my parents because of the drugs in our house. They then stopped fighting.

The next day, I was on my way to school when a girl crossing the street with me asked with an attitude, "Wasn't your mother and father fighting in the yard last night?" I got so angry. I threw my books at her and tore into her and we started fighting. The other classmates also walking across the street gathered around us as we were going at it. The crossing guard came over. "OK girls, stop fighting or I will report you to the principal." We then stopped fighting.

I was so embarrassed they knew about my parents' fight. I did not want to show my face in public again. The only way I could bear my life was to pretend and dream about being grown, married and with my own family. I was a constant daydreamer. Some of my teachers were concerned about me because of my lack of paying attention in class.

My first-grade teacher sent a note home and it said, "What is wrong with Arden? I had to physically shake her back to reality after I tried to get her attention by calling her name. I would not be concerned if it was only one occasion. However, she does this all the time." Every time I saw my parents do something and it hurt me, I swore I would never treat anyone the same. My imagination was my way to block out my horrible existence because in my imagination I am happy.

Once, my father and my mom were fussing and fighting. My dad said, "Geo, I'm tired. I'm going upstairs to get the gun and end everything." He went upstairs. My mom followed him as she was carrying my little sister in her arms. The next thing I knew, my mom was running down the steps looking back at my daddy and she was crying and saying, "Clayton, please don't do this. Put the gun away." I looked up the steps, and my dad was at the top of the steps pointing the gun at my mother.

I ran up the steps, hugged my dad, and said as I was crying, "Daddy, please stop!" My dad held me tight in his arms and said to my mom, "Hey Geo, Arden's really frightened. Come feel her. She is shaking all over." My dad then put the gun away. He looked at me and said, "Now baby, don't be afraid, you know I was playing with your mother."

Soon, we moved out of the row house projects and moved into the sixteen story building which took years to build. Those projects were called the Robert Taylor Homes and we were excited because we were going to live on the fourth floor. We thought it would be fun living up so high. They were still the nasty filthy projects, but they were brand new apartments and we would be the first family to live there. I was eight years old when we moved there. The whole time we lived there, it was pure hell. My mom was a complete wreck. She was always high on heroin, cocaine, alcohol or pills. Most of the time she was high on a combination of them all.

There were times when my dad's girlfriend came over to buy dope from him. Also, there were many times when my dad would stay out all night. I heard my mom tell her sister, "I'm tired of crying every night about Clayton and his whore." When my dad would come home after staying out all night, my mother would start cussing and threatening to kill him. My dad would start singing, "A well a hello Geo a well a what do you know, oh well I just a gotta back a from a hell of a show a well a taking a chance, a jig and a jag and a rap tap tap..." and he would start tap dancing around the house.

We would laugh, and my mother would go crazy. My mother would try and hit my dad with something. She would throw things at him. If she had too much to drink, she would grab a knife or get the gun and chase him around the house. My mom would be so serious, and my dad would be saying, "Geo, you look so pretty when you're mad. Come give me a kiss."

I overheard my mom tell everyone -- even my dad -- how his girlfriend Connie was a prostitute. My mom would cry and say, "Clayton, you better stop seeing her because one day I'm going to kill you and her." My dad would respond by saying, "Geo, you should be glad you are my wife and not the whore because you don't have to get out in the streets to make money. Baby, I am bringing the money home to you. Connie is taking care of us." My mother would eventually calm down and everything would seem okay.

One day, my mother was high. She had been drinking, taking heroin, plus she had taken some pills. She was out of it all day and locked up in the bedroom and would barely wake up to talk to us when we tried to get her attention. It was Thanksgiving Day. My dad's friend, Miguel, the gourmet cook, would cook meals for us in exchange for his heroin fix. He had prepared a nice traditional holiday dinner for us, but my father had been out all night and all day. My father finally came home late in the afternoon.

My dad was about to do his song and dance and asked, "Where is your mother?" Little Clayton said, "She's still sleep." My dad then went into the bedroom and closed the door behind him. We were listening at the door because we thought they were going to start fighting and we wanted to be ready to go to my mother's rescue. Instead I heard my dad shouting "MIGUEL! MIGUEL! Come help me!" I ran and got Miguel and he ran to the bedroom door and when the bedroom door opened, I could see my mom hanging out of the window in the nude.

My dad had caught her by her arms as she jumped out of the window trying to commit suicide. My siblings and I were screaming, hollering, praying and crying. "What's the matter with our mother?" We lived four stories up, and if my mom had fallen, she would have died for sure. Miguel came into the bedroom and helped my dad pull my mother back in. All I can remember is turning to Miguel and saying, "You bastard you saw my mother naked." I could not think about the fact he helped save her life.

My friends were down below looking up at my mother hanging out of the window. Most of those looking were my schoolmates because directly below us was the playground where all the children in the building played. The school I went to was also in the building we lived in. The lady who lived below us rushed up to our apartment to see if everything was okay. She could see my mom's legs dangling in front of her window. I was so embarrassed because she had some sons who were cute. I liked the son who was in my classroom. I did not want to show my face ever again. I was devastated.

After they pulled my mom in from the window. I was so frightened. I ran out of the apartment and called my grandfather on a public phone. Crying, I said, "Granddaddy, my mother tried to kill herself by jumping out of the window." I was hysterically trying to explain what happened. My grandfather said, "Don't worry and calm down Arden, your grandmother and I will be there as soon as we can get there." About five o'clock my grandparents arrived to see if everything was okay. My grandfather took my mother in the bedroom and they talked for thirty minutes.

When they came out of the room, my grandfather looked at my grandmother and said, "Come on Ruby, let's get back. Everything is okay." I said, "No granddaddy, don't leave stay here with us for a little longer?" My grandfather stayed a little longer talking and playing with us. I had a Barbie doll and I remember my grandfather trying to make her stand up on the table. She kept falling and I thought my grandfather was going to get mad. An hour passed, and my grandfather said, "We have got to go because it's getting late and we have a long drive." "Granddaddy, can we please go with you?"

"We'll see you all in the summer when we come to pick you up when school is out." I hated to see my grandfather go. I was afraid my parents were going to fight again, or my mother was going to try to commit suicide again. However, all seemed normal between my parents and we all sat down and had our Thanksgiving feast as if no trouble had occurred.

My classmates harassed me daily by teasing me, saying, "Your mother was hanging out of the window naked and she is ugly and skinny like Olive Oil." I was so angry. I went home for lunch and got a big butcher's knife. I hid the knife under my sweater and took it to school. After school, a couple of girls kept following and teasing me and this time, I turned around and pulled the knife out on them and screamed, "None of you better not say anything about my mother again or I will cut all of your heads off." They all took off running and saying, "She's crazy. Let's leave her alone." I was in third grade and serious about using the knife. I hated living in those Sixteen-Story projects. There was trouble all the time. Some men broke into our house one day and held us all at gunpoint and took everything of value, including my dad's drugs.

I could not wait until summertime when my grandparents would pick us up to spend the summer with them. I loved going there. On our three hour drive, we had fun counting cars on the way there. Sometimes we would count Volkswagens, or yellow cars, or red cars, or whatever Grandma Ruby wanted us to count.

They raised Black Angus cattle, hogs, horses, chickens, ducks, sheep, goats, and they had a big garden. They would sell the vegetables and fruits. In the cow pasture, there was an apple orchard. In the gravel pit, there was a little lake, which people fished in. Down a little further were the woods. My grandparents would charge people to go in the woods where they would hunt deer and squirrels. My great-uncle, my grandfather's brother, owned a restaurant in Battle Creek, Michigan. Battle Creek was about eleven miles from Climax and was considered the big city -- population, about fifty-thousand. My uncle's restaurant was located at what was informally called "The Corner."

On the Corner was a pool hall, my uncle's restaurant, a club called the El Grand, and across the street from my uncle's restaurant was a small place where the number runners ran their gambling shop. People would win money at the end of the day if their numbers came up. It was illegal, but everyone knew about it, and everyone played the numbers. The Corner was the hottest spot in town. We would help the workers in the restaurant. It was so much fun. All the young guys would come in and buy candy. We would play the jukebox, laugh and have lots of fun.

Mom and daddy

Ida B. Wells Projects we lived in

CHAPTER 4
WHAT A DREAM TO DREAM

My daddy started making more money by getting more customers and selling more drugs. We moved out of the projects by the time I was nine years old. We moved into a nice neighborhood on the south side of Chicago, enrolled in a good school, and some of our family problems were being worked out, it seemed.

My father would hand me a large stack of cash. He called it his bankroll. "Count it," he said. It was so much cash! I would spread the money across the bed, putting like bills together and all facing the same direction. On most occasions it was about $10,000 a day or more. My dad would then take the money to a safe deposit box at the bank. He could not deposit it because, I remember my dad saying, if he put the money in the bank, the government would make him show how and where he earned the money. If he could not prove he earned the money legally they would confiscate it. My dad stopped keeping his money at home because either the police or stick-up men would take all his money and drugs.

Usually, if the police came and found some dope, they would proposition my father. "Hey Clayton, if you give us all your cash and all your drugs, we will not take you to jail." If he did not have the money, they would take him to jail. However, money can buy a good crooked criminal attorney, which is what my father had. His attorney was one of his customers. He always found a way to get out of the charges brought against him.

One Saturday morning, I went to the store to get a box of cereal. As I was walking home, I happened to notice two white men signaling to each other. One was in front of our house and the other was on the corner. We lived in the middle of the block. I thought they must be the police. Chicago is very segregated, and I remember Doreen saying, "If you see white men in our neighborhood, they are either the police or an insurance salesman. There are no white people who live in the city of Chicago. They all live in the suburbs."

I ran upstairs. My mom and dad were still asleep in bed. It was eleven o'clock. I woke my father, "Daddy, daddy wake up. I saw two white men signaling to each other and I think they might be the police." My dad and mom hopped out of the bed and started cleaning up and hiding all the drugs. Sure enough, about five minutes later, the police started banging on our door. They did not ring the doorbell or knock on the door. They banged on it like they were going to break it down and on many occasions; they did break it down.

"We have a search warrant to search your premises for possession of narcotics" is what the officers said at the door. Of course, my father let them in with a smile because he knew they were not going to find any drugs. The police officer looked at my father and said, "You bastard, you must have known we were coming because why are you so willing to let us in?"

Little did they know the little girl reading the back of the cereal box was the one who told they were coming. My dad became so proud of me. "Arden, you are so smart. Thank you for noticing the police." It turned out to be a big thing for many years to come -- how I was so smart for being so alert. When I received an "A" in math it was not as big a deal as me noticing the police.

Sometimes, we would get a violent visit from the stick-up men. It was hard to tell the police from the stick-up men because they all looked alike. They wore suits and looked like businessmen. The only difference was the police would identify themselves at once and show their badges. The stick-up men would make us believe they were the police to get in, but when they said, "Get down on the floor and lay your face down," and then they started moving everything out of our place, we knew they were not the police. The stick-up men would take all my dad's dope, all his money, and any other values we had.

On another occasion, the police came in the afternoon. We were all about to go shopping for Christmas and were waiting until my daddy finished shooting dope, so we could leave. A sudden loud knock on the door was the police. I knew my daddy didn't have enough time to hide his dope, so I held the police at the door shouting "Daddy, it is not the police. I think it is the stick-up men." I was blocking the officer and he could not get around me. The officer said, "Get out of my way, little girl." Soon, my daddy came out of the bedroom.

"Are you a police officer? I do not have any drugs. What are you here for?" I gave my dad enough time to throw his dope down the laundry chute which went straight to the basement. I was saying the police were stick-up men because I did not want the police officer to think I was being defiant. The police officer said to my dad, "You got your daughter trained. She held us at the door while you cleaned up the dope." My dad smiled.

One time, the police came at a time when my father did not have enough money or drugs to pay them off, and they took my mom and dad to jail. If my father got a new supply of dope, he would exhaust his funds and would have to sell the dope before he could make his money back. The police left us children at home by ourselves. We called our grandfather and he came to Chicago to get my parents out of jail. My grandfather said he would take Clayton and Gia back to Michigan with him because it was time for us to go to Michigan for the summer and they had not started school yet. However, Ava and I were unable to go to Michigan because we were in summer school and had friends we did not want to leave for the summer. My parents were supposed to pick up Clayton and Gia after the summer, but they never did. Finally, since my grandfather did not want them to miss school, he enrolled them in school there in Climax. They never came back to live with us in Chicago. It was never planned my parents never went to get them; I am not sure why.

Ava and I wore good expensive clothes. All our clothing came from Chuppy, a longtime family friend and one of my father's best customers. She was called a booster; she stole anything she could get between her legs and sold it to my father in return for her heroin fix. She wore a big dress over huge bloomers she stuffed with all sorts of stolen merchandise. She went into a heavily secured fur company and stole two fur coats. She walked into a department store and walked out with a television set in her bloomers. We never could figure out how she did it.

Through Chuppy, my mother had diamond rings, mink suits and coats, and a lot of expensive clothing. Chuppy did not steal anything cheap. She went for the biggest and the best. She would always say, "The reason I go for the best is because if I get caught, I want it to be a federal offense, because federal prisons are much better than state prisons." From time to time, she lived with us. She and my mom fought all the time about everything. They fought about age, hair, dress, how to raise children. I mean everything.

Ava and I met some friends in our new neighborhood, and we all had fun. We still jumped double Dutch rope and played all types of games. A lot of our friends were boys, but none of the boys seemed to like me. They liked Ava. I always had my finger stuck in my mouth, so they made fun of me. However, we still had fun.

In my third grade class, I met Barbara Lee. She was new, and I desperately wanted her to be my friend. She lived around the corner from us. Barbara Lee and I walked home from school together. Ava and I were never allowed to bring any of our friends to our home because of what went on there, so we went to their house or sat on their porch or our porch and listened to music and danced.

Once, when Barbara Lee and I walked home from school, she could not get into her place because no one was home. She asked if she could use my bathroom. I hesitated because I never knew what to expect when I got home. But since she was only going to use the bathroom, I thought it would be okay.

When we walked through the door, my mother was slumped over in the chair. I lifted her head up and she was out of it. The needle was still sticking in her arm from where she had been shooting dope, and blood was dripping everywhere. I leaned her back and took the needle out of her arm. My friend asked, "What is wrong with your mother?" I told her, "My mother is sick, and you need to leave right now."

A few minutes later, when my sister walked through the door, she and I had to bring my mother out of her highness. She was on her way to taking an overdose. My father was not home to help us. We walked my mother around to keep her awake. We gave her milk, and we put ice on her body. We revived her and saved her life. It was a good thing we had seen my father revive so many people many times, so we knew how to save her life. When my dad got home, I was scolded for bringing someone home with me. I was sorry I let my friend come in, and I was embarrassed she saw my mother's condition. I prayed she would not tell anyone. I swore to myself I would never bring a friend home again.

I met another friend at school. Victoria and I would walk home together, and a few times, I went to her house. Her parents were so nice to me. Every time I went over there, they would want me to stay for dinner. Once, Victoria's mother asked me, "What kind of work do your parents do?" I thought a minute and said, "My mother is a telephone operator and my father's a police officer." When Victoria would ask if I could have company, I always told her, "No" because my parents are at work and I can't have company when they aren't home."

Victoria had an older sister named Joyce. She was in high school when Victoria and I were in the third grade. Joyce asked me, "Have you ever seen the Temptations sing?" I said, "Who?" She said, "You don't know who the Temptations are?" "No." "What about Smokey Robinson & the Miracles?" "I never heard of them, either." Victoria asked her sister, "Can Arden go with us to the Regal Theatre to the concert?" Joyce said, "Of course she can go with us." I said with much excitement, "I would love to go!"

I have always loved music. My father had bought us the Beatles *I want to hold your hand* album. My father had a big record collection, and I would listen to his music: Count Basie, Duke Ellington, Ella Fitzgerald, Sarah Vaughan, Billie Holiday, Nat King Cole, Miles Davis, Jackie Wilson and Sam Cooke, to name a few. Sam Cooke and Jackie Wilson were my favorites because I did not like jazz as much as I liked singing along with the record.

I remember when I was about four years old, my father took me with him to the Regal Theatre to see Sarah Vaughan. It was so boring. The only thing I remember was crying because the man in the seat next to me was using the whole armrest. I remember my father apologizing to the man because of my behavior.

I was so excited because I am going with my friend and her sisters. About a week later, we were at the Regal Theatre. The Temptations were there, Smokey Robinson and the Miracles were there, Billy Stewart was there, and many more, but I only remember those. It was so exciting. People were dancing in the aisles and singing along with the groups. When Smokey Robinson came on stage to do his show, I was in a trance. I totally enjoyed his show. He was easily the best performer.

There I was, a little girl only nine years old, and I was in love with Smokey Robinson. I imagined myself grown up and married to him. I thought going was the best thing ever in my entire life. I was so grateful my friend took me with them. The next day, I asked my father for money and went to the record store to buy all the songs they had by Smokey Robinson and the Miracles and the Temptations. I went home and listened to them over and over again until I knew all the words. I found something I could be happy with, an imaginary dream. I always wanted to be alone, so I could daydream about my new fantasy --- singing Smokey songs.

Soon my world turned upside down. On our way home from school, Victoria stopped walking with me and said, "I can't walk home with you anymore. My mother told me to stay away from you because your parents are dope fiends." I was absolutely devastated. I cried all the way home. Even my friend Barbara Lee told me her mother said she could not associate with me anymore.

I found myself to be a loner. I would walk home from school alone. I will never forget my ex-friends were walking behind me and I could hear them talking about me. It was four of them. When I heard one of them say, "You should see her mother's arms. You can tell she's a dope fiend." I turned around and threw my book at the group. One girl ran up and grabbed me, and I went crazy. I knew I could not beat up four girls at one time, so I grabbed one and tried to kill her.

My mother told me, "If you find yourself in a crowd of girls fighting and you can't win; beat one of them to a pulp." I did because I beat up one of the girls bad. The next day at school, even though the fight did not happen at school, I got suspended. I remember the teacher saying, "Arden, it's a shame you beat Sheila up as bad as you did. Her mother had to take her to the emergency room." My life was now turned inside out. I had friends who could not be my friends anymore. I loved them too. They were like my family. Now I had no one. I did have Smokey Robinson's songs to listen and sing to, then I would forget all the pain.

CHAPTER 5
THE ACCIDENT

For fun and excitement, I looked forward to going on the West Side where my grandmother lived. We had so much fun over there because we had lots of friends. When we came around, they would crowd around us and say, "Hey, look at y'all nice car and your pretty clothes. You guys are rich, aren't you?" We had started going over to my grandma's a lot because after my daddy got robbed by the stick-up men and busted from the police so many times, he started keeping his dope and most of his money at my grandmother's place. No one suspected it was there.

We had double Dutch jump rope, hopscotch, and hula hoop contests with our friends. We would call it a match against the West Side girls and the South Side girls (us.) We felt we were the more intelligent group and more lady-like than the tomboyish West Side girls.

We also would spend the night with my Aunt Doreen and her son Erick. They lived down the street from my grandmother. My mom would say to Doreen, "Don't feed them too much junk." Doreen fed us cakes, candy, potato chips, and soda pop all the time. She said, "Don't tell your mother I gave you so much junk food." She would fix us some of her special sloppy joe burgers. We had fun at Doreen's. Erick was so funny. He kept us laughing until three o'clock in the morning with good, funny, and sometimes dirty jokes. We would sing and dance to the latest songs, put on talent shows -- those were truly the good times I looked forward to.

I can recall my mom took all four of us on the bus to Doreen's. When we got off the bus a man snatched my mother's purse and ran. My mom took off running after him and turned to us and said, "Y'all hold hands and don't move. I'll be right back." A few minutes later my mom was coming back to us with her purse cussing and mumbling. She grabbed us by our hands and said, "Come on let's go." Once, after spending the weekend on the West Side, we went home on Sunday afternoon to find a big fat lady lying on our couch. Ava and I snickered, "Look at the fat woman sleeping on our couch." We started to walk towards her when my dad said in a stern voice, "Don't go over there by her." We knew something was wrong.

Later, Ava and I saw my father and two of his friends carrying her out of the door. We were laughing at them struggling to carry the big fat lady out until one of my dad's friends said, "This woman is already heavy, and dead weight makes her heavier." Ava and I looked at each other with big eyes; "She's dead!" We jumped up, ran to our bedroom and put the covers over our heads. The next day, I heard my mom tell Doreen, "Haddie OD'D here last night. Clayton, Billy and Snuggie dumped her body in the alley." Later, I asked my mother, "Why did they have to dump her in an alley?"

"Because If they had taken her to a hospital or called the police, then they would be responsible for her death. Had they said she died here then we would be called murderers." Several times people almost died in our house and got revived, but it was the first time someone died.

One of my father's friends had come over and bought dope. I remember him sitting on our couch, waiting for his drugs. He was sweating and rocking from side to side. My dad asked, "Man, what's your problem?" He said, "I just offed a man." Meaning he killed someone. We were surrounded by all kinds of despicable people who spoke freely in front of us and discussed any matter. Most of the women were prostitutes or boosters. I remember one of my dad's prostitute friends saying, "I make $200 a night turning tricks." The men were hit men and hustlers. They did whatever they had to do to buy dope and survive. Some of my dad's customers were big stars and businessmen. I hated the lifestyle we lived. I wanted a normal life where I could play with my friends, but I did not see it ever happening.

Three years after we moved to our nice place, my father was making even more money. He had a friend in the real estate business who was one of his customers. My dad came home one day and said, "We're moving. I bought a two-flat building." Our new place was bigger and better than the one we moved from. My father also bought a brand new 1966 Buick Electra 225. It was like we were rich. I had turned eleven years old when we moved to our new place.

At our new place, the police were always busting my father. It would happen when we were about to go shopping or to a movie or something. We would be waiting on my father and bugging him all day. "Daddy, when are we leaving?" "I'm waiting on my shipment," he would say. "As soon as it comes, we're leaving." But at the end of the day, the police would come and clean my dad out, so we had to wait until he bought and sold enough dope, and he would then give us money from his profit.

Even though my father made a lot of money, there were many times when the cash was low. Every Christmas, we would be warned we were not getting presents. However, my daddy always found a way. We were never disappointed. My parents had us believing in Santa Claus. Sometimes, on Christmas Eve, we still had not gone Christmas shopping. I was sure we were not getting anything for Christmas -- but on Christmas Day, "Ava look! It's the dolls we wanted." We always had plenty of presents and toys. We were sure Santa brought them. I was twelve years old when I realized there is no Santa Claus.

Ava and I remained in the same school from the other neighborhood. Our new neighborhood was a gang area, Blackstone Rangers territory. The Stones, as they called themselves, were Chicago's most notorious gang. Ava and I had met new friends in our new neighborhood, but none of them were in gangs. We had gangs in our old neighborhood, too, but they did not kill people like the Blackstone Rangers were rumored to do.

The worst that happened in our old neighborhood was Ava and I was walking home from the store, when a young man was approaching us. I said, "Boy if you touch my sister or me, I hope God strike you dead." He turned around and went the other way saying, "Ain't nobody gonna mess with y'all."

The school we stayed in was a good school. Midway through the third grade, our teacher took sick and had to quit, so our new teacher was Mrs. Rita Whitlock -- the meanest person in the world came to Dixon Elementary School on February tenth, which I remember clearly because it was my birthday. I had my mother fix my hair like hers, in a grown-up hairstyle. I usually wore a ponytail, but this morning, my mom put curls in my hair and pushed it up in the front.

Mrs. Whitlock said, "I'm going to come around to each of you and see your notebooks." She went to each student and looked through their notebooks and made various comments. She would say something like, "Oh, Janice you're a good student. Look at how neat your papers are in your notebook. Janice, I'm proud of you." When she got to me, she asked, "Arden, where is your notebook?" "I don't have one." She yelled at me at the top of her lungs. "What do you mean you don't have a notebook!? You will never come to my class again without a notebook! Do you understand?"

Then she said, "You are much too young to have your hair styled the way it is." She took a brush out of her purse and brushed my hair back and made me a ponytail with a rubber band. I started crying and said, "My mother does not allow me to put rubber bands in my hair." She said, "You are a Miss Smart-mouth, and if your mother has anything to say about what I did, then she can come see me." I was so angry because Mrs. Whitlock was not as mean to anyone else. She turned to the class and said, "Arden is going to be my worst student. None of you better 'Not!' take me lightly because I'm not to be played with." I could not believe I went from a teacher I liked very much to a teacher who was mean and hated me from the first time she laid eyes on me.

At the end of the third grade, we learned Mrs. Whitlock was also going to be our fourth-grade teacher. Mrs. Whitlock stayed extremely hard on me. She harassed me all through the fourth grade. When we were 'disobedient' she had statements' we had to write, and they were a paragraph long. Every day she said I did something, and it got on her nerve. I was always writing statements in her class. Once I smiled at her and she suspected I had something up my sleeve and she made me write fifty statements. She grabbed me by my arm one day because I talked back to her and put scratches on me. I would tell my parents at home how mean she was to me, but they never did anything about it.

Because of their involvement with drugs, my parents did not like going to the school because they thought someone was going to arrest them. They were afraid of their own shadows: always fearing being busted by the police or robbed. Whenever they had to sign a paper, they would sign another name as our guardian. They were afraid someone would notice their name or something. It was not like when we were in Catholic school and my mother threatened the nun.

It was mostly embarrassing when my parents did come around. We had an assembly in our auditorium where the students put on a show, and I was in the show. One of my classmates came to me and said, "Your parents are nodding out in the audience?" They would sit there asleep with their heads bobbing and weaving back and forth. Or if it was Parent's Night at school where parents came to meet the teacher and see their child's progress, the next day, my folder was the only one still sitting on the desk because my parents did not make it to the open house. Other kids would ask, "How come your school folder is still on the desk? Your parents did not come to Parents Night. Your parents don't care about you, do they?" I had so many fights because of what people said about my parents.

At the end of the fourth grade, I was happy Mrs. Whitlock

was not going to be my fifth-grade teacher. On the last day of school before the summer, we were itching for the bell to ring, so we could get out of there. Mrs. Whitlock announced to the class, "You have all passed to the fifth grade and you are all going to be in the same class." She then told us, "Go report to room three-thirty to meet your new teacher." We all assembled in our new classroom. A few minutes later, Mrs. Whitlock walked in and sat down at the teacher's desk.

"Let me tell you who your next teacher will be." She looked at a list and said, "What a big surprise for this class because I will teach this fifth-grade class." She tricked us. I thought I would die when I found out I was going to have Mrs. Whitlock for another year. She harassed me more in the fifth grade than she did in the third and fourth. I finally did get rid of her in the sixth grade.

After we moved to our new place, my father was in a bad car accident. We got a call from the hospital saying, "The family needs to come soon because this man is in critical condition." He was on his way to my grandmother's house to get his stash of drugs. We all rushed to the hospital. The doctor told my mother; "Your husband broke both of his legs, his ribs, and his hips. He will have to be in this body cast for quite a long time."

My mom told Doreen, who was with us, "I know Clayton nodded out while driving because he was so high when he left." My dad's whole body was in a cast. My mother would bring drugs to the hospital for my father. He soon wanted to come home -- it was hard to use dope in the hospital -- so they arranged for a hospital bed in the middle of our living room. It was like a hospital room.

My father was hard to live with. He was impatient and often yelled. His body cast had only one opening around his private parts. I could never stand it when I had to clean his bedpan, especially after he had taken mineral oil to soften his stool. I did not have to do it much thanks to Herbert, one of my father's live-in dope-fiend flunkies.

CHAPTER 6
HEY, I KICKED THE HABIT

I sucked my thumb from birth. My parents tried extremely hard to get me to stop. First, I started sucking my thumb on my left hand. When I was about six years old my parents wrapped my thumb up with a cloth and put hot sauce and pepper in it for about two weeks. When they thought I had stopped, they said, "Arden, you're getting so pretty since you stopped sucking your thumb." They came into my bedroom when I was sleeping and noticed my other thumb in my mouth. The next day, they were angry with me and said, "We saw your other thumb in your mouth last night. We thought you were getting prettier, but you are uglier now more than ever. You look like a monkey."

Somehow, I could not stop sucking my thumb as much as I wanted to. I mean, there I was twelve and still sucking my thumb. Well, I started sucking my finger next to my thumb on my right hand. It would be turned upside down with my fingernail to my tongue, and I would roll my hair with my left-hand finger next to my thumb. It was quite a funny sight. My classmates would say, "Look at the baby sucking her thumb. You are going to have buck teeth." Everyone laughed, made fun of and talked about me.

We went to Michigan when school was out for the summer, as we usually did. I told Grandma Ruby, "I want to stop sucking my finger," My grandmother said, "It's a habit you've had since birth. It is like trying to get off heroin or coke. You're no better than your mother and father, who are drug addicts." I thought she must be

36

right because I did not feel I could survive without sucking my finger. My grandmother said, "I want to help you stop before the Ogg gets to you." "What's an Ogg?" "He's a little man about the size of a chicken, with a beak on the top of his head. He travels through the night and kills kids who suck their fingers, wet the bed, and disobey their parents. He strikes between the ages of seven through thirteen."

I told her, "I do not believe you, so stop making it up." She said, "I didn't believe my mother either. When I was a little girl, I disobeyed my mother and she made me stay in the closet. I could see under the house through a crack in the closet floor and I saw the Ogg looking and pointing his finger at me - as if to say, 'You bad girl, you'd better straighten up.' From then on, I never disobeyed my mother again."

She then said, "The Ogg's job is to turn bad kids into good kids. He will give you a warning sign, and if you are not good, he will kill you." I asked, "Grandma Ruby, has the Ogg ever killed a kid before?" She said, "Sure he has." I did not believe her, but the way she told the story sent chills throughout my body. I found myself afraid. I wanted, so bad to stop sucking my finger because I thought, "Soon I might find a boyfriend, and what boy is going to put up with a big 'O' person like me sucking my finger?" For the first time, I was aware I was sucking my finger and aware I wanted to stop. Every time I caught myself putting my finger in my mouth, I would take it out.

A few days passed, and one morning I woke up and there was a piece of red tape on my arm. I showed it to Grandma Ruby, and she said with a surprise voice "Oh no! The Ogg is here!" I thought she had gone crazy. She was screaming and everything. My brother also had a piece of tape on his arm. Nothing was on my sisters' arms nor my grandparents; only my brother and me.

A couple of mornings later, my brother and I found tape on our arms again. We figured Grandma Ruby was doing it. However, no one ever woke and caught her. One morning she had tape on her arm. When she woke, she got angry and snatched the piece of tape off her arm and said, "I don't like the Ogg lurking in my house at night." She yelled at my brother and me. "Little Clayton, you have to stop wetting the bed, and Arden, you need to stop sucking your finger or else the Ogg is going to get you." I told her "Please tell me there is no such thing as the Ogg because I'm terrified."

Climax, Michigan is spooky anyway. It is very dark and has a lot of open land. There were giant trees. They moved with the wind at night and brushed against the windows. They reminded me of monsters. Most of the land in the area is wooded - all trees. My grandmother assured me it was not her doing. She said, "It's the Ogg, and he is angry with Clayton and you." She then said, "I would not frighten a child with a lie." I could not understand why a small man about the size of a chicken would lurk in the middle of the night to frighten little children to death. If all he wanted me to do was to stop sucking my finger could he see, I was trying as hard as I could to stop?

I found myself throughout the day catching myself sucking my finger and taking it out, but at night I could not sleep without my finger in my mouth. I did it unconsciously. We had gone to town in Battle Creek and worked in my uncle's restaurant. When we returned home, my grandmother grabbed me by the arm and took me into the kitchen. Outside the kitchen door was a stairway to the attic. There was a drop of blood on every step. She said, "I caught the Ogg in the house today and I shot him, and he hopped up the steps."

She told me, "You and Clayton might be killed tonight because the Ogg is angry." I could not sleep because I did not want to make the mistake and put my finger in my mouth. I put my hands under me to remind me I did not want to put my finger in my mouth. I never thought of putting my finger in my mouth again. Finally, I broke the habit. Years later in my life, I told my grandmother, "It was great psychology you used in creating the Ogg because I stopped a habit, I thought I would never break."

My grandmother told me, "The Ogg is very real. I did not make him up." I am not sure if she was telling me the truth or not, but how come she is the only person to ever see him? She never denied the Ogg to her dying day. She died when I was thirty-three years old. Grandma Ruby was an exceptionally clean woman. She did not allow anything out of place. She had drawers full of beautiful little gifts her patients had given her. She was a nurse and had lots of gifts she had folded in drawers.

When my grandmother would leave us in the house alone, we would look through her drawers and put on her pretty hats and shoes. She had little dolls and they were so cute. She did not even allow us to sit down on her bed. When she returned, she would tell us -- even before she entered the house -- all the things we had done while she was gone. Sometimes it was impossible for her to know some things, but she knew everything. We never could figure out how she knew. Mysterious woman she was. She had a well-earned reputation for being mean. She would do the opposite of what everyone else wanted. If we wanted to watch something on television, she would not want to watch the same. We always had to watch what she wanted.

She knew I hated going fishing with her, so she would wake me up at six in the morning to go fishing. As we were getting ready, she was cooking breakfast. She had a plate she ate out of, and we all had our plates we ate out of. However, she confused me because she put two sausages on my plate and one on hers. She knew I could not eat two sausages, so I grabbed the sausage out of her plate and started eating it. She went crazy, took the plate, and threw it across the room. She said, "I can never eat out of my plate again because your dirty little hands touched it." I still have a scar on my leg where the glass from the plate cut me by ricocheting off the wall and landing on my leg.

When we went fishing, she would make me sit there all day and would not let me talk. She said, "Shush, the fish can hear you and you will scare them away." We would be there fishing all day. She loved to go fishing in the rain because she could catch catfish, which she loved to eat. She said, "Arden, put this worm on the fishing hook for me." I said, "But Grandma it's alive." I hated it when she would say "Here Arden, take this hook out of the fish" because I could hear the insides tearing out of the fish. Fishing was relaxing to her, but it was awful to me.

At home, she would make me play Chinese checkers with her. She would beat me every game. She would want to play game after game after game. I would pretend to fall asleep while she was taking her turn. Thinking she was going to wake me and tell me to go to bed, she would wake me and say, "It's your move." I will never forget the time when she piled some pork and beans on my plate. I hated pork and beans. She was forcing me to eat them. I was pretending to eat them.

I tried to put the beans from my plate back into the pot on the stove. She heard the top to the pot scrape across the pot and she came into the kitchen and saw me trying to put the beans back and said, "Arden, if you wanted more, you could have asked me," then she piled even more beans back onto my plate. I sat at the table for hours refusing to eat the beans until my grandfather finally said, "Go get in the bed."

Another memory of mine in Climax was when my grandfather would kill the chickens and make us hold the legs while he chopped the heads off. We had to hold them by their feet because after the chicken's head was cut off, it would still run around in the yard. While we were holding the chicken, it would try to squirm out of our hands. Blood spattered everywhere. They would kill it so my grandmother could cook it for dinner. I found it hard to eat Harvey or Audrey for dinner. We named the chickens and they were our friends we played with.

Those days were when I was younger. Now at twelve years old, I was grateful to my grandmother because I had finally stopped sucking my finger. The summer was over, and Ava and I had to return to Chicago for school. I was looking forward to going back to Chicago and school. I wanted everyone to know I had finally broken the habit which made everyone laugh and make fun of me.

CHAPTER 7

BOYFRIEND TERROR

After we got back home life was still the same. My father was lying in the hospital bed in his body cast and getting high hour after hour. My mother was drinking up a storm and my parents fought all the time. My father had his friends sitting around all day long. We had no peace from them. If my daddy were asleep, they would bump up against the bed, shake my dad to wake him up, to say, "Oh I'm sorry Clayton. I didn't mean to wake you up." They knew he would wake up and start getting high and they would be able to get their morning fix. My dad's flunkies could not wait until my father got high and started to nod out so they could rip him off. Many times, my dad's friends would steal his dope and his money. He would know they had stolen it, and they could come back later and get a favor. My daddy was not even shrewd enough to be in the business of drug dealing.

I went to the playground down the street from where we lived. Some guys were playing baseball. I watched and set my eyes on one guy. He was cute. Of course, he did not pay any attention to me. I was skinny and homely. I overheard some girls teasing him, saying, "Hey Bob, Sherry is about to have the baby." I figured he had a girlfriend who was pregnant. I thought he was too old for me. I was a virgin and sex never entered my mind. My imagination could not take me beyond a kiss.

The only guy who ever paid any attention to me during

41

primary school was Cedrick Davis from my sixth-grade class. He sent a friend to me who said, "Cedrick said, "Will you go with him?" This happened at the beginning of the lunch period. I told his friend to tell him "Yes." At the end of the lunch period, Cedrick sent his friend who said, "Cedrick said to tell you it's quits." I did not really care; I only wanted a boyfriend because all the girls in my school had one.

In school, all my friends had boyfriends. I wondered why no boys ever asked me to go steady with them. It never bothered me too much because ever since I was nine years old, I was in love with Smokey Robinson. I knew I would meet him and become his wife someday. The love I felt was too strong for me not to believe it. I was not crazy. I had an imagination and it took me away from the ugly reality of my life. When I was daydreaming, it was the only time I could feel happy. Even though there was no one in my life who liked me, and I did not want anyone, I still wanted someone to want me and care about me. Even though I was young, I felt grown.

Bob lived down the street from us on the same block. I started seeing him all the time. I was twelve years old, and he was a lot older. One day, I was on my way to the store. Bob stopped me as I passed his house and said, "You are kind of cute. Do you have a boyfriend?" I said, as I giggled, "Hee, hee, hee no I do not."

"I saw you pass by a few times." Then he asked, "Have you ever had your thing taken care of?" "I don't know what you mean," I said. "You're not stupid, are you?" "No, I'm not, but I don't know what you are talking about?" He asked, "How big is your snake hole?" I said, "I don't know what you're talking about." "I want to try you out for size," he said, "I can fix you up right. I can make your vagina big enough to take the whole size of my penis."

I said, "Oh, I never did it before. I'm afraid to try sex and I need to talk it over with my mother first." My mom had always said to me, "If you ever come to the point where you can't say 'no' to sex you should discuss it with me and I will tell you how to protect yourself." Bob said, "I will show you what to do and you don't need to let your mother know. In fact, you should never tell anyone."

He told me, "Meet me on your front porch at eight tonight. I am going to introduce you to the snake eye." Bob came to my porch. I was excited because I felt grown, and a man was paying attention to me. I suddenly felt romantic and the only way I could fulfill the desire was by petting my little kitten. I told Bob, "I'm going in the house for a minute, and I will be right back." I wanted to get my kitty.

When I got upstairs, my father would not let me go back out. I screamed and hollered and fell all over the floor. My father said, "Arden, you're almost a teenager and you are too old to act this way." I asked him if I could go to tell my friend I could not come back out. He would not let me. I felt so angry with my father for not letting me go back out. My father was never so firm with me. It was as if he knew I was about to lose my virginity.

The next day, when I saw Bob, he asked "What happened to you last night? Why didn't you come back?" We were standing on my porch and a few other people were standing around. Most of them were Bob's friends. I told him, "Would you believe my father would not let me come back out." Bob eyes got big and he took his hand and slapped me in my face and told me, "You will obey me for now on, not your father." I do not know why I did not go tell my father he slapped me. I was embarrassed, too, because of the people standing around looking. I took off running to the back of the building. Bob came running after me.

When he got me in the back, he said, "Let's do it." I told him, "I'm scared of you." He took me into his arms and said, "I'm sorry. I really wanted to see you last night and I was so disappointed when you did not come back." He then convinced me. I asked Bob, "Where will we go to do it?" He said, "Right here." We were in the basement door entrance. I could not understand because I thought we were supposed to be in a bed behind closed doors. If our neighbors had looked out of their window, they would see us. He told me, "I will teach you how to do it."

He said, "Take off your clothes." I said, "I don't want to take off my clothes." He showed me his fist and laid it on my face and told me, "This fist is the eye and it goes with the snake, now shut up and you better do whatever I say." The next thing I knew, I was butt naked and standing up against the wall. Bob did not take his clothes off; he took it out.

I started crying and he hugged me and told me, "I will not hurt you if you do what I tell you to do." So, I surrendered to him. I was with my back to him and he was behind me. I had my hands against the wall and the lower part of my body pushed out. As he was starting to put his snake in as he called it, I got scared and told him, "Stop because you are hurting me."

Bob pulled my hair while showing me his fist and told me, "You are not a virgin and you better not try and pull one over on me." I suffered through the terrible incident. When it was over, Bob said, "Go upstairs and get cleaned up." I went into the house and went straight into the bathroom. I got myself together. Then, Bob came to my back door. He asked me, "Are you okay?" I told him, "I'm bleeding and I feel kind of shaky." Bob's eyes got big and he said, "Where is the blood?" I said, "In my panties." He said, "Can I see the blood." I started crying and told him, "Bob you really hurt me." He said, "Now since we have been together, you belong to me only and you better watch yourself from now on."

He said "You are forbidden to talk to any men. You must have my permission to even say hello to them. Even if I am not there, I better not hear tale of you saying one word to a male." I thought he must be right because my mother always told me, "Only have sex with one man all throughout your life. Never cheat on your man." She also said, "A woman who has babies by more than one man is a slut." I assumed I was his forever. The next day, Bob slapped me in my face again in front of everyone. He said, "You are like my puppy dog. Now get on your hands and knees and bark." I did it because I was scared. He threatened to hit me with his fist with all his might if I ever disobeyed him. All Bob's friends started laughing at me. It was a big joke to everyone. Bob did not laugh at all. He stood over me with his fist balled up and told me,

"Get up off the ground. I'm going to train you, so you obey all my commands as my dog at home does."

Every night, I had to have violent sex with Bob. He was a sadist. If I told him he was hurting me, he would slap me while we were having sex and say, "Shut up." Bob and I never had sex in a bed together. We always "did it" in abandoned buildings, basements, old cars, and back porches. I hated it when I had to have sex with him. I always hid what was going on from my family. Ava would say to my dad, "Bob hit Arden yesterday." My dad would say, "Arden, did Bob hit you?" I would scream, cry and shout and say, "Bob never put a hand on me. Leave my boyfriend alone." Bob never put any visible marks on my body, so whenever he was confronted about hitting me, he would say to me, "Tell your family I never hit you or I will beat you again." All my marks were either hickeys in my head or if I pulled my lip down, there were cuts and bruises from him slapping me in my mouth.

My father started getting better and was beginning to walk again. His business had started picking up. When my father was down on his back, business was slow. My dad was always getting ripped off by one of his "friends." He was always out of it because to deal with the pain he stayed doped up while he was healing. My father was doing more drugs than he was selling. He became his own biggest customer.

Bob would come over to my house every day. When he was leaving at night after he beat me up and made me have sex with him, he would say, "Call me at nine in the morning." I had to call him at the specified time he said, or I was in trouble. I could not call him a moment earlier or a moment later. It had to be the time he specified. After I talked to him on the telephone, he would say, "Be standing in the window so you can see me walk up." He would never tell me what time he was coming. I better be in the window when he came. He never wanted to ring the doorbell because my father always answered the door. We had a built-in intercom system. We could ask who was at the door from our telephone. In 1966, it was a luxury. Now of course it is common.

If Bob had to ring the doorbell, I would get a slap or two in the face from him. If something should happen and I was not standing in the window waiting, I would get a slap or two. Bob would come into the house. The first thing he might say using an extremely low voice, one I could not hear, "Go get me a drink of water." I would say, "Bob, I can't hear you." He would get angry and say even lower, "If I have to repeat myself, I'm going to slap you." Then he would say in an angry voice while talking with his teeth shut tight as he was yelling at me, "I said, go get me a glass of water."

I would get the water and when I gave it to him; he would take the glass and look me right in my eyes and say, "If I look in this glass and see one spec in the water, I owe you one." meaning he owed me a slap or two. "I would give it to you now, but I don't want your father to know." Then perhaps he would say, "Sonny Boy, don't talk to anyone for twenty minutes." He always called me Sonny Boy. He never called me by my name. My mother could ask me a simple question, "Arden have you seen the TV Guide?" I would answer, "Here it is." Bob would tell me he owed me another one for speaking to my mother. Many times, to keep from getting another slap added on to the ones I had already accumulated, I would totally ignore her or anyone else talking to me.

There were so many ridiculous requests Bob demanded from me throughout the day. When he left, he would make me walk him downstairs. First, we would find a secluded place. While we were having sex, he would say "Sonny Boy, you know you messed up several times and I owe you thirteen (or seventeen or five or eight) times today." Whatever the number was is how many times he would hit me.

He would slap my face and knock me in the head with his knuckles and count that as two. If I begin to cry, he will add more. After we got through with sex, he would hug me, kiss me, and say, "Sonny Boy it hurts me to hit you more than it hurts you, but I've got to get you trained right." He would then hit me about five times without stopping. I still was not allowed to cry. He would then finish giving me all the hits he owed me.

Sometimes, he would say, "I'm going to stop hitting you at

eight, but Sonny Boy you know you still have five more coming."
He would save the other hits for the next day. I had to keep track
of how many he owed me, and if I happened to miscount them,
he would add more.

On days he saved hits he asked me, "How many do I owe
you from yesterday?" I had better say the right amount, too. He
always threatened me, saying, "I will hit you with my fist with
all my might if you tell anybody about what I'm doing to you."
He said, "You think I'm hurting you now, but tell someone and
you'll see what it is like to really be hurt."

Bob even had another girlfriend who had a daughter by him
a couple of months after I met him. He would call her from my
house. He would make me sit next to him while he talked to her.
He told me, "If you make one sound she can hear, I will make
you sorry you were ever born." He would say things to her, like "I
can't wait until I get some of your Snake hole later tonight." I had
to sit and listen. Sometimes, he would put the phone to my ear
so I could hear what she was saying to him. Her mother worked
nights, so Bob spent all day with me and all night with her. Bob
made it clear to everyone and me Sherry was his number one girl.
I was only second place in his life. He also treated Sherry badly
too. I do not know to what extent, but I heard he beat her with a
combat boot when she was pregnant.

I was forbidden to ask or inquire about her. If Bob and I were
going somewhere together and had to walk to get there, I had to
walk on the opposite side of the street because someone would
tell Sherry they saw Bob and I together. He claimed she never
knew about me and she never will. He told me, "I will definitely
marry her one-day." Sherry's family moved to New York. I was so
glad she moved because I thought, "Now I've got him." However,
Bob would write her letters. He would give them to me to mail.
They would not be sealed so I would read them. He would tell her
how much he missed her and their daughter. A couple of times,
I wrote her as an anonymous person.

I would tell her all about Bob's and my relationship. I even
wrote Bob letters and would make up stories about men she

was seeing in New York. Bob would ask me, "How does Sherry know about us?" I always played dumb and told him, "I don't understand how anyone knew." He also told me, "I'm getting letters telling me she is having a relationship with another man in New York." I had a friend at school write the letters for me in case he wanted to compare my handwriting to the writing in the letters.

CHAPTER 8

PREGNANT AT THIRTEEN
YEARS OLD

My father was back on his feet again. At least he was taking care of his own habit and my mother's. He was not making as much money as he had made in the past, but we had enough to live on.

During my father's illness, my mother started seeing one of the neighborhood drunken bums, Mitch. I hated him so much. I would think of ways to kill him. I thought he was breaking up my family. My mother would let him come over while my father was not home. I would say, "I hope my daddy catch you in our house and shoot you." He would say, "Arden, you're dumb and stupid. Don't talk to me." My mother would not say a word. She let him talk to me like I was a dog. My mother was always stoned out of her mind drunk and high on heroin. She was always out of it.

Many times, my father would be coming in the front door and Mitch would be going out of the back door. My father caught on and tricked my mother and went to the back and caught Mitch leaving. I heard many gunshots. I went into the bathroom and prayed with tears in my eyes, "Please God let my dad kill him." Unfortunately, my dad missed. There was always a gun in the house and many times either my dad would threaten my mother, or my mother would threaten my father.

To add to all the confusion, when I turned fourteen years old,

I was two months pregnant. Bob had me stand in front of him with my clothes off and he touched my stomach and he said, "You know you're pregnant." I said, "I better tell my mother." He said, "Don't tell anyone yet." Two months later, I finally told my mother. "Momma, I think I'm pregnant." She asked me, "When was your last period?" I told her, "In December." It was April, which made me four months pregnant. My mother started crying and said, "You are stupid. Didn't I tell you to let me know when you couldn't say no?" She then said, "Don't worry; I will take you to a good doctor." My Aunt Doreen was eight months pregnant, so she got me an appointment with her doctor.

My mother went with me to the appointment. The doctor confirmed I was four months. My mother said to the doctor, "What about an abortion?" He told my mom "She is so young and too far gone to have a safe abortion." His suggestion was "She should have the baby and put it up for an adoption if you are not prepared to take care of it." My mother said, "Oh no, we ain't giving this baby up for no adoption." I realized I was going to have a baby. I thought it would be a way to grow up and live on my own. I was so tired of the living situation I was in. I was embarrassed I was pregnant.

I never told anyone. I did not have any friends. My only friend was Bob, and he did not allow me to associate with anyone. At school, all the people thought I was a weird person because I stayed to myself. I never talked to anyone. I did not even talk to Barbara Lee, and she had been my friend since the third grade.

Bob gave me a certain time to be home from school. He would say, "Sonny Boy, I want you home at four-forty-five on the dot every day from school. I will be standing in my window and when I see you walk by; I will call the time and it better say it is four-forty-five exactly. Don't let it say four-forty-five and ten seconds." When school was over, as soon as the bell would ring, I would take off running. Most people walked home, but I moved out of the district, so I had to take the bus. There were a couple of other classmates who took the same bus, but I never talked to or walked to the bus stop with them. One of the girls was one I beat up when I was in the third grade. She still was mad at me.

Sometimes, the bus might be too crowded, and the driver would not stop. I would have to catch the next bus, which meant I was going to be late getting home. I would cry at the bus stop in front of people because I knew I was going to get it from Bob. I had to catch two busses, so when I missed the first bus, I was going to miss the second bus. The next bus stop was close to home about eight blocks away. If I missed the second bus, I would run those eight blocks trying to meet my deadline. When I got home, I would be out of breath and might say, "Someone was chasing me." This was to account for me being out of breath when I entered the house.

I would be running past people crying and sometimes screaming. I know the people I would be running past wondered why I was screaming and running. I was trying to make my deadline because I was very terrified of what Bob would do to me if I were late getting home. He would slap me around and treat me bad. However, I still was afraid he would kill me or really hurt me as he threatened to do.

One time at school, we were having a girls' volleyball game. I was four months pregnant. No one knew I was pregnant because I had not started showing. I lost about five points for my team because I kept missing the ball. My team captain came to me and said, "Change places with me." I said, "No I'm not changing positions with you." She then said, "If we lose this game, I will kick your butt after school."

I got so mad until I shouted out, "I quit" in the middle of the game, and I stormed into the dressing room to change my clothes. I yelled so loud until the teacher came to the dressing room and asked me, "Arden, what is the matter with you?" I had my blouse pulled up as I was changing my clothes when she walked into the dressing room. Some of the girls followed her to the back to see what punishment I was going to get.

One girl told the teacher, "Miss Clark, look at Arden's stomach. Is she pregnant?" I got highly angry and shouted, "All you silly girls, mind your own business because I don't have time for any of you." Tracy, the team captain said, "You better make time for me because I'm going to take care of you after school." She wanted to fight me. When we got back to our classroom, I told the teacher, "Tracy wants to fight me after school." The teacher talked to the both of us and she decided I was wrong, and I should apologize. I did not want to apologize, but I did because I did not have time to fight after school. I had to hurry and get home; or else I will get it from Bob.

Rumor had it I was pregnant. I was in the eighth grade. Every student I passed in the hall would look at my stomach while talking to me trying to figure out if the rumor were true. I was never going to tell. Barbara Lee came to me and asked, "Arden, I'm your friend. Tell me the truth -- is the rumor true? Are you pregnant?" I said, "Barbara Lee, it's not true." She said, "Because girl, it would be awful if you have to drop out of school to have a baby."

I told her, "You will see me at Hirsch High School in September after the summer, and then everyone will know I'm not pregnant." My baby was due in October, so I really did not expect to return after the summer. I survived the rest of the school year and when I graduated from the eighth grade, I was five months pregnant. Still, no one knew for sure because I still was not showing much and did not tell anyone.

The summer finally came, and I could not go to Climax as I usually did because I was pregnant. I could not tell my grandfather -- I knew he would be hurt -- so I told him I was not coming because I had a summer job. I knew I was not going to keep it a secret long. I thought it would be easier to tell people I have a baby instead of telling them I was pregnant.

During my pregnancy, I was always upset. My dad always had his friends over. As soon as I woke up every morning, there were men everywhere. I remember waking up one morning, and my father's friends were all watching television. They were watching the Cubs play baseball. It was a playoff game and they were excited watching the game. I got so angry and shouted at the top of my lungs, "All of you dope fiends get the hell out of my house right now," and I turned the television off. My father came into the television room, yelled at me, and said, "Arden, you have no right to treat my friends this way."

I was so upset, I said, "Daddy, you don't know how it feels to wake up and find a bunch of zombies in the television room. What if I wanted to watch something on TV?" Ava had moved out of the house and was living with some friends of hers. Also, with my younger sister and brother living in Michigan, I was in the middle of everything, and no one was there to help me or to be on my side.

When I was six months pregnant, my mom and dad were fighting. My dad had gotten a new supply of dope in. Of course, all the zombies were crowded around waiting for their fix. My mom went off as usual and grabbed the gun. She was running behind my dad with the gun, "I'm going to shoot your ass." I said, "Momma put the gun down or I will call the police." I grabbed the telephone. My mother and I fought for the telephone while she had the gun in her hand.

I took the telephone and I hit her with it. She fell to the floor and I ran down the hall into my bedroom to use the phone. My aunt and one of my father's friends ran behind me. When I got a hold of the other phone in the bedroom, I called the operator. By the time the operator answered, my aunt and my father's friend tackled me onto the bed. They were holding me on the bed, and I was yelling, "help." I threw the phone across the room and I screamed to the operator the address and to send the police right away. My mom was still threatening my father with the gun while my father was mixing up the dope to sell.

In about five minutes, three police cars came. Everyone was looking at me with blood in their eyes. Even my father, He said, "Why would you call the police Arden when you know all this dope is in this place?" I shouted, "I don't care about the dope. I'm concerned about mamma shooting you." My father laughed and said, "You know your mamma ain't gone shoot me."

I yelled out, "I hate everyone, and I wish you would all drop dead." My aunt ran to the door and told the police, "I'm sorry, she is a teenager out of control. She is fourteen years old and pregnant. Her mother is taking care of the situation." The police believed her, and they left. The confusion continued. I felt so helpless. I locked myself in my bedroom, and I did not care who shot who, who took an overdose, or what other trips they went through. I wanted to listen to my friend Smokey because he would bring me out of depression or calm me down faster than anything else would.

A few days later, I was babysitting for the lady who lived in the apartment downstairs from us. I bought Smokey's new album, *Special Occasion*. I played the song "Give Her Up" repeatedly. Bob was there with me, "Why are you playing the same song over and over?" "Because I like the way I feel when I sing it." He said, "I'm the only person who should have the power to control those feelings inside of you." He then took my album and broke it in half.

I was so upset, I started screaming and crying. I told Bob "I hate you." Bob grabbed me by my neck and started choking me. He told me, "I'm not going to beat you now because you're pregnant. However, when the baby is born, I will resume beating you and I will hold this against you." I was going into my seventh month of pregnancy. All I did throughout my pregnancy was scream, holler and cry. I was so miserable.

From four months to seven months of my pregnancy, I did not gain one pound. On my seventh month visit, my doctor was concerned about my weight. He said, "I don't understand, you weighted one-hundred-twenty-four pounds on your fourth month visit and at your seventh month visit you are weighting the same." My doctor questioned my eating habits. He knew something was wrong.

I would not dare tell my doctor about all the problems I was facing at home. The doctor said, "Your baby has a strong heartbeat and there is no reason for you not getting any bigger. By your next visit, if you do not gain any weight, I'm going to hospitalize you."

The next day, I was watching television, and I felt something wet running out of me and when I stood up it was running down my legs. I did not know what was happening. I was rushed to the doctor's office. He examined me, and a portion of my water bag had busted. My doctor told me, "Go home, rest and wait to see if you'll either go into labor or if the water will stop on its own. Call me if anything changes."

Two days passed and nothing changed. I called the doctor and he told me to go to the hospital the next day and he would be there to help me. Bob stayed with me. He was not supportive though. He said, "I wonder what your snake hole looks like with water running out of it?" I told him, "Bob I don't want you to see." He said, as he was showing me his fist, "I said open your legs, so I can see."

Bob stopped hitting me when I was about seven months pregnant. He said, "I will start back hitting you again as soon as the baby is born. And, what you do now, I will not forget about later." I then opened my legs, so he could see. Then, he wanted to do it to me. "Bob the doctor said not to have sex because it could be dangerous." Bob told me, "Your doctor doesn't know what he is talking about. You better listen to me, not your doctor." So, I had to have sex with him while I was dripping wet so he could see how it felt.

The next day, I went to the hospital, which was a Saturday morning. I weighed three pounds less than I weighed when I went to the doctor's office. Going to delivery, I only weighed five pounds above my normal weight. I never even developed growth in my stomach. At seven months, no one could tell I was pregnant.

As I was checking in to go to deliver my baby one of the nurses said, "What can I help you with?" When I told her, "I'm here to have a baby" she started running around getting all she needed to take me to labor and delivery. I had a shot every thirty minutes. The doctor was inducing my labor. No pains came. Sunday morning, my doctor came and said, "I'm going to deliver your baby in about thirty minutes." I said to him, "Dr. Jordan, I'm scared." He asked me, "Do you want a girl or a boy?" I told him, "A boy." However, deep inside myself, I wanted a girl.

Bob said, "I already have a daughter and you better bring me a son." I was afraid to bring home a girl because I thought Bob would try to kill her and me. When I told my doctor I wanted a boy, he said, "A boy?! Why didn't you tell me you wanted a boy?" He said it as if he could have changed it. My doctor kissed me on my forehead, grabbed a newspaper and relaxed in the empty bed next to me. As he was lying there, he said, "I'm right here if you need me."

Thirty minutes had passed and still no labor pains, my doctor told me he was going to try something different. He put an IV in my arm and at once my pains started to come. All I could do was cry and scream. I started thinking about the time when Bob called my baby "the thing." He said once when I was five months pregnant, "When that 'thing' is born, you know I won't be buying it any shoes." I replied, "Bob, you don't have to." He also told me, "If the baby's complexion is dark, I will never say it's mine." Suddenly, I hated Bob more than I had ever hated anyone before. If he were there, for once, I would have told him exactly how I felt. I also wanted to tell everyone about the horrible way he treated me.

My mom and aunt were at the hospital with me. The nurses had thrown them out a couple of times because there were no visitors allowed in the labor room. My mom was very persuasive and could talk herself into or out of anything. When my mom realized I was in pain, she went to the gift shop and bought me some comic books. She knew I enjoyed reading them. I said, "What am I supposed to do, read these and laugh or something?" She could not stand to see me in pain. I could see how much my mother loved me.

My grandmother, a little old lady of sixty-four, came to the hospital by bus to see me. I was in so much pain; I did not want to see anyone. When I saw my grandmother, there was blood all over my sheets. They kept giving me all these shots to try and help me to ease the labor pains. They were using these gigantic needles which had scissors on the end of them. They inserted the huge needle into my uterus to deaden my feelings from pain.

The delivery was taking longer than the doctor had expected. When my grandmother came into my room, she saw the blood and started crying and cussing at the doctor because she did not think he was properly taking care of me. I said "Grandma, why don't you leave." I made her feel bad because I could not show appreciation for her taking the bus so far to see me. She never went anywhere, especially if she had to take the bus. She could hardly walk. However, she felt it was her responsibility to see me. I appreciated her.

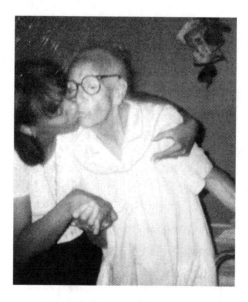

My grandma
She lived until she was 105 years old

CHAPTER 9

THE BIRTH OF A BEAUTIFUL GIRL

In the delivery room, the nurse grabbed my hand and said, "I'm here to help you through this." I grabbed her hand and she was screaming louder than I was because her ring was turned the wrong way as I was squeezing her hand. During the delivery, they had a mirror up above my head, so I could see the baby come out. However, one nurse's big head was in my way and I could not see anything. Seven hours after my labor was induced, I had a three pound thirteen-ounce baby girl. As far as the doctors could see, my baby was normal. Only small which is expected of a premature baby. I felt so happy and felt a big release of frustrations. I felt strong. My doctor said, "We are going to take you to your room now, so you can rest."

I said, "Can I go home? Why do I have to stay here?" I asked him, "Where is my baby? Can I see my baby?" He said, "Wait until tomorrow morning." Early in the morning I walked to the nursery. I was looking for my daughter. I did not see her there at all. All the babies were white. I asked the nurse, "Which baby is mine?" She said, "Oh she was transported to another hospital which have better facilities to deal with her. She has pneumonia and it's dangerous for a child her size." She also said, "We baptized her as a Catholic because there is a good chance she will not survive." I was so angry because they did not consider my feelings or my input into the matter. They did not even let me see my baby before they took her away. If she had died, I would have never seen her.

The people in the hospital treated me like I was poison. I wanted to leave. The reason I wanted to have my baby there is because they brought the new mothers congratulation cakes. They were cutely decorated little sheet cakes. Doreen had her baby at the hospital. When we visited her, they brought the cake in. I wanted to get a cake and was convinced to have my baby there.

The lady who was in the room with me had a ten-pound baby. They brought her a cake. They also brought her all kinds of gifts like diapers, safety pins and rattles. They did not bring me anything. They treated me as if I did not have a baby at all. Even when they brought the woman's baby to her, they would close the curtains around me as if I were contaminated. Finally, my doctor said I could go home. I wanted to see my baby. I named her Chelle.

The day I got out of the hospital; Bob came with my father to pick me up. I could not believe my father and Bob were riding in the same car. When we got back to the house, my father hugged me and said, "I will now accept Bob if you love him." He was telling me he wanted peace. I was thrilled my father was trying to make things better.

I wanted to tell my father, "I hate Bob." I wanted to tell him how bad he treated me, and now since the baby was born, I felt doomed. However, I had a love/hate relationship with Bob. I always wanted to defend him. He had a way of charming me and then putting more fear into me than I thought was possible.

Bob wanted to see my stitches. I told him, "Not now, and please leave me alone." I was in a lot of pain. Bob reminded me by saying, "Hey, Sonny Boy, I can start smacking you upside your head again." I wanted to pick up something and destroy him. I held myself back many times. Bob said, "I want to have sex with you to see if I can burst your stitches." I was so afraid of Bob I did whatever he wanted me to do.

Bob and I went to see Chelle at the hospital they had taken her to. The first time I looked at her, it was through the nursery glass and she was inside an incubator, lying with her head to one side. I noticed her ear lobe looked like it was split in half. I started shouting to the nurse, "Something is wrong with my baby's ear!" The nurse showed me it was pressed down and stuck from her lying on one side too long. The nurse said, "Don't worry, mom, it will pop back to normal." I was so relieved. For a minute, I thought her ears were deformed. The nurse said, "Your baby is doing very well. She should be able to come home in about four to six weeks, or when she weighs four pounds, nine ounces."

After Bob and I returned from seeing Chelle, Bob said, "I have somewhere to go, so sit in the window until I return. If you are not in the window when I come back, you are going to really get it. I owe you, anyway, for all those months you were pregnant." I stayed in the window from six to ten at night. Bob had not come yet. I had to go to the bathroom. I hurried as fast as I could because I was afraid Bob would come while I was away. When I returned to the window about five minutes later, it was my worst nightmare, Bob was standing outside looking up with his arms crossed. When I saw Bob there, I knew I was doomed.

Bob knew my father was not home because his car was not there, and he knew my mom was off drunk somewhere. And even if she had been there, she would not have done anything about the way he was treating me. He knew it was the right time to beat me up, or "get even with me," so he called it. "Where were you?" Bob asked me from the window. I told him, "I had to go to the bathroom." He said, "You're in trouble." "Bob, I was waiting four hours for you."

He said, "I don't care what your reason is for not being there. You were not there, and you disobeyed me." He then told me, "Stick your head out of the window." He walked up to where he was directly under the window, and as he was looking up at me, he said, "I'm sick and tired of you messing up all the time." He picked up a rock and threw it at me. I ducked from the rock and he said, "Oh! Sonny Boy, I know you did not duck. Now I'm going to make you jump out of the window."

We lived on the second floor, and I could have been hurt or

even killed if I had jumped. I said, "Bob I'm not going to jump out of the window." He said, "What did you say?" I knew had I repeated what I said, I could kiss myself good-bye. I kept quiet and stared at Bob awaiting his next command.

Bob said, "Sit in the window with your legs hanging out," which I did. He then said, "I order you to jump." I was sitting there positioning myself to jump, until Mars -- one of Bob's friends who was standing and watching everything -- told Bob, "Man, if you tell her to jump again, I will beat your ass." Mars saw I was going to jump. I know he saved me because Bob was getting a real thrill watching the power and control, he had over me.

Mars saved my life. Bob was awfully upset with me. He slapped me around quite a bit. He told me, "I should make you throw yourself in front of a moving car in the middle of the street." I would have killed myself if he asked me to. How weak I was. I could not wait until my baby comes home from the hospital. I called or went to the hospital to see her every day. I had dreams of running away and taking my baby to a better life. I did not want to bring her home to such horrible surroundings.

My baby and me

CHAPTER 10

STARTING HIGH SCHOOL

When school started in September, I was in the ninth grade, my first year in high school. I went back to school on time. All my friends were surprised to see me. I ran into Barbara Lee. We had a class together. She said, "Arden, I thought you were pregnant." I said, "Girl, I told you it was a rumor." Chelle had not come home from the hospital yet, so I did not have a babysitting problem, but when she comes home, I was not sure how I was going to continue school.

I was going to Hirsch High School, which was a good school. I came in as a freshman. Whenever anyone looked lost or asked where a certain classroom was, the students would encircle them and chant "freshie." So, freshmen had to find our classes without asking. I was lucky because Ava had been there for a year already, and she helped me get around until I found my own way. Also, if a student dropped anything on the floor in the classrooms, cafeteria, or hallway, and it made a noise, everyone would yell out "freshie." It was fun.

One time, Ava asked me to go to the basketball game with her and her friends. I lied to Bob and told him I had to go with my mother to the doctor. The game was so much fun. I loved the excitement of everyone cheering, laughing and having fun. I wanted to participate in all the sporting events. I asked one of the cheerleaders, who was my sister's friend, "What do I have to do to be a cheerleader?"

She said, "Come to a tryout, and if you get picked, all you have to do is come to practice every day after school." My excitement died then and there because Bob would never let me go, and I could not lie to him every day. I wanted to go so bad, but I feared the thought of what would happen to me if I were to disobey Bob. I hated Bob so much. I needed to get away from Bob and my family so I could take care of myself and my child and finish school.

I wanted to stay in school because I really enjoyed going. I went to the office and talked to my counselor, Mr. Carroll. I told him, "I'm having a tough time at home because my parents don't have any money to give me, and I go all day without eating."

He took a liking to me. He said, "I do have a job for you -- working with the Neighborhood Youth Corp." I worked in the program office. I did not make enough money to make a difference, but I needed money for when my baby comes home. My daddy was still supporting me, but I wanted to have enough money myself to buy my baby something.

Mr. Carroll was also my science teacher and he would let me get away with a lot he did not let other students get away with. His class was my first, so I was late all the time. He never wrote me up or gave me a hard time. He even gave me special instructions on exams coming up by telling me what pages to read. I thought he had a crush on me. He made me feel uncomfortable the way he would look at me and stand close to me when we were talking. He never made a pass at me. I believe had he known I had a baby, he would have. I did not tell anyone. It was my secret I kept to myself.

Working in the program office was fun. I had records of all the students and what classes they were in. Everyone started becoming my friend. A student would come in and say, "Hey Arden, what class is so and so in?" These were students who had crushes on certain guys or girls, and they asked me to tell them what time the student would be in a certain class, so they could "accidentally" run into them. I was enjoying school; it was my way of escaping my living conditions.

Finally, after two months, my baby came home. Our living situation was chaotic as usual. Bob would take all my money when I got paid. I told him I was saving so I could support my baby. He told me, "What do you think your father is for?" The day after Chelle came home, my father brought a friend home. It was early in the morning when my father came in my bedroom and said, "Get up, Arden, and fix my friend something to eat." I had to fix him lamb chops with three over easy eggs and fried potatoes (my father's favorite breakfast.)

My dad said, "This man is going to make us rich." Dexter was a singer, and my father was going to be his manager. I saw in my father's face the happiness he would feel if he were out of the life he was living and doing something legal. My father was caught like I was caught. He was a good man and wanted to do what was right.

My dad never meant to cause any harm to anyone. Dope is fast money, but the environment and reconditioning are not worth it because it takes generation after generation to straighten up the mess it causes. I wanted to support my father one hundred percent in taking a chance on trying to change his lifestyle.

Ava came to see my baby and we had fun. Bob saw right away an attraction between my sister and Dexter. Dexter was about twenty years old. He was a very good-looking man, and he knew it. He would say "I'm tall, slim, pencil trim, neat in the waist and cute in the face." He was quite a show-off. He did have a good voice, a Marvin-Gaye-style singer.

Since Bob knew Dexter was not a threat to him as far as I was concerned, then he allowed me to take part in the fun everyone was having. I still had to keep a certain profile. Certain words I could not say, or certain ways I could not put my legs. I could have fun but within my limits.

When Ava was twelve years old, she came to me and said, "Arden I'm addicted to heroin and momma and daddy gives it to me." I said, "Ava stop lying." She said, "I asked momma what it made her feel like and she then asked me if I wanted to try it. She gave it to me, and I liked it." I then understood why Ava was so emotional. She said to me, "The reason I moved is because I was trying to get off drugs and live a drug free life." When at home, she was always having violent fights with my parents because she wanted more than they were giving her. They knew the pain of wanting it and not having it.

I did not see the power of heroin until my parents could not get any. I was about ten years old, and it was the first time I had ever seen them sick because they did not have dope. My mom and dad were screaming, hollering, and moaning. They were making these horrible sounds as if they were trying to throw up. They were saying, "Oh my legs ache, oh my back ache." This went on for hours. I had never been so glad to see their stash of dope come in. I hated to see my parents in pain. I prayed many nights to God to please never let them run out of dope, so they could stay well. Heroin is so powerful even those who do not use it, but are around loved ones who do use it, will pray for the all-mighty heroin load to come in. I hated to see anyone sick because they could not get dope.

Dexter and Ava got into a big argument. I was sure then they were enemies. The next thing I saw, they were hugged up on the sofa together and a love affair was born. Ava moved back into the house because of Dexter. Dexter was also staying there. The situation around the house was starting to get bad. Not only did Dexter turn out to be the man who did not make my father rich, but he turned out to be the man who made my father unhappier. There went my father's dream of getting out of the dope business and into the music business.

My father was against Ava and Dexter seeing each other. Dexter was twenty years old and Ava was sixteen. Dexter was also a heroin addict and wild. I can recall an incident when he flipped out and was running through the house screaming "Kill me, kill me!" It took three men to hold him down while he gained control of himself. He was very violent.

Some months after Dexter moved in, he was drafted into the Army. My sister and he were married the day before he left for Ft. Polk, Louisiana. My father did not know about their marriage until Dexter had been gone for a while. They were married at City Hall, and their marriage ceremony took about fifteen minutes.

They had to stand in a long line for about one hour. Only my mother, my daughter and I attended the ceremony.

After Dexter was finished with his basic training, Ava left and joined him in Louisiana. Ava and I always kept in close contact. We were like friends. Our age difference is only fourteen months apart. We were almost twins. I hated to see my sister go so far away, because she was my strength most of the time. However, I was used to her being gone because she had only moved back into the house because of Dexter. Shortly after Ava left, my father was arrested and stayed in jail for seven months on a $250 bond. All my mom had to do was come up with the money, and my father could have come home. When my father was home, there was always money because my daddy was a hustler. He always found a way for us to be comfortable.

In jail, my father could not make money. While my father was in jail, my mother was slowly getting off heroin by drinking three or four bottles of Richard's Wild Irish Rose Wine or Mogen David Twety/Twenty (known as Mad Dog Twenty/twenty) a day. Sometimes, she could not think for herself. Wine made her simply mindless. Most of the time, she was slumped over in a corner somewhere.

My mother broke up with Mitch and started dating Mars, who had moved in while my dad was in jail. I hated Mars so much. Even though he did stop Bob from making me jump out the window, I still could not like him. The first time I saw Mars and my mother in bed together, I nearly went crazy. I walked into her bedroom, saw they were in bed together, and screamed, "Mom, wake up! I can't believe you're in bed with this man!" I called her a tramp and a slut. She called a woman who cheated on her man sluts. "Some example you are setting. You told me not to cheat on my man, and here you are cheating with a bum. My dad should be here. I'm ashamed of you."

Bob had moved in also when my father was in jail. I had him full time. He would beat me if Chelle pooped and it took me too long to change her diaper. He was totally flipped out. I found myself surrounded by flipped out people.

CHAPTER 11

FED-UP WITH HIM

The summer came and school was out. I do not know how I made it through. Mr. Carroll said, "You missed a lot of days and somehow you passed all your classes except Algebra. You will have to take it again." I could not concentrate on school. I went because I got paid and I needed the money. Mr. Carroll then asked, "Do you want a summer job? I can help you find one." He helped me get one in the office of a daycare center. I had fun working there, and all the teachers really liked me.

When the job was over, I went to visit my family in Climax before school started. Gia called and said, "We want to see Chelle. She's a year old and we have not seen her since she was born." I really needed to get away because my father was still in jail and living with my mother was not so good.

Since Bob did not mind if I went to Michigan and I wanted everyone to see Chelle. I took my baby and we went. I did not have much money, but I still had two checks coming to me from the Board of Education for my summer job. When the checks came in the mail, my mother was going to mail them to me. Both checks were over $100 because I worked full time during the summer. A few times I could take Chelle to work with me, so babysitting was not a problem.

While in Michigan, I waited and waited, and I never received my checks. I called my mother and she said, "Those checks never came in the mail." I stayed in Michigan for the month of August, which is a long time to be without money. My grandfather helped me a little, but he said, "Everyone should take care of themselves." I said, "Grandaddy, I promise I will pay you back."

When I returned to Chicago, my checks still did not come. Also, upon my return, my mother informed me, "We have been evicted and I'm expecting the Marshalls to come any day and put our stuff out in the middle of the street." My mother got on welfare and found an apartment. The apartment was small, nasty, filthy, dirty and infested with mice and roaches. It was located upstairs from where the Blackstone Rangers held their meetings. I did not want to live there, especially since Mars was going to live there. I stayed in the old house by myself with my baby. I was going to stay there long as I could; however, there was no heat, so I could not stay there because the weather was starting to turn cold.

It was time for school to start again. I was to be in the tenth grade. I wanted to return to school. I wanted to make up my class credits, and I wanted to become fully involved with my schoolwork. But I had a problem -- I did not want my mother to babysit for my daughter anymore -- so I was unsure of what was going to happen.

Bob was going through some changes because Sherry ironically met a guy in New York and was expecting to have a baby by him. Bob told me, "I think we should get married." I thought, I could live with Bob then I would not have to live with my mother and Mars. However, I could not bear the thought of living in Bob's house of morbid. Whenever I went over there, everyone sat around and did not say anything to anyone. They never talked to me at all. Sometimes, it was as if I was not there.

I went to Bob's place and he said, "Let's go get the blood test, so we can get married." I started telling him about what happened when I went to the Board of Education to report my missing checks. I said, "The Board of Education said they mailed my checks and they had been cashed." I told Bob, "They took samples of my handwriting and said I will get my money back as soon as they get the handwriting analysis back. They also said they will make an investigation and prosecute who ever forged and cashed my checks."

Bob said, "I stole your checks." I got so angry! "Bob, I had to live off my grandfather with my baby for four weeks!" Bob started getting mad at me and said, "You better watch your mouth before I slap you." Chelle was sitting on my lap. I then said, "Bob, I hate you for taking my money." When I told Bob I hated him, he looked at me and said, "You are in a world of trouble." Bob had a family dog who was vicious. He told me, "Since you are brave and can talk to me this way, then you better go outside and pet Lacy," his dog.

Bob's dog did not know me, he was a huge German Shepherd and he would have attacked me. I told him, "I'm not going out there and pet your dog." His family was sitting on the front porch taking in the last few sunny days before the hulk came. Bob and I were on the back porch when he started coming toward me as if he were going to beat me up. I ran into his den and tried to run out of the door. Bob caught me and sat me down on the couch. I still had my baby in my arms. As he was sitting next to me, he started looking me in my face and balled his fist and pressed it on my eye. I screamed and started hitting him.

He was surprised, and so was I because I had never fought back. His grandmother came into the den because she heard me scream. When she got back there, with her southern accent, she said, "Bob, na why is you beatin on dhat dhere gal?" She made it possible for me to make it to the front door to get out.

Bob ran behind me and when I got to the front door, as I was walking out, he took his foot and kicked me out of the door. His family was still sitting on the front porch. I went tripping out of the door with Chelle in my arms. I was so embarrassed for them to see me being treated so horribly. I was so angry. I could not put up with it anymore.

I walked around the neighborhood with my baby. She was beginning to walk. People stopped me and said, "Oh, she is so cute." I wanted to do some thinking. I wanted to go to school, which meant I had to live with my mother, and I could not put up with her. I was fed up with drunk and disorderly people.

I was forced to live with my mother. Little did I know moving there was my exit cue from Bob. The neighborhood we moved to was Blackstone Ranger Territory, and the area was off limits for Bob. When I told Bob where my mom had moved to, he said, "I can't come over there because the Black Stone Rangers will beat me to death." "But Bob you are not in a gang." "I can't be caught in their territory. You will have to visit me." Sherry came back to Chicago to have her baby. By Sherry coming back, it took Bob's attention off me because he started spending a lot of time with her. He still demanded I see him, but I really wanted to totally break away from Bob.

Shortly after moving in with my mother, Bob received his draft papers and had to go into the Army. Also, Sherry and Bob were married. Bob said, "When I told Sherry I was drafted, she cried, and when I told you; you didn't cry, so she loves me the most, so I married her." Hurrah! I was finally rid of Bob.

All the time Bob and I were together, the thought of us being apart simply terrified me. I knew I would have died if Bob ever left me. Well, to me and everyone else, I was glad he was OUT OF MY LIFE!! With my daughter, I had a lot of responsibility and work to do.

Bob

CHAPTER 12
MOVING OUT AND MOVING ON

After the summer, I could go back to school, but it was extremely hard for me to concentrate on schoolwork. Many days, I could not go to school because there was no one to watch my baby. My mother would not drink some days and could watch her, but it was seldom. It was impossible for me to continue school.

One day when my mother was babysitting, I came home to find my baby with a huge burn on the side of her face. I screamed, "What happened?" My mom said, "She was trying to blow the light bulb out, and it fell over and burned her left cheek." It was a horrible burn. Her skin was still stuck to the light bulb. I was so angry. I had to figure out something because I did not want my baby home without me anymore.

I went to look for a part-time job. The first place was a Walgreen Drug Store. They needed a cashier. They gave me and two others a series of tests but only one of us was going to be hired. I did not have enough money to take the bus back home and it was too far to walk. I was fifty cents short. In training for the job, they let us work with real change. The bills were monopoly dollars. I took fifty cents out of the cash register and put it in my shoe. I was so frightened because I thought they would know.

After the testing was over, I started walking out of the door when the lady who was training me called me back. I was so afraid. I thought she knew I had taken the money. I knew I was going to jail. However, she said, "You did well on the test, and I want to offer you the job." I said, "Can I work every day after school?" She said, "Oh I'm sorry, the job is for full time only starting tomorrow morning at eight o'clock sharp. Will you be here?"

I wanted to continue to go to school, but I needed to work too. I took the full-time job and become a high school dropout. I thought it was best because then I could make enough money to put Chelle in daycare. At fourteen months, she was already potty-trained, walking and talking. I did not think it would take long to find daycare for her. For my first few weeks at work, my Aunt Doreen babysat for Chelle.

Doreen had gone through a drug rehabilitation program. Her husband found out she was using heroin, and he talked her into getting help. Her daughter, whom she named after me, was four months older than my daughter, so my aunt had to straighten up her life and become a good mother to her child.

After my mom's brother was found dead from an overdose, Doreen became a born-again Christian. In fact, Doreen suddenly became so saved until all she talked about was Jesus and God. She became a religious fanatic. It did not take me long to find a daycare center for my daughter. They would pick her up in the mornings and drop her off in the evenings, which was perfect because if I had to take Chelle on the bus she would cry and scream trying to squirm out of my arms so she could roam on the bus. It was embarrassing but I did what I could.

At my job, I was starting to meet friends and to really enjoy my life. I still had the situation at home with my mother. My father had gotten out of jail and was trying to get himself back together. When he got out, he immediately started using heroin again. He was in jail for seven months and had been drug free.

He could have walked away clean, but the desire to get high was still there. My father could help me out a little, financially. He did not have a lot, but he had twenty or thirty dollars here and there. Also, he was trying to get his dope business back in the swing. My dad got a small place not too far from where we lived. I went to his place to visit him and he told me as he was crying, "Arden, I'm so very hurt because while I was in jail, I lost everything. I lost your mother, our home with all my possessions. I lost all my customers too." All I could do was hug him and say, "I love you daddy. You did not lose me, and everything will be OK."

At home with my mother, things were very chaotic. I never knew what to expect when I got home. I hated every moment of living where we lived. My mother had made friends with some of the Blackstone Rangers, and they would be in our apartment when I got home from work.

I brought a friend home with me, a co-worker. I knew I should not because as soon as we went inside, there was a strange and very tall man there. I did not know him. Even my mother did not know him. He walked up to me and said, "I want to do it to you" – but not in those words. I told him, "You are crazy and get the hell out of my face." The next thing I knew, he was taking off his clothes and trying to force me to lie on the bed. I started yelling, "Mom this man is taking his clothes off and trying to rape me."

Mars came into the room and said to the man, "Put your clothes back on man what's wrong with you?" The man started yelling obscenities at me. Mars said, "Arden, leave the apartment," because they could not control him. I left. Again, I was sorry I had brought someone home with me.

I went to the public telephone across the street and called the police. Whenever the police were called, it was a miracle if they came. Since we lived in the same building where the Stones held their meetings, it was an area the police department did not deal with. The blacks were killing each other. However, because I sounded sincere, they came.

I went up to the apartment with the police. When we walked in the door, Mars had tied the guy up. He was in the nude and still yelling obscenity. The police could not reason with him, so they called an ambulance and had him taken to a psychiatric hospital. We found out later he had taken some acid and was "trippin." Once again, Mars saved me. Had Mars not stepped in the guy could have overpowered me.

I soon left Walgreen's and got a better job working at a shoe store. I had a terrible experience working at the shoe store. A woman came in to exchange her old torn up boots for a new pair because she fell down the stairs and the heel broke. The boots were over a year old. She was very indignant. My boss was going to exchange the boots to get her out of the store. She overheard me telling my coworker with an attitude, "Hum if I was him, I wouldn't give her nothing." I did not mean for her to hear me. She walked up to me and said, "What did you say?" I repeated myself and she slapped me in my face and said, "I will be here when you get off to kick your ass."

I prayed to find another job where I would not have to work with angry people. I did find a job at Spiegel's, which I considered to be a step up from a store clerk. I was happy with my new job. I met some friends and they invited me to a bar everyone went to after work. It was my first time in a bar. I was only sixteen years old and I did not want anyone to know I was so young. The bartender came and asked me, "What would you like to drink?" I said, "I'll take a strawberry pop." The bartender giggled and said, "We don't serve strawberry pop."

My friends told me, "Get what we are getting, a screwdriver." I did not know what a screwdriver was, but I ordered it. I thought I would die when I took a sip out of the glass. I did not have the slightest idea the drink was going to have alcohol in it. I said as I was spitting out the drink, "This has alcohol in it." They laughed at me. It was the first time in my life I had ever tasted alcohol. It was so nasty. I do not see how anyone could drink it. I then said to the waitress, "Excuse me, I will have a Coke please."

There was a man in the bar I kept my eyes on. He was cute and he seemed to be looking at me too. My friend Jamie said, "I have a date for you and he's going to give us a ride home." When we got into the car, the front seat was reserved for me because I was being set up with the driver, Larry Shaw. I looked in the back seat and there was the cute guy who I was admiring all night. He was Larry's running buddy. I was a little disappointed because I did not think Larry was cute at all. Jamie was telling

Larry's friend Billy, the one I liked, "I'm going to fix you up with my sister." He seemed excited to meet her. I wished she were fixing me up with him and her sister up with Larry, but Larry did have a car.

When I got out of the car, he said, "I definitely want to see you again." I was not anxious for a man or sex. Bob was enough for a lifetime. I kept seeing Larry. I had a problem being late for work almost every day. I was on probation for my tardiness and my boss said, "If you're late one more time, I will have to fire you." I took after my mother because her boss said the same thing to her. So, to help me, Larry started picking me up for work in the mornings. He lived four blocks from me, and we worked at the same company. Jamie and Fred, Cheryl and Billy and Larry and I all started going out on dates together. We had lots of fun. I enjoyed being with them.

I never wanted to be bothered romantically. Larry and I fought all the time about sex. I was not ready. I had a coil inserted for birth control, so I knew I was not going to get pregnant. Larry was patient with me; he was nice to me also. Finally, I did indulge in sex with him. He asked me while we were in the middle, "Arden does this feel good to you?" I was puzzled and said, "Is sex supposed to feel good?" Larry said, "You have a two-year-old baby and you don't know sex is supposed to feel good?" Bob always made having sex with him the worst part of my life. When it became time for sex, I knew it was time for me to get beat up. I could not imagine sex feeling good.

I kept dating Larry because of the ride to work. It was much better than taking the bus. I was sixteen when I met Larry and he was twenty-four years old. I did not dare tell him how old I was. I told him I was twenty (the age on my ID.) Larry would come over and I did everything I could to keep him from finding out how old I was.

Larry liked my daughter a lot and I wanted to keep him because I thought I needed him. However, every time we had sex; I did not enjoy it. An older lady at work said, "Honey, it is all in your mind." She did not say it to me, but I overheard her say it to someone else. I tried to put it in my mind to make it feel good. It took practice, so I always pretended to enjoy him because I thought he would beat me if I did not.

When Larry and I would talk, if he moved him hands around, I would start shaking and jumping. I kept watching his hands because I thought he was going to smack me. Larry said to me once, "Why are you so jumpy and nervous all the time? Do not worry. I will never hit you." I did not tell him about Bob. I kept it to myself.

Larry and my mother never got along. My mother was hard to understand; one day, she could be the nicest, sweetest person in the world to you, and the next day, she could threaten to kill you. Many times, Larry would come over and end up leaving in anger because of something my mother said to him. For example, once my mother found some old torn-up coat in an alley. When Larry walked in, she asked, "Larry, do you want to buy this coat for $50?" "No, Geo, I don't want to buy it." "What the hell do you mean you don't want to buy it. This is a good coat." The next thing I knew, my mother was cussing at Larry and throwing things at him. I was so angry with her.

Larry knew all the problems I was going through at home because I told him. He lived with his sister, but on weekends, he would rent a hotel room. I would bring my daughter and we would stay together. Sometimes Larry would not spend the night in the hotel, and it was Chelle and me. Larry had four sisters, and every weekend, we would go to one of their homes for dinner. One of his sisters, Dana, asked Larry, "Is marriage in your plans?" Larry said, "Perhaps." Then he added, "First, we are going to look for an apartment." The two of us had never discussed living together. Later, I told Larry, "You will have to marry me before I will live with you." I had in the back of my mind what my mother once told me: "Never live with a man first because he will never marry you."

Larry would go to the horse races and make bets. He would borrow money from me because he had lost all his at the track. I did not have much money to give him, but I did help him out a few times. He would get angry with me if I did not give him money when he asked. He never tried to hit me, but he would ignore me or annoy me. Larry was not demanding; neither did he put fear in me like Bob did. Also, I knew Larry would take me out to some place nice and spend his money on me.

We all went out and Larry got drunk. I did not know how to drive, and Larry was too drunk to drive me home. I got behind the wheel and I drove home. I did not do too badly. I only sideswiped a couple of parked cars. I did not even stop to see if any damage was done. I kept driving until I made it home safe. I had the hardest time getting Larry to the apartment. It had been raining and it was real slushy and muddy. I did not want to take a chance on parking out front because the street we lived on was a busy street. I did not know how to drive-less known-how to parallel park, so I parked in the backyard. There was so much mud in the backyard. Larry and I fell a few times while helping him up the stairs. We were a funny sight. We were completely covered with mud.

When Ava left her husband and moved back home, she and my mother started dealing and using heroin together. I hated to see Ava get addicted to heroin again. I prayed she would stop using. Ava and I would always argue. She told me, "You think you're a real Miss Goody Two-Shoes." She would really tear into me trying to fight me. Ava criticized how I took care of my baby. She would say, "Arden, you are not a good mother," and other harsh things when she had been drinking or using dope. She gave Chelle a drink of wine and got my baby drunk when she was fourteen months old. I was so angry with Ava for giving my baby wine.

Ava said to me, "You should toot some of this heroin up your nose. It will make you feel really good." I did try it. It was pure heroin. It was the "P-Funk" uncut. The P stands for (pure) I tooted the heroin in my nose, and I got so high. However, I was fortunate because it made me sick. I could not determine where or how it felt good. I hated feeling like something was controlling me. I could not stand up straight. Everything seemed to be going in slow motion. I could not control my baby who was running around the house. I threw up and broke out with red dots all over my face. Even my eyes had red dots in them. I was sure I would never try any again.

Despite all the problems Ava gave me, I was glad she was home. She had been gone for about six months. We were talking in bed -- the bedroom had twin beds -- and were about to go to sleep when she reached to turn the light off. I said, "Ava, can we leave the light on? I'm afraid of the dark." "When I was in Ft. Polk, Louisiana," she said, "I would never turn the lights off, either, because I was afraid of the dark until once I was rolling over in bed at three in the morning, when I noticed a man peeping at me through the window."

She screamed, and the man started laughing and hitting the side of the house. Her husband was not in the barracks because of an assignment. She said, "There were about four apartments in the little hut where we lived." All the women from those apartments would sleep together because the 'Peeping Tom' had not been caught yet. Ava said the man would come every night to terrorize them.

She said, "The house was on stilts so sometimes he would get under the house and beat on the bottom, and he always knew which apartment we were in. He never came around when our husbands were there. He was never caught." She said, "Because of him, I would never again sleep with the lights on. The only reason he looked in my window is because he could see me because the light was on." Since Ava frightened me, I never sleep with my lights on.

I noticed my mother hiding money in my closet. Later Larry came over. He was desperate for money. He asked, "Can I borrow some money from you?" I said, "I don't have any money Larry." I then mentioned, "I saw my mother hide some money in my closet." Larry talked me into giving him the money by saying, "I swear I'm going to win the Daily Double and I will bring the money later." It was $110. Well, to no one's surprise, he lost my mother's money and did not have any way to pay it back.

I was hoping my mother would not notice the money was gone until I was able to put it back. A couple of days went by, and finally my mother went to get her money. She started crying and asked me, "Arden have you seen my money I hid in this closet the other day?" I said, "I never saw the money. Maybe Mars stole it." My mother said, "I know Mars would never take my money." I then said, "Maybe one of your drunken friends found it and stole it." Somehow, I could not fool my mother. She said, "Arden, I know you took my money." She was so angry with me. I could not lie to my mother.

The situation reminded me of a time when I was five years old, and I took two nickels out of my mother's coin purse. I hid them on the inside of my dresser. I took the drawer out, rapped the nickels in some tissue and hid the money. I then put the drawer back in. The next morning, I woke up and went to get the money and it was gone.

My mother came to me and said, "Arden, I couldn't find the nickels in my coin purse yesterday. I cried all night and was upset. Then suddenly The Good Fairy appeared and told me where my money was and who took it." I believed her because there is no way she could have known where I hid it. My mother knew I had taken the money. I said, "I'm sorry Mommy. I promise to pay you back."

My mother became furious with me, she said, "Leave my apartment and I don't want you to ever come back again." I called Larry in tears, "Because you can't give me back the money, my mother is kicking me out of the house, and I have to leave now." He said, "I'm on my way to get you." He came to pick me up and we went to the cheap hotel we always went to. He told the clerk, "We want to rent a room for a week." They charged us $21. Larry and I were both working, and we thought we would save up enough money to move into an apartment. There went my dream of being married before I lived with him.

I did not call my mother for a while. I wanted to have the money for her the next time I saw her because I was too embarrassed. She finally called me at work and said, "I want you to come back home." She also said, "Dexter is now home from the military." When she told me he was back, I did not want to go home. I told her, "Larry and I are going to get married and find an apartment together." I was away from all the drunken bums, the dope fiends and the fights. I did pay my mom back.

A few days after my mother told me Dexter was back; she called me and told me, "Ava stabbed Dexter seven times. She didn't kill him though." I was glad I was away from all the commotion. However, there were some people who lived down the hall from us and they would fight all the time. Turns out they were men dressed like women. I do not understand how the men could not tell the women were men because even dressed as women, to me, they still looked like men. They were tacky, dirty and ugly. I never understood their tacky wigs they wore. Their real hair had to look better.

The transvestites would lure men into their hotel room, and when the men discovered the women were men, the fighting and cussing would start. I was grateful I had no part of the violence.

CHAPTER 13
THE SO CALLED "MARRIAGE"

Larry and I lived in the rattrap hotel for months. There were many nights when he did not come home. Larry once told me, "If I ever stay out all night, call the morgue because I'll be there." I thought he was saying, the only way he would stay out all night is if he was dead.

The first time Larry stayed out all night, I thought he was dead somewhere. Crying, I called his sister, "Dana, Larry is dead." She said, "Oh God what happened?" I said, I'm not sure because I have not called the morgue yet." She said, "I don't understand." "Larry said if he stayed out all night to call the morgue." Dana laughed at me and said, "Girl, Larry is okay. He'll be home soon." Three o'clock in the afternoon, he finally came home.

I fussed at him and said, "Larry, I'm humiliated and embarrassed because you said to call the morgue if you stayed out all night. I called your sister because I thought you were dead." Larry laughed but then started yelling at me because the laundry was not done yet. I felt awful because I knew I had trapped myself into a living situation I did not want to be in. However, I did not want to go back home, so I put up with it.

I was afraid of being alone. The place was infested with mice and rats. The crack under the door was so wide the mice ran back and forth all night. In fear, I would feed them so they would not eat my baby and me. I thought, at least they were full. It did not occur to me feeding them meant they would keep coming back. Who does not like a free meal?

Whenever Larry came home, we argued. I wanted to move out. Larry gambled all his money away. I saw we were never going to save enough money to move. Mind you, though, it was better than living with my mother. I was fired from Spiegel and got a job at the University of Illinois Hospital working in the cafeteria. I made more money there — not enough to make a big difference, but enough to pay rent in a better place. I had to be at work at six o'clock in the morning, which meant I left the hotel at four-forty-five. Larry never took me to work, though he could have and still gotten to work on time himself.

I was afraid walking alone to the train station so early. It was dark. I usually made myself aware of everything around me. One day, however, a man appeared from nowhere and said, "I have a gun, so you better do whatever I tell you to do." I was too frightened to say a word. He started taking me up some stairs to a building. I thought to myself if he takes me to the top of the steps, I am going to scream my head off because I could see people at the top of the steps. It was as if he read my mind because he started taking me back down the steps.

I knew he did not know what he was going to do to me or how he was going to do it. He started walking me around the corner and he motioned for me to go down a dark spooky-looking alley. I signaled back with body language, I am not going down an alley. For some reason, he did not make me. Instead, we walked past the alley. I then started talking. I said, "You know, I had a baby two weeks ago." He did not comment. Then I said, "I have cancer and I'm going to die soon." He asked, "When are you going to die?" I told him, "Soon." My intentions were to tell him since I am dying soon, it does not matter when. I was then going to start screaming and running.

However, it did not happen. He took me into a hallway of an apartment building. Before he had a chance to do anything to me, I thought about a woman I worked with who had epilepsy. She had fits and always needed her medicine. I mimicked her by lifting my purse and slurred, "My purse! My purse!" Then I stuck my tongue out of my mouth and starting hissing. I said, "I need air, and medicine from my purse." I remember him asking, "What is the matter with you?" The next thing I knew, I was out the door and running away. He ran after me and caught me. I screamed at the top of my lungs. He let me go and I started running again.

I ran straight to the hotel. I was expecting to be shot in the back, but I did not hear any gun shots. I did not even turn around to see if he had a gun or if he was chasing me. I was running as fast as I could – screaming and crying. I was passing people walking down the street. I know they were wondering what the matter with me was.

When I got back to the hotel, which was about three blocks away, I ran in screaming and yelling to the clerk, "Call the police." The police took a report. The police asked me if I was still going to work. I was upset, but I still had to go to work because it was a new job and I was trying to make a good impression.

The officers drove me around to look for the guy. He was nowhere to be found, so they took me to the train station and waited with me until the train came. I had a big bruise and scratch on my face. My other injury was I was so frightened. I was grateful he was not able to rape me or hurt me. I now wanted to move more than ever.

Another incident happened on my adventures to work early in the morning. I saw a man waiting for a ride. I saw him get picked up a few times. One morning, I passed him, and he was masturbating. I started running as fast as I could past him. The next morning, I did not want to encounter the same experience, so I decided to cross the street before I reached the point to where he would be waiting. However, before I got to cross the street, there he was in a different spot, playing with himself again. I was worried because I thought he was going to try me next.

I called my mother and mentioned the situation to her. She said, "Call the police and tell them." The police said they would check the situation out at that time. The next morning, I never saw the police or the man again. I wanted to move out of the hotel so bad. I told Larry I was very tired of living there and we needed to move immediately. Larry criticized everything I suggested. I had hoped he would try to look for a place or help me look, but he never did anything about where we lived.

An awful thing happened to my mother. She had to move because the Blackstone Rangers broke into her apartment. They raped my mother and beat Mars and one of his friends up. Ava and her husband were not there. Mars' friend had to be hospitalized. They broke one of his legs and some of his ribs. Mars was okay, but his face was disfigured. For the first time since I have known Mars, I felt sorry for him.

Mars knew where one of the gang members lived. He went over there and kicked their door in. He had a gun. He said, "There were two people lying in the bed sleeping. I took the gun and shot at both people in the bed. I am not sure if I shot the people or not. I'm not even sure if they were the right people." My mom and Mars had to flee the apartment immediately. My mother did not even take all her belongings. They were afraid, and they had to get out.

My mother said to me with tears in her eyes, "I lost all of my baby pictures of you kids." Those pictures were her prized possession. She lost everything of importance to her. I comforted her and said, "At least you still have your life. And you know you'll find something better." My mother found an apartment in a nice area of Chicago called Hyde Park. She was better, but still drinking a lot and found more alcoholic friends. Her friends were so disrespectful. Mars was there too. My mother told me I could live with her, but because of her friends, I would not live with her. Meanwhile, I had to figure out how I was going to move because I was so very unhappy where I was.

I went to the garbage room to empty my trash. On top of the garbage bin was a rat about the size of a cat. It stood up on its hind legs and sniffed at me. I screamed and fled. I could not wait until Larry got home because I was going to tell him I am moving, and he could stay in this rat trap if he did not want to move with me.

Of course, he did not come home until the next morning. I told him, "I'm going to find me an apartment today." He looked at me all mean and said, "You ain't gonna do nothing but talk. All you do is run your mouth." I was so angry with him.

After Larry left for work, I went to see my mother. "Mom, I need to move today." My mother said, "Don't worry, I'll help you." As we walked all over Hyde Park looking for an apartment, we ran into one of her friends. Mom asked him, "Do you know where we might find an apartment to rent for my daughter?" He told us there was an apartment for rent in the building he lived in. It was also in Hyde Park and the rent was $95 a month. I knew I could afford it; I paid the rent in the hotel by myself because Larry always gambled his money away. I paid $21 a week.

My mother and I walked to the apartment building. She took the "for rent" sign off the door to the unit. We knocked on the manager's door, and he showed us the apartment. My mother did all the talking for me. Larry still did not know my real age, and we had been together for a year.

I had changed my age from the moment I went to take my baby to the clinic for her three months' check-up. One of the nurses asked me, "How old are you?" I said, "I'm fourteen years old." She got upset with me and said, "You are too young to have a baby. You could not take care of a baby at your age. Have you considered putting your baby up an adoption?"

I told her, "Absolutely not." While I was sitting there talking to her, she picked up the telephone, called someone, and said, "I have a young girl in my office with a baby. She is only fourteen years old. Is it possible for me to take this baby away from her because she cannot take care of this child? She should be in foster care herself."

I was scared and left there as fast as I could. I told my mother, "She wanted to take my baby because she said I was too young." My mother and I went to a notary and swore under oath I was born in 1950 in Water Valley, Mississippi and there was no record of my birth. They made up a document which became my new birth certificate. I went from age fourteen to eighteen.

The manager rented me the apartment. I went straight to the hotel and started packing my things. Larry did not come home as usual. Like a dummy, I called his friend Billy and gave him the address. I knew he would tell Larry.

Larry came to the place after I moved, though I really did not want him to. I wanted to be alone. Before I met Larry, my biggest fears were being alone at night and not being able to support my child and me. Over the last eight months, however, I had paid all the bills and Larry did not come home at night, so I did not need him. Still, I could not bring myself to throw him out of my life, so I let him stay.

After we moved into our new apartment, I thought things might get better between us. My next-door neighbor was married, and she was very much in love with her husband. Whenever we talked, he was all she talked about. They had been married about three years. She was twenty-five years old and he was younger than she was. They had no children. When I saw them together, I could not dare tell the truth. I told her we were married and Chelle was his daughter. I told Larry I was going to tell everyone we were married to spare me the embarrassment.

I did not like not being married and having a child. People always looked at me differently when they knew I was so young with a child. Most comments would be, "You must have been a young hot thing." Most of them assumed I did not know who my child's father was.

Larry criticized everything I did. He said things like, "I will never marry you because you stink, and you never clean the house." He always complained about my cooking. He compared me to his mother. If I cooked a pot of spaghetti, he would look in the pot and start shouting at me because I did not cook anything else along with the spaghetti. He would say, "My mother would cook pork chops with spaghetti." I would get angry and yell back, "Well, my mother would only cook spaghetti with no pork chops." We fought every day about the same things.

I was determined to make everyone think I was married. I worked in the university cafeteria with a lot of older women who would say, "You're living in sin. When are you and your man going to get married?" After I had gone on a week's vacation, I came back to work and told everyone "Guess what, I got married." To make the lie stronger, I changed my last name to Larry's.

My co-workers were angry with me, "Why didn't you invite us to the wedding?" The next day when I came to work, they had a surprise wedding shower for me. I convinced Larry to pick me up from work because I had too much stuff to carry. When I explained to Larry why I received all these gifts, he became furious with me. He said, "I'm going to tell everyone we are not married. Arden, why would you tell a lie?" He even became angrier when he found out I changed my last name to his.

If Larry and I were not fighting about us, we were fussing about my family. He hated my mother, my father and my sisters. Ava had gone through so many changes and lived in so many places, trying to make her marriage work with her crazy husband. For a while they lived in the same building as Larry and me. They moved there after Ava had a beautiful little girl named Asia. I was so happy she was there, but it did not last long; they soon moved.

My father was living in a nice apartment and had a new car. Ava moved in with him, and her husband moved back to California. I was happy to see Dexter go. He had orders to go to Vietnam, but after they found out how crazy he was, they did not even want him in the military.

My mother, Mars, my daughter and I had all been in the car with Ava and Dexter when they brought their new baby home from the hospital. There was a lot of traffic, so Dexter drove down the sidewalk doing fifty miles per hour.

My mom said, "Dexter, why don't you slow down and drive on the road?" He would laugh and say, "If you don't like it – get out." We became frightened of his driving and took his suggestion. We got out and took the bus the rest of the way home. I begged Ava, "Will you please come with us or give me the baby? What if you get into an accident?" She said, "I can't get out or let you take the baby." I said my prayers and hoped everything would be okay.

I hated Ava was strung out on dope by the time she and Dexter separated. My father knew it and still supplied her with drugs because he knew the pain of not having it. Ava was very violent when she could not get any dope. My mother and Ava were on the warpath because my mother and my father were on the warpath.

My daddy was dating our longtime family friend, Chuppy -- the one with large bloomers who used to boost stolen merchandise. My mother felt double-crossed by this, even though she was living with Mars. My mother and father were always close because he still supplied her with dope. Also, my mother was welcome to come to my dad's place anytime she wanted to.

But now my father did not want my mom around because she always started a fight with him, Chuppy or Ava. Ava was having tough times. I was upset every time I went over to my father's apartment because Ava was always yelling and screaming at someone. She and I had a talk. "I'm sad because I love my husband and I miss him and I'm considering moving to California to be with him."

I told Ava in excitement, "I would love to move to California myself because, you know, Smokey Robinson now lives in Beverly Hills!" I thought if I went to California, I could meet him and tell him how I love his music, and I could thank him for being an encouragement to me while I was growing up.

Ava decided to move to California, so we all went to my grandmother's for Easter dinner to say buy to her. Shortly after my mother and I arrived at my father's place, Ava and my mom got into a big cussing fight. "Hey, you guys, it's Easter. Do you have to fight?" They never paid any attention to me. Ava grabbed a knife and stabbed my mother in the arm. About a week later, she left for California. I was both sad and happy to see her go. She had already been gone four months when she finally called to tell us how she was doing and how we could contact her in California.

CHAPTER 14

TO CHEAT OR NOT TO CHEAT

Larry was still up to his old tricks, staying out all night and gambling his money away. He was starting to get weird. He would wake up in the mornings and say, "I feel great because I slept with my eyes opened all night. There was a lot of dust and bugs in my eyes but after they cleared away, it felt great." I thought, 'okay?'

When Larry was gone, I often talked on the phone with his best friend Billy. I liked Billy from the moment I laid eyes on him and it was before I saw Larry. He knew it, too, because I told him how much I admired him the night I met him and Larry. Billy said he had wanted me, too, but we did not dare cross a line we may regret. However, whenever Larry was gone, Billy and I talked. Most of the time we would hang up as Larry was walking in the door.

It was about a year since I had been hired as a food service cashier at the University of Illinois Hospital. I often served food, too, but I was tired of working in the cafeteria. I wanted to work in an office. I remember going around the hospital, staring at a secretary typing and answering phones and wishing it were my job. I applied for every clerical position available. I could not type, so I knew I would never qualify for a secretarial position. Finally, I interviewed and got hired as a file clerk in the medical records department. I was the happiest person in the world.

Prior to getting the job, I had written a letter to God and asked him to please give me the job. Larry read the letter and laughed at me for writing it. He said, "Do you actually think God read your letter?" "I got the job didn't I." At least Larry was reliable in one way: I could always count on him to discourage my efforts and bring me down about whatever I did.

Unlike the cafeteria job where my co-workers were a lot older and we had nothing in common, the people I met at my new job were young and around my age. We had a lot more in common – we liked the same music -- and became friends. When I first started, Carol, Jerrie, and I had so much fun together on the noon to eight o'clock shift. I loved going to work. Larry resented my friends and continued to stay out all night with his friends. As I grew closer to my new friends, I grew further away from Larry.

Larry got into an accident with his car. He was okay, but the car was totaled. I said, "Larry, you know I have some money I have saved in the credit union, and they said if I ever need a car loan, they could help me." Larry said, "Will you buy me a car?" I said, "Under one condition; you teach me to drive." He said, "I promise I will teach you." I knew how to drive because my mother let me drive all the time when I was as young as ten years old and I had the driving experience when Larry was drunk. I needed to practice so I could get my driver's license.

I went to my credit union and they gave me a $400 loan. Larry took the money and bought a car. It was important for us to have an automobile because Chelle had to be picked up at daycare by six and I did not get off until eight. Larry would pick her up and keep her until I got home. He would never come to pick me up from work. There were many nights when I was totally frightened to take the bus home. I had to go through the subway plus catch a couple of busses in bad neighborhoods.

I met a guy one day on my way to work. He was not cute or anything, but I was looking for a way out of the relationship with Larry. He said his name was Dennis and he wanted to give me a ride to where I was going. I said, "I'll take the bus but thank you." He followed me with his car as I walked to the bus stop. "Dennis, I'm on my way to work and I'm married." He said, "I only want a friend. I am not looking for a girlfriend because I am married too. They had a newborn son. He once again asked me, "Can I please take you to work?" I told him, "No," and I went to work on the bus. The next day when I was on my way to work, I saw Dennis again. He was waiting for me. He said, "I thought about you all night. Won't you let me take you to work?" I said, "OK." After he dropped me off, he said, "Can I pick you up?" I said, "Yes" because I knew Larry was not going to.

Dennis and I became friends. I always told people Larry was my husband, so he thought I was married too. One day, Dennis picked me up for work at the bus stop, and instead of taking me to work, he pulled up into a motel. I told him, "I do not want to go into the motel with you." However, I found myself in the room with him. We were about to have sex, but I could not do it. I told him, "There is no way I can cheat on my husband." He said, "Don't worry I understand." He then took me to work.

When Dennis picked me up, I said, "I don't want to see you again." I did not mind being his friend, but I did not want to have sex with him, and I did not want him to try again. A few days later, Dennis called me at work. He said, "I really like you. Why don't you let me pick you up?" "No, Dennis, and please don't call me again."

It was about seventeen degrees below zero. I wanted a ride home because it was so cold, but I did not want to be bothered with Dennis. So, I took the bus. After I got off the second bus, I waited over an hour for the third and final bus. Even my brain was frozen. I was a human icicle.

Finally, I could see the bus coming. I did not have far to go, only about ten blocks. As the bus was coming Dennis pulled up. He stopped and said, "Girl you better get in this car and out of the cold." Sternly I said, "I told you I did not want you to pick me up, and I have been waiting for this bus for over an hour. I almost died standing here waiting for this bus. Do you think after waiting so long for the bus in the cold and now I can see it coming I am going to get in the car with you? I would be stupid." I am sure he thought I was crazy. If he had pulled up before I waited a full hour, then perhaps I would have let him take me. I got onto the bus. At first, I could not sit down because I was frozen. When I got off at my stop, Dennis was waiting there. He said, "Can I please talk to you for one minute?"

I was mean to him and said, "What do you want with me?" He said, "I really want to be with you, sexually." I told him, "I am not cheating on my husband, and I don't want to see you again." I then went home to not-really-my-husband, Larry -- the grouch. Every night, I hated going home.

I was not much of a drinker of alcohol, because I hated the smell of it. Whenever I smelled alcohol on someone, I hated them. It would remind me of my mother and all her friends I disliked so much. Alcohol is so powerful. When my mother was high on heroin, she was okay after she stopped nodding out and falling all over everywhere. But when she was drunk on alcohol, she became mean, hateful, and evil. Alcohol destroyed her sense of thought and control.

I got drunk with my friend Carol at work. I called Larry and asked him to pick me up because I had been drinking. He said, "No." When I got home, after taking the bus drunk, Larry was on the couch sleep. I woke him and said, "Larry, wake up. I am hungry. Take me to get something to eat, right now!" Larry said, "You're drunk. Go sleep it off." I got angry and told him, "You are going to take me to get me something to eat, right now." He refused to budge. I told him, "I bought the car, and you better take me right now or I will take it myself." Ha ha - he laughed at me.

I then took the car keys and went for a drive. It was my first time driving alone, plus I was drunk. I made it to my destination and out of all the people to see, I saw Dennis at the store. He asked me, "Do you still feel the same about me?" I told him, "Yes." We then went our separate ways. Even though, I did not want Larry, I still could not cheat on him. Not with Dennis anyway. I wanted Larry out of my life. He still gambled all his money away every week. I paid all the bills. I figured, what is Larry here for? I did not love him, and he only complained about me. Each day I hated Larry more and more.

I would call Billy every time I got upset with Larry, which was quite a bit. I was usually glad when Larry was gone because then I could talk to Billy. He was my fantasy next to Smokey. Billy told me, "As soon as you and Larry break up, I will be glad to have you for my girlfriend." We all went out to a club. Larry was sitting next to me on one side and Billy was on the other side of me. Billy and I arranged it so we would be sitting next to each other. I pretended I was with Billy, and he pretended he was with me. We were holding hands under the table. I turned around and asked Billy to kiss me, and he did. It was quite a passionate kiss too. I did not even care if Larry saw us.

I ran into the mother of my childhood friend Barbara Lee and got her phone number. Barbara Lee had friends and they had fun going out to parties and dancing. I started hanging out with them. Larry hated me going out with my friends and we argued about it. I would yell at him, "You go out with your friends all the time. I am not looking for another man. I want to have fun with my life." When Larry and I would argue, I would scream at him, "I hate you, I hate you, I hate you, I hate you, I hate you..." until he would leave the house.

The situation between Larry and me was not getting better. I would hate it when he compared me to his mother. I do not care what I did; his mother would never do it the same. When Larry's sister was going to be married in Pine Bluff, Mississippi, he asked me "Do you want to go to the wedding?" I told him "No I don't want to go." He became angry with me. He called his mother and put her on the phone with me. She said, "I'm dying to meet you so I'm personally asking you if you would come to the wedding." I told her, "Yes Mrs. Richards. I will be glad to meet you too." Well, at least I will meet the woman whom I am compared to.

We drove to Mississippi from Chicago without stopping. It was a long and miserable drive. I hated every moment of it. The car was hot and crowded. When we finally arrived at Larry's parent's house, the first thing I saw was a dead squirrel on their porch. I asked, "Are you going to leave a dead squirrel on the porch?" Larry's father came out and said, "Girl shoot that there is my dinner for tonight." I knew then why Larry complained about my cooking. I was not about to kill, clean and cook a squirrel for him.

The house Larry's parents lived in was the nastiest house I had ever been in. In the bathroom, his sister's baby diapers were in the diaper bucket. They smelled bad. I could see maggots crawling in the baby's diapers. Larry suggested we should move to Mississippi. I did not agree with him at all. I wanted to go home. I am from Chicago. I could never get used to country life. It was more like backwoods life. We stayed there longer than we had expected. I did not bring many clothes with me because we were only going to stay for two days for his sister's wedding and we stayed a week. We went out to a club. I did not have anything to wear. Larry's sister said, "I have an outfit you can wear." It was a cute outfit. I put it on, and we went out.

All night, I smelled something bad. It smelled like spoiled fish. I thought it was the person sitting next to me. But later when I went to the bathroom, I realized it was the outfit Larry's sister gave me to wear. I felt awful. I went back to the table and said, "Larry, take me back to the house right away." He was angry with me because I did not want to stay. He said, "Why do you want to cause problems? We are all having fun." I told him, "This outfit of your sister's stinks really badly and it's making me sick." He even got angrier and could not believe it was his precious little sister's outfit smelling so bad.

After we got back to Chicago, our situation started getting worse. Larry was starting to act very weird. He would come home late and go into the bathroom and clean the sink for about an hour. Once I asked him, "Why are you cleaning the bathroom sink at three in the morning?" He got furiously angry and slapped me, and I fell into the bathtub. I told Larry, "I want you to move out." He went crazy. He started turning over the furniture in the apartment. He said, "I will kill you first before I will lose you." Right away, I knew I had to get away somehow. I thought if he did not move then I would.

I secretly started looking for an apartment. Larry found out I was looking because he saw my newspaper with certain apartments circled. He went crazy again. I said, "Larry I love you and I promise I won't look again." I did not mean one word of what I was saying. I neither needed Larry nor cared for him. I wanted out. I was still going to look for a place; I was not going to let him find out. My friends at work were helping me look.

There was a guy I worked with at the hospital, Victor. My friend Jerrie liked him. She would talk about him all the time. I found out he lived down the street from me. I knew Jerrie had a boyfriend, so I knew she did not want Victor. I got off at eight o'clock at night and Victor got off at nine.

Victor asked me, "Will you wait for me to get off work and we can ride the bus together since we only live a block away from each other." I waited, and we rode the bus together. I felt safe with a man on the bus late at night. I started waiting for Victor every night.

Larry was furious one day and asked me "Why are you getting home so late every night?" I said, "I'm getting a ride from someone who gets off at ten at night and I wait for them to get off work." I told him I was scared to take the bus home at night all by myself. He would not take the time himself to come to pick me up, so I wanted company on the bus.

I told Larry, "My coworker takes me home in his car. He is married, and his wife works there, and she is in the car with us." I would not dare tell him the truth we were taking the bus together, and Victor was not married. However, the truth was, I was starting to have a serious crush on Victor. I thought he was so smart.

Victor said, "Would you like to come to my apartment?" I decided to go over. He was an interesting person. He was reading several books at the same time. They were college books, and I had never seen a college book before. He even taught me how to play chess, a game I wanted to learn. I spent the night. We did not have sex, but I did not get home until six in the morning.

Larry had to go to work. Walking home from Victor's, I was saying to myself, "I'm not going to lie to Larry. I'm going to tell him how much I hate him, and how much I want him out of my life." I thought I would tell him I spent the night with Victor. I wanted to tell him the truth about Victor. I wanted to tell him I deserve to be happy and it was time for me to search for my happiness.

When I walked into the house and saw Larry crying and he looked at me and said, "You better not have been out with another man or I will kill you," I hurried up and thought of a lie. "I'm sorry Larry I got drunk last night and had to spend the night at a friend's house." Good thing I said another friend other than Carol because he had gone over to her house at three in the morning looking for me.

Before Larry went to work, I somewhat convinced him I was telling the truth. He said he believed me but wanted to meet the friend I claimed I was with. I played it off and said, "Okay, you'll see I'm not lying. I even got angry with him and started crying and said, "I can't believe you don't trust or believe me."

No sooner than Larry walked out of the door for work, I took Chelle and we went to visit Victor. We spent the entire day with him. He liked Chelle and she liked him. After we left his place, Chelle kept singing, "Victor, Victor, where are you." He was playing hide and go seek with her, so she was singing the song they had been singing all day. I told Chelle, "Do not sing it around Larry." Larry knew of Victor, but he knew of him as the man who gave me a ride home from work with his wife. If he found out we were friends, he would have gone crazy again. Suddenly, I felt more fearful of Larry than I did Bob because I felt he would kill me. I did not think Bob would have killed me. He would have instigated me killing myself, but he would not have done it himself.

I played up to Larry. I told him, "Larry I love you and I think it's time for us to get married and have a baby." Larry always wanted me to get pregnant by him, but I would not remove my I.U.D. birth control coil. I was hoping to make him forget about everything. Larry said to me, "I don't care how sweet you are, I'm still going to investigate your story and meet this friend whose house you were at last night." I still did not get worried. I knew I would think my way out of the situation. I still played up to Larry. I told him we would never part and I would love him forever. He told me the same. In fact, we had a very romantic night.

The next morning, we awoke to a rainy Sunday. The first thing Larry said to me was, "Are you ready to take me over to this friend's house you were at Friday night?" The look in his eyes told me he was crazy, and I should try and get away from him. I still led on like "Okay, let's go." Chelle was three years old. While holding her in my arms, when Larry and I stepped out of the apartment, I took off running. If I could make it down the street to my mother's place, I could be safe. However, Larry caught me. He slapped me around and made Chelle and me get into the car. Chelle was screaming and crying, so he stopped hitting me.

Larry picked up a screw driver from the floor of the car and put it into my hand and showed me a thick vein in his neck and shouted, "Stab me right here in my vein while you have a chance because I'm going to kill you!" He then said, "We are going to take a drive to the Lake. It was winter and pouring rain. I knew no one would be at the lake. I was so afraid.

I told Larry I did not want to go to the lake. We drove around the same block about fifty times. I saw a police car and I wanted to signal to the officer Larry was going crazy. I could not get the police officer's attention. Then Larry turned down another street and, it happened to be the street Victor lived on. Larry was starting to cool down until Chelle (who called me Arden) said, as she was pointing "Arden, Victor lives there. Can we go over to his house again?" Larry got furious and asked me, "You took Chelle to Victor's place?" I said, "No." He said, "Then how does Chelle know Victor?"

He started going crazy again. He was swerving the car down a busy street. It was wet and slippery on the road. I told Larry to please stop because I did not have anything going on with Victor or any other man. I told him, "Larry I love you." He soon calmed down. However, he kept getting excited and would find a reason to threaten to kill me. To get through the situation, I had to keep telling him there was not another man in my life and I loved him.

We soon started back home. For a few days, Larry was holding me hostage. Whenever my telephone rang, he would not let me answer it, or he would hold his foot in my face and tell me, "I will bash your face in if you mention what I am doing." He did not even let me go to work, nor did he go to work.

After three days, he finally let me go to work. I told my friend Carol he is crazy, and I do not want to go home to him. For a week, he would not go to work, and he would be waiting for me at the job when I got off. Only when he suspected I was seeing someone else did he finally take me to work and pick me up. He never gave me a ride before. When there was no competition, he did not care how I got home.

Even when his car broke down and he could not drive me to work. To my surprise, he took the bus with me to work, and he met me after work and took the bus home with me. He was not going to let me out of his sight for one minute. He felt something was going on between Victor and me, and he was not going to give me the opportunity to ride with Victor again.

He even asked me to take him to Victor, so he could meet his wife and they could give us a ride home. I told him, "Victor doesn't work here anymore." He was really giving me a hard time. One day, Larry went into the building Victor lived in and rang the doorbell because he wanted to ask if my story was true about him and his wife giving me a ride home. I was grateful Victor was not home. My only concern was how to get away from Larry.

Finally, Larry came to the realization he could not make me love him. He left and moved in with a guy he worked with. After Larry left, I did not even want Victor. I dropped him like a hot potato. Victor was angry with me because I refused to see him again at work or visit him at his place. I did not want anyone. I needed to be alone.

As far as the new love in my life, it was "*Smokey*," Smokey

Robinson's new album. It was his first solo album without the Miracles. I listened to it again and again and again. The last album I had prior was "Special Occasion," the one Bob broke.

Smokey's singing made me forget all my problems. I would fade into my imaginary world; a world where I was happy and had someone who loved me as much as I loved him. I could only dream about the man who would come into my life and take me away from heartache and misery.

CHAPTER 15

ON MY OWN SO I THOUGHT

I was confident I would survive on my own. My life was simple. I never thought much about buying clothes. I was not into any of the latest styles. I liked to wear suits and dresses. My one struggle was to maintain a decent household for the welfare of my child. I did not spend money on myself except for the one thing I enjoyed more than anything else in the world: buying records.

Chelle is beautiful. She was tiny, impudent, and bossy. Always into something. If she was not biting the neighbor's kid, she was diving off the second-floor porch (escaping with minor bruises.) She was a holy mess to keep up with. She did not stop playing or talking until seven o'clock at night. She would start to wind down, and then would be out like a light and no noise could wake her. She would sleep until six o'clock in the morning and was go, go, and go until seven. I coud time it every time. When putting her to bed, I would tuck her in, give her a kiss, and say, "I love you and have a nice sleep and a sweet dream." She would say the same to me. Ava and I said the same to each other every night when we were kids.

When I got into bed, I would lie there and fantasize while hugging my pillow before I could go to sleep. It seemed as if I resisted going to sleep because I could not control my fantasy when I was asleep. I wanted to lie there and go through what ever adventure my imagination would take me through. I would imagine Smokey was hugging and kissing me and telling me everything is going to be okay.

My friend Barbara Lee started visiting me more. We started going to parties together and having fun. I realized I am a beautiful woman and deserved the best because I had plenty to offer. I still could not dare date more than one man at the same time. I was looking for someone special. Occasionally, Billy would call and try to get something going on, but I could not date him. All the time I was with Larry, I really wanted Billy. However, now since I was not with Larry, I could not date him. The two were still best friends. It would not be right to date Billy when Larry and I broke up on bad terms.

Larry was still calling me and wanted to see me from time to time. Once, Barbara Lee and a couple of her friends and I all went to visit Larry at his new place. Larry asked me, "Would you take some acid?" Barbara Lee and her friends Valerie and Judy all indulged in taking the acid. I tried a little because Larry begged me. He said, "Please try it and you will see it is not bad. It will give you a chance to know how I feel when I take it." I only took a speck on my tongue. I was scared because I knew people were killing themselves. Also, all I could think about was the guy who tried to rape me while he was 'trippin.' I was lucky because I did not feel any effects from what I took.

While everyone in the apartment was high and 'trippin,' as they called it, Larry was in the bathroom cleaning the sink. I then understood his weird behavior. I knew Larry had been taking acid for a long time. All those days when he came home and started cleaning the sink, and talking about sleeping with his eyes opened, it was because he had been taking acid.

Shortly after I got my freedom and was starting to enjoy my life, my mother got evicted from her apartment and I let her move in with me. She was drinking more than ever. We also learned Ava was in prison in California. I hated to hear my sister was in prison. She also did not know where her daughter Asia was. I felt bad for my sister because I did not know how to help her. When my father found out about Ava's imprisonment, he started crying.

He said, "I've been a criminal all my life and never went to prison. My innocent little daughter does one small crime in her life and has to suffer in prison."

I felt my life starting to turn upside down. My apartment was small. The bed pulled down from the wall. My mother was staying with me. There were times in her life when she would drink more than ever, and this was one of those times. Her friends were all the neighborhood drunks. I hated all of them.

My mother came in at four in the morning with about six bums. I had only a few hours to sleep before I had to wake for work. When my mother walked through the door, she pulled the cover from over me and said to her friends, "See, I told you I had a fine beautiful daughter." I screamed at the top of my lungs, "Mom, you and your friends get the hell out of my place right now." She got angry with me and left.

In addition to all the problems I was encountering, my father got evicted from his place. He also came to live with me in my little small apartment. I simply cannot describe the horror. I was a victim of being with parents whom I loved very much but hated at the same time. They needed me to survive. My parents were good parents when they were not on drugs or drinking. They never mistreated me or hit me ever. I was always well taken care of.

I owed my parents what they needed to survive. Even so, I wanted them out my life as soon as they were strong enough to take care of themselves. I wanted the American dream: a nice husband, family, house, car, etc. I was hurting so much inside because I knew I could never have those things if I had to take care of my parents.

I had new friends at work because Carol got a promotion to one of the clinics and Jerrie joined the Air Force. Casey and Duke took their places. The three of us had a wonderful time working together on the noon to eight o'clock shift. During the day, Brian and Steven worked from eight to five, so we would get together and have fun. Mrs. Fleming, our boss, knew we were a good crew; however, she went crazy trying to deal with all of us. Most of the time, we finished our work early so we would leave and go somewhere fun like bowling. We were not given permission to leave; but we left.

We did not have to be at work until noon, so sometimes on payday, we went in early to pick up our checks, went downtown to cash them, and then we would go to work. This one day, we decided to pick up our checks and cash them, but then we all called back to tell Mrs. Fleming we would not be able to come to work. We pulled it off perfectly. We met up and went to the movies to see *Claudine* with Diahann Carroll. Turns out it was the best movie I ever saw. Later, we went to Casey's place and got drunk and partied all day long. I realized I had a crush on Duke. Duke and I had the same last name. If we got married, I would not have to change my last name. I got the impression he liked me too. Steven was cute, but he had too many girlfriends for my taste, I was not at all attracted to Brian, but Brian did like me.

I talked to Casey all the time about Duke. I told her, "I really like Duke and wish he and I could get something going on." It was not long before Casey came to me and said, "Duke and I are starting to date and I hope you don't get mad at me because I know you like him." I did not care. They remained my friends and I never felt angry. I figured if they could have a wonderful relationship, then I was happy for them. Once they came to me and said, "We are in love and want to get married." I said, "Let's go to the Justice of the Peace and you can get married on our lunch hour. My sister got married there." They asked, "Arden will you be our witness?" After they got married, we went back to work.

Duke and Casey would give me a ride home from work every night. I lived quite a distance from the hospital, and they only lived a few blocks away, and yet they would take me home even though it was out of their way. As Duke and Casey gave me a ride each night, I started telling them about the changes I was going through at home. They never believed I was telling them the truth until one day, when they brought me home from work and I invited them in. My mother was watching Chelle for me.

When we walked in, the apartment was all smoked up and a TV dinner was burning in the oven.

My mother was laid out sleep across the bed and Chelle was lying next to her. Chelle was awake. Chelle was four years old. My mother had been taking pills and drinking. She was drunk and had fallen and knocked the TV tray over. The leg of the table ended up in her mouth and had cut the root of her mouth. There was blood everywhere. I was embarrassed my friends saw my mother this way. I was as ashamed at seventeen to bring someone home as I was at five or ten. "This place is too small. Let's find a larger apartment." I wanted to live alone, but I could not turn my back on my parents. A larger apartment would eliminate all problems, so I thought.

After looking for two weeks, I found the perfect three-bedroom apartment. It was still in the Hyde Park area, which I liked. The rent was $175 a month. We would all be able to have our own room. I asked, "Can we please be one big happy family? And please, daddy, don't sell drugs out of this apartment." He said, "I promise I will not sell drugs here." I asked my parents to please not fight each other. They both said, "We won't fight." My mother promised she would not bring her friends to our apartment. I went to work and told my friends they could come over and we could have lots of parties. I told them, "I am going to throw myself the biggest party for my eighteenth birthday. I had all the best music and we are going to have fun."

Steven and I started playing with each other every day. When it became time for him to go home, he would say to me "Bye darling, see you later tonight." I would say, "Okay honey, don't be late." We would never see each other later. We would joke every day with each other. He was complaining about his two girlfriends to me. He said, "My girlfriends are driving me crazy and I don't know what to do." One of Steven's girlfriends lived with him and the other one saw him when it was convenient for him. I told him, "Why not give up both and take me?" I did have a crush on him but something inside of me would not let me pursue him. He was the one thing I did not want: a boyfriend who had several women. However, he came over to my place. He said, "Let's put the joking aside and let's get it on Arden." He ended up staying until four-thirty in the morning.

We slept together. It was not especially great or anything, but Steven sure did turn me on. I was hoping he was taking my advice when I suggested to him to drop both of his girlfriends and take me. The next day at work, he was nice to me. I thought, maybe this is the guy for me. A few days had passed, and Steven asked, "Will you come to a hotel and spend the night with me tonight?"

All day, I was looking forward for the moment when Steven and I would go to the hotel. We enjoyed ourselves. He was very gentle with me and he treated me as if I were special. I was convinced I had fallen in love. A few days passed, and we made another date to go to a hotel after work. And to my surprise before we got off work in walked his girlfriend. Not the one he lived with, but the other one. He then came to me hoping she would not see him talking to me and he whispered, "We have to cancel our date for tonight."

I was furious because I wanted to be with him. She did not know anything was going on between Steven and me, and I never led her to believe anything was. She was there waiting until work was over, so she could leave with him. She was confiding in me about their relationship. She said, "You know he is living with another woman." She told me she and his other woman had physical fights before. I could not see myself caught in the middle. I wanted to be respected more than a woman he took to the hotel.

I started backing off from Steven and let him do his own thing. I found myself arguing with him and I did not feel I was going to win him, so I stopped trying. We did remain friends; in fact, we were good friends. I did not want to have sex with him anymore because when he ignored me and had other women in my face, I could not bear it. Sometimes when we partied together, we might spend the night because of the distances we lived from each other. Once when I spent the night at Steven's place, He said, "Arden, will you sleep with me tonight?" I would not sleep with him. He was truly angry with me, but he knew he was not going to use me for his sexual pleasure.

Two weeks after we moved into our new apartment, a knock came at my back door. It was eight in the morning. I got up to answer the door when a man I had never seen before in my life asked me, "Where do you want this dresser to go?" I said, "You have the wrong apartment." My dad then woke up and said, "Oh Arden, Mickie is going to move in for about a month." Mickie was my father's dope partner. I said, "Daddy, you know this is wrong. You're about to turn my apartment into a dope place." I then said, "I'm throwing myself a party for my eighteenth birthday in two months, and I want her out of this apartment before then." My dad promised me she would be out by then.

We learned Ava was pregnant. I wondered why they would send her to prison when she was pregnant. All she did was forged her signature on a check she stole out of a mailbox, so she could buy herself and her child something to eat. When they found out she cashed a check not belonging to her, she was arrested, and her child was taken away from her. It was her first offense. I did not know exactly how, but I knew I was going to help my sister one way or another.

I do not care what my family went through; we were on each other's side. I would die for my child, my brother, my sisters, and my parents. Nothing was more important to me than my family's happiness and well-being. I started communicating with my sister more. My major challenge with helping my sister was first helping myself.

I remember coming home from work and finding Don asleep in my bed. Don was one of my mother's drunken friends. He never took baths and he smelled like a wine factory. I went into my bedroom, jumped on him, and started beating him. I said, "You nasty bastard, get out of my bed!" He pulled me close to him and said, "I like this, Arden. I didn't know you wanted to go to bed with me." I said, "If you don't let me go, I will get a knife and stab you." I screamed, "Momma, get him out of my house right now!" My mother cussed at me. My father would tell me to control myself and not to get so excited. I did not have no say-so in my own apartment.

I came home from work one-night tired and wanted to sit in my front room, relax, and play some music. I felt good as I walked home from the bus stop. I was singing and wanted to hear the song when I got home. When I walked in, the regular bums were there, dancing and playing my records. I was furious. My mother knew I did not allow anyone to play my records when I was not home.

I stayed cool and walked into the back to complain to my daddy about what was going on in my apartment. My daddy and his friend were laid out on some pure un-cut heroin. I could not get any help from him. I then went back into the front room where the party was going on and yanked the record player cord out of the wall socket. Mars started yelling at me and said, "Arden, you are acting ugly, and God don't like ugly." All the bums started laughing and falling all over the floor. I said, "Mars, you're a bastard. Shut your mouth."

Don took the cord out of my hand and plugged it back in and started walking around saying, "I don't get no respect around here." I told my mother, "Please leave and take your bums with you." She started crying and asked me, "Why are you treating my friends so bad?" She said, "We were having fun until you came through the door. Why don't you leave?"

I started screaming at the top of my lungs. I said, "Daddy if you don't get these bums out of my place, I will call the police and I don't care about the dope in here." My daddy found the strength to walk to the front room, looked at Don (mind you, he couldn't completely open his eyes as they were awfully heavy,) and said, "Don, Man, why don't you get out of here."

Don walked up to my father and told him in a nasty way, "Go back to the back before I kick your crippled ass." My father turned around and went back to the back as if he were obeying Don's command. Every bit of strength left my body. I had sunk to the floor. I had no power, and no one was on my side. I was a prisoner. I would have done anything to change places with my sister, a real prisoner behind bars.

I had met a married couple who would baby sit for Chelle until I came home from work. I would tell them about what went on in my apartment. They felt sorry for me and they volunteered to watch Chelle after she got out of school and until I came home from work. Their daughter went to the same school as Chelle. They helped me a lot by watching her because I did not get home from work until nine o'clock at night and the school bus dropped Chelle off at six.

I left and went to the married couple's apartment and asked if my daughter and I could spend the night. They took me in and told me to make myself comfortable and I could stay as long as I needed to. I only wanted to stay one-night because I knew the situation at home would be different. It would be as if the incident never happened.

Mars

CHAPTER 16

"CALIFORNIA HERE I COME" TO GET THE BABY

I started thinking how easier my life would be if Ava came home. I know she was tired of prison. She wrote me a letter every now and then, but she never told me anything. I knew she was pregnant, but I did not know how many months. I did not know what was going to happen to the baby. I wanted to know the answers to all these questions. I sent her money to buy stationery and stamps, so she could mail me a letter to answer my questions. And she would write me, but she did not answer my questions.

About six months after we moved into our apartment, we got some good news: my sister found out where her daughter was, and she was safe. Ava wrote in her letter, "They put this old lady in my cell, and she told me my daughter was with Dexter's sister, and she was okay." She gave my sister the phone number to where her daughter was. Ava said, "The next day the old lady was gone. It can't be explained except it was a miracle."

I was leaving for work when I met the mail carrier, who had a letter from Ava. I was so excited to get the letter and stopped to read it right away. The letter left me puzzled. Ava told me some negative things. She said she lost her children. She said she will have to put her unborn child up for an adoption, and she is sure her daughter will not remember her. She also said she had nothing to live for.

I felt so bad for my sister. I called the prison to see if I could talk to her. I was going to beg them to let me speak to my sister. But to my surprise, I happened to call the prison hours after they had taken Ava to the hospital to deliver the baby. I asked, "What's going to happen to the baby?" They told me, "Arrangements have already been made to put the baby up for an adoption."

I told them, "No, you let me speak to my sister, right now." I told them I need to hear personally from my sister if she wants to put her baby up for an adoption. They finally told me to talk to her counselor. He was off work. Probably because of my sincere and relentless determination, I was given his home telephone number; information never given to anyone. Fortunately, when I called him, he was happy to talk to me. "I'm glad you're concerned about Ava. She needs the love you are showing her. I didn't think anyone cared for Ava."

I told him, "I love my sister very much and the reason she had no visitors is because she has no family in California. It is a mistake Ava is in prison. She is a nice and good person who never meant any harm to anyone. She was desperate for food for her daughter and herself after her husband was arrested." The counselor said, "You should write a letter and send it to the prison board. It would be in her favor for the board to see she has someone who cares about her."

I asked the counselor, "Is it possible for me to come and get my sister's baby?" I did not want my sister to lose her baby. Her counselor told me he would talk to Ava the next day and would get back to me. I waited very impatiently for his call. He called the next day and told me, "Your sister had a healthy boy. And Ava is happy you're coming to get her baby."

Of course, I could not afford to go to California to get the baby, but I knew I had to go. I worked and paid all the bills. My father sold drugs and made a little money and could help here and there. He was a hustler and he produced $200 towards my airline ticket. My mother had no income only what we gave her. My father and my mother had a strange relationship. My dad took care of her, but he did not love her. His pride would not let him because of the condition she was in all the time, and because of the people she kept company with. My grandfather was my only hope to get the rest of the money I needed. I thought my grandfather did not like me much since I had a baby so young. To his friends and his side of the family, I was a disgrace. My whole family was a disgrace to him, even his own daughter, my mother.

My grandfather resented supporting Clayton and Gia. My father did not send money regularly. I always looked forward to Gia coming back to Chicago every school break. Clayton stayed in Michigan because he worked, plus he was on his school football team and had to stay for practice. Sadly, Clayton's football career ended when he lost his eye. He and his friend were playing with BB guns when a BB shot through his glasses and a shard of glass got wedged into his eye. He had surgery about three times, but he lost the vision.

My grandfather paid all the expenses for the medical cost for Clayton's operations. Although my grandfather did not want to help his granddaughter who had a baby when she was fourteen years old, I called him anyway and asked him for the money to go to California and get my sister's baby. Of course, I did not know how I was going to manage to take care of a new baby.

Since my sister sent me Dexter's sister phone number and she was the only person I knew in California, I called her and told her I was coming to get Ava's baby. Virginia said, "You are welcome to stay with me for as long as you need to." I was not planning to stay any length of time. I wanted to stay for one day. I wanted to get the baby and come right back. However, since Virginia made the offer, I decided to take my vacation and stay in California for a week. I knew Smokey had moved there, and I thought I can catch him in a concert. I had not seen him perform live since I was nine years old and prayed, I would be able to see him there. I thought it would be great to tell him how much his music inspires me. I could not wait to get to California to see my sister, the baby and my niece.

I had so many obstacles getting to the airport. When it came time for me to leave to catch my plane, my father said, "I can't take you to the airport right now because I am waiting for a phone call, so I can cop." Cop is what he called getting his stash of drugs. He could not leave the house to take me to the airport because he had to be there for his dope call.

He finally got his dope supply in. I said, "OK daddy, take me to the airport so I can get on my flight." He said, "Wait until I make these few sales, so I can give you money for California." I canceled three flights waiting for my dad. I was angry I had wasted three days of my vacation before I finally caught an early morning flight. I wanted to get there in the evening after six o'clock because they could not pick me up until then. I got to LA at eleven o'clock in the morning.

When I got off my flight, there was no way I was going to stay in the airport until that evening. I rented a car, got directions and attempted to drive myself. I drove around in Los Angeles for two hours and never found the street I was looking for. I stopped the car alongside the freeway where there were some guys working and I asked for directions. I could not even find a person who spoke English. When I did, they had never heard of the street I was looking for.

I thought I had driven out of California. It was a hot day. Hotter than any Chicago summer day I had ever experienced. I was so aggravated because I was so hot. I could see why the women in California dressed so skimpy. I was hotter than I had ever been in my whole life. Also, my eyes were burning and running. I could not understand what was happening to me. I wanted to find a place and take my clothes off and take a shower or jump into a pool. I did not dress for such hot weather.

I was crying in the car because I was lost. I finally stopped at a gas station. I was trying to get directions from the attendant. He showed me a map and said, "Locate where you are going." I cried, "I can't read a map. I need directions." I could not tell north from south. I stood there crying because the attendant could not help me.

I spotted a man pulling into the gas station He was the first black person I had seen since I arrived in Los Angeles. As I ran to him, I said, "Excuse me, please. Can you give me directions?" He called Virginia to get directions to where she lived. "Not to worry pretty lady, follow me." I asked him, "Do you know if Smokey Robinson is performing anywhere.?" He said, "No" but I know a place I can take you to tonight." He picked me up later and took me to the Baked Potato" When I finally arrived at Virginia's place and was happy to see my niece. Virginia was a nice person. She said, "I'm sorry I couldn't pick you up from the airport. My husband left the car for me to pick you up when you arrived, but I was too scared to drive."

I thought how weird she was afraid to drive, but I did not let it bother me because I was there, in California! I noticed Virginia was drinking a glass of gin and talking loudly. She was on her way to getting drunk. When her husband, Calvin got home that evening, he was surprised I had rented a car. He said, "I left the car with my wife to pick you up." Virginia and her husband started yelling at each other. The next thing I knew, Virginia was crying and said, "I was in a car accident ten years ago and it is hard for me to drive."

I told them, "Please stop arguing about her not picking me up because I made it here fine." I could not get away from drunken insecure people. I told them, "I only came for the baby and I didn't want to cause any trouble." I told Calvin, "Give me directions and tomorrow I'll go get the baby and go straight to the airport." Calvin said, "I will take you. As long as you are here, you don't need a rental car because I will take you every place you need to go."

Everything settled. I called Laura, an old friend in San Francisco whom Ava and I knew when we were nine and ten years old. I told her I was in Los Angeles, and she took the next flight out and came to see me. When we went to pick her up at the airport, Calvin told me to take the rental car back. I had no problem because it was scary driving on the freeway in Cali. - quite different from the Dan Ryan Expressway in Chicago.

After we picked up Laura from the airport and took my rental car back. We went back to Virginia and Calvin's place and partied all night. Everyone was getting drunk. I was having a good time playing with my niece. She said, "Auntie Arden, I'm glad you are here. Are you going to take me to see my mother?"

I felt bad and all I could do was cry. She then asked, "Auntie, can I go back to Chicago with you?" I told her I would love to take her back. I asked Virginia, "Can I take her back with me?" Virginia started yelling and told me, "You better not even think once about taking Asia away from me." I did not want to argue with her, so I decided to let Ava deal with it when she gets out.

Laura said, "I will go to the prison with you to help you with the baby." It was a long and hot drive. Near the prison, we saw cows crossing the road. I thought how much Corona, California reminded me of Climax, Michigan, with the dirt roads and farm life.

When we arrived at the prison, we approached a huge white steel wired fence covering the entrance of a building surrounded by a big wall. A guard stopped us and checked a list, which had my name on it. He said, "The other visitors are not allowed, and they can wait for you in the waiting room." I became emotional and told the guard, "You don't understand, sir; I'm not strong enough to see my sister without my friends. I need them to help me with the baby." I was shaking all over and crying.

The guard must have had a heart because he let Calvin and Laura go with me. We walked into the building and down a long narrow corridor. About one-fourth of the way down the corridor, I saw a sign with an arrow pointing and it said, "HOSPITAL." The arrow pointed straight ahead. My heart started beating fast. Inside the hospital, a nurse went to get my sister and the baby while we waited in a little room. I was watching the door waiting for my sister and the baby to walk through it. There was a prison guard in the room with us. I did not want him there because I wanted privacy with Ava.

When I saw my sister walk through the door with her beautiful baby, I broke down and cried and said to my sister as I hugged her, "Ava, when are you coming home?" The situation was so touching until everyone there was crying, even the guard and the nurses. Calvin and Laura were also crying. It was the most emotional experience of my life. The guard left the room to give us privacy. They let us stay two hours when visiting hours were only thirty minutes in the hospital.

It was a great visit. Ava and I used our pet names for each other; she was Sasha and I was Tasha, or sometimes I was Sasha and she was Tasha, or sometimes we would both be Sasha or Tasha. We laughed about a lot of times in our childhood. We did not talk about a single bad thing. We wanted to remember only the good times. I said, "Ava, I want you to come straight to Chicago as soon as you get out." I told her, "I am going to get rid of the problems so when you come home, we can live a decent life."

Ava said, "I thought I was going to have to lose my baby because I could not find the strength to ask you a question like would you come to get my baby and take care of him until I get out of prison?" I said, "Ava it was meant for me to come to get this baby. If I had not called the prison the day I did, I would not have known you were in labor. The next time I would have heard from you; the baby would have been put up for an adoption. This was meant to be." I told Ava, "Don't worry because I will treat your baby as if he is mine."

My sister and me

CHAPTER 17

MY NEPHEW, MY BABY AND NAM MYOHO RENGE KYO

Finally, it was time for me to leave Ava. The departure was as emotional as the arrival. I absolutely hated leaving my sister behind. They slammed the thick iron doors which separated us. Ava peeped through the little window on the door, and I walked backwards all the way down the corridor until we could not see each other anymore.

I made up my mind I was going back the next day. I did not want to stay a few more days as I had planned. Virginia got drunk again and started complaining about everything. She and her husband had a big fight. I could not wait to get the hell out of their place.

All I could do was cry as I was looking at Ava's beautiful children sleeping next to me. My sister was innocent. All they had to do was make her pay restitution. It was her first crime. She cashed a welfare check she stole out of a mailbox due to desperation after her husband got arrested, leaving her and their child with no money. She had a baby to take care of – plus, she had a heroin habit and she did not know anyone in California.

Ava's husband had a long record of all types of crimes. He robbed a store and was sent to prison. Being in California with no family, and being on bad terms with her parents, Ava did not have much to work with as she fought to survive. I deeply wanted to take Asia back with me. I was tempted to leave in the middle of the night with her and head straight for the airport. But I knew it was in Asia's best interest if she stays in California because Virginia was the only person she knew, besides her mother. I was a stranger. She knew I was her aunt, but she loved Virginia.

I pleaded with my family, "Please let's get this place fit for living. I do not want any drugs around this house." I had a baby to deal with, and I needed their support. Everyone promised to help me make things easier around the place. Also, a week later, Gia came from Michigan for the summer.

Gia helped me a great deal with Chelle and the new baby, Dexter, Jr. However, we nicknamed him Bear. By the time Bear was two weeks old, he had been in three different States. He was born in California and came to Illinois when he was four days old. Also, we took him to Michigan when we went to pick Gia up for the summer.

I wanted my sister Ava home because I knew she could help me get some order in our place. My mother said to me, "I'm going to straighten up my life and support you in taking care of the baby." Still, the dope was there. I wanted the dope out because when Ava's home, she could be sent back to prison or use drugs again due to the environment. I could not change any of my situations. I felt so trapped. I needed a way out.

Gia and I were on our way to the grocery store. I noticed an event going on at the high school across the street from where I lived. A man walked up to Gia and me and asked, "Do you want to attend a free show? The Startells are going to be there." I thought who are the Startells? I then thought he must mean the Stylistics (a popular singing group,) so I said, "Okay, we will go."

We walked into the auditorium full of people and saw a good talent show. Suddenly everyone started chanting strange words. Nam Myoho Renge Kyo, Nam Myoho Renge Kyo, Nam Myoho Renge Kyo... We then realized we was somewhere we did not understand. We wanted to get up and leave but we were afraid to. We hoped if we sat there, no one would notice us. I did notice the people in the auditorium smiled and seemed happy. However,

I did not understand what they were chanting or why. Though I noticed some good-looking men, I still wanted to leave.

The chanting was lasting for a long time. I looked at Gia and she looked at me. As we were getting up to leave, I recognized a guy from my third-grade class with Mrs. Whitlock. Taylor is his name. He said, "You can chant the words Nam Myoho Renge Kyo and overcome all your problems." I looked at him as if he were a nut, and we left. I never thought about chanting again, until two weeks later. I saw Taylor walking down the street in a neighborhood I am never in. I looked up and saw him running towards me shouting, "Arden Hey Arden. Would you attend another chanting meeting with me on Friday night? Then I can teach you about Buddhism and what chanting those words can mean to you."

I thought he was weird. I said, "I'm sorry but I'm Catholic and I can't go to a Buddhist meeting." Two weeks later I was in a completely different part of Chicago when I looked up and Taylor was running towards me yelling, "Hey Arden. You want to go to a meeting and learn about Buddhism and chanting?" I asked him, "Are you following me? Because again, I'm in an area I'm never in and I run into you." I told him, "I don't want to go to a Buddhist meeting." He asked me for my phone number, and I gave it to him.

He called every week to ask me to attend a Buddhist meeting with him. Each time he asked, I said, "No, I can't go." I was sorry I gave him my number. I never discussed any of my problems with him, but he was so sure I was suffering and needed help. I was, and I did, but I thought I covered it up well. Taylor knew something was troubling me. He could see below the surface.

Taylor said, "You don't have to be unhappy. Don't you deserve to be happy?" "Of course, I think I do," was my response. He told me, "Chanting Nam Myoho Renge Kyo will assure happiness in your life." Anyway, all I needed was a Smokey Robinson song and it will wash away all my sorrows.

Barbara Lee and I were in close contact with each other. She was my best friend. She came by all the time, which is how she got involved with one of my father's friends; he sold cocaine, and Barbara Lee liked it. Barbara Lee was like a family member. She had her own place. She had a good job and she was a very smart person. Barbara Lee was always one of the smartest students in the class. She always got straight "A's" on all her test papers. Her mother was a school librarian and she was strict about Barbara Lee studying and doing her homework.

One day Barbara Lee called me crying. She said, "Arden I feel so bad, sad and blue because I got fired from my job." I told her, "When I'm sad my 'Oldies but Goodies' songs I play brings me out of any depression, and perhaps they will help cheer you up. I'm on my way over." We had a good time singing, dancing and snapping our fingers. We smoked a joint a police officer had given her. We were silly and laughing and falling all over the floor. I had so much fun with her. It was like having another sister.

I spent the night at her place and took the bus. It was not until I was home when I noticed I did not have my records. I called Barbara Lee. "Did I leave my records at your place?" She said, "I don't see them." "Oh no! I left my records on the bus!" I thought I was going to die! All my Smokey Robinson songs were gone. I had other songs by various other artists missing too. I walked around in a state of misery for a week.

Losing my records was like losing my best friend. However, one day, while at work, the radio announced Smokey's new *Anthology* Album was at the local record stores. I had the songs back I had lost on the bus plus songs I did not have before. I was elated. I fell in love with Smokey all over again. I would fall in love with him for a while then it would go away, and something would happen to stir the love back up. My fantasy of him was a role model for the type of man I wanted to attract in my life.

We learned Ava was not getting out of prison for about another year. It was hard taking care of the baby. I was hoping they would let her come home sooner, but when her current sentence was up, she was going to be prosecuted for welfare fraud. I wrote all kinds of letters to the governor of California. I wrote letters to the prison warden. I also wrote letters to the parole board. I pleaded for them to please release my sister. I kept sending letters. Gia was writing as many letters as I was.

Larry came by and asked, "Arden, will you go out with me tonight?" I did not mind going out with him; I did not want him to ask me for sex, but sex was the only reason he wanted to take me out. Larry was waiting for me to answer if I would go out with him when the telephone rang. It was Taylor, asking me if I would go with him to a meeting. I told Taylor in a very mean voice, "I'm going to go to your crazy meeting, but I will never go back to another one and please do not ask me again." Taylor got excited and told me he was happy I agreed to go, and he would pick me up.

I told Larry, "I'll go out with you when I get back from the meeting." I complained to Larry about going to the meeting. He said, "Why are you going if you don't believe it?" "I don't know, but something is telling me to go." Larry said, "I heard how mean you were to the guy about going to the meeting. I don't understand why you're going." I told Larry what time to come back and pick me up for our date. I called Barbara Lee. "Come to this Buddhist meeting with me." She did not want to, but I talked her into it.

On the way to the meeting, Taylor showed me a picture of the car he was driving. He said, "I chanted for this car." It was yellow. I was skeptical and told him, "Anybody can buy a car if they get the money." I could not understand where chanting helped him. When we arrived at the meeting, I decided to keep an open mind. There were so many beautiful people with nice smiles who were singing and having a fun time. Some people shared their experiences, and they were all sincere and interesting. An experience or benefit is what one receives when we chant and is designed to fit your life. I was encouraged by the experiences I heard. A woman said, "I have a six-year-old daughter, and I'm teaching her to chant. While I was cooking dinner, I peeked into her bedroom and was thrilled to hear her chanting in the right rhythm."

Later, her daughter asked, "Mommy, can I have some money to buy ice cream?" The mother felt awful because she had no extra money to give her daughter. They say you can get anything you want by chanting. She got angry at the whole concept of chanting because her daughter had chanted for the first time, probably for ice cream, and now she could not have any. The mother had been ready to stop chanting, but the little girl did not think much of the situation and went outside to play. The mother said the daughter came in the house five minutes later and said with excitement, "Look Mommy I found a dollar outside." The mother then realized the power of chanting Nam Myoho Renge Kyo, and she decided to never stop chanting.

Another woman shared an experience where she had been robbed, but the robber did not take all her money. She said he only grabbed what was on one side of her wallet, which was about thirty dollars, and on the other side of her wallet was two hundred dollars, which he did not see. I thought these experiences sounded great, and I was encouraged to try the chant for myself.

The meeting room was filled with approximately three-hundred vigorous, brilliant and energetic people. Everyone was so nice to me. There were people from all walks of life and of many nationalities. They were chanting in unison. I had a good positive feeling inside. People there encouraged me to chant to change my problems.

I was having a conversation with a lady. I told her, "I am not sure if chanting can help me because my problems are my parents and my family. My sister is in prison and I have her newborn baby, and I want to live my own life. I want to go back to school to get my high school diploma, go to college and accomplish something meaningful in my life." She then asked me, "Out of all your problems, which do you want to change the most?" I told her, "My sister's situation is my biggest problem. I want her to be home with her family." "Then you need to receive a Gohonzon," which is a scroll, "and start chanting Nam Myoho Renge Kyo for ten minutes everyday for your sister to be home soon."

Since they did not ask me for money and I did not have anything to lose, I decided to receive my Gohonzon and try the chant. When I told the woman, I was going to try, she started jumping up and down and congratulating me. She said, "I can not wait to hear about all the benefits you will be receiving! Watch all your sorrows turn into joy!" I thought she was crazy because she was all excited, but I knew I needed help and chanting seemed so easy and promising for my future.

At first, I was scared to try the chant because I thought God would punish me. I was not sure about chanting. I had been devoted to God. There were times when I would go to church and pray to God to please help my situation, but I never saw my life change. I only saw my life get worse and worse.

I figured I would try chanting. The Bible says God is very understanding, so I figured if I chanted and realized it was the wrong thing to do, God would forgive me if I asked him to. Besides, I was angry with God. Why didn't he help black people for four-hundred years of slavery? We were taken away from our families, beaten, raped, hanged and burned. I do not think God likes black people because today we still suffer with poverty and environmental injustice.

The Buddhist practice consisted of chanting as many Nam Myoho Renge Kyo's as I could. I would try to do it for an hour. I also had to recite a thirty-one page book called the Lotus Sutra. I had to repeat those thirty-one pages five times in the morning and three times in the evening. It is done in a rhythm; if someone else was chanting with me, we would be in unison. Even if the person did not speak my language, we would still chant in the same language. It is a Universal religion. We chant for world peace through individual happiness.

Frankie said, "The practice takes at least forty-five minutes in the morning and thirty minutes in the evening, which is hard because you have to get up earlier and chant before work and take thirty-minutes in the evening. You must shut off the radio and your television. Chant when you are sick. Chant until your dying day. Chant or pray for your happiness. You get out of it what you put into it."

On my way home, I told Barbara Lee and Taylor, "I am looking forward to chanting and I'm excited to try." Barbara Lee said she, too, would try. I was scared, but I was going to try anyway. I said, "OK I don't want to go out with Larry tonight or ever again."

CHAPTER 18
CHICAGO BYE

When I got home, my mother said in a mean voice, "Ava called today." I nearly fainted because I did not know she could call from prison. She had never called before. Larry was there, waiting to take me out. I was so excited about the meeting. I told Larry, "The meeting was really good. Next week I'm going to another one and you should go with me."

Larry said, "You're crazy. What was the last thing you said before you went?" The last thing he heard me say to Taylor was I would never go back to another meeting with him, and there I was trying to recruit Larry only after my first meeting. Larry said, "I never want to see you again," and he left. I could already see Nam Myoho Renge Kyo working in my life because Larry was finally out of my life. I was looking forward to my sister calling back.

The next day I woke up to try the chant. The phone rang, and it was Ava. She said, "Arden, I'm out. They opened my cell and told me I was free to go. Due to several letters received on my behalf, I was released from prison and sent to a halfway house in Hollywood." I was happy my sister was free. The baby was four months old. Gia had gone back to Michigan for school.

Ava said, "I want to come home, but if I can't bring Asia, then I will have to stay here in California. I do not know how I am going to get home anyway, because I do not have any money. I am happy because I went to see Asia and she was as happy to see me as I was to see her. I do wish I could stay in California because it is so beautiful here. Also, I know I can't legally leave the state because I'm on parole."

I said, "Ava, I will send you the money to come home." Ava said, "I don't want Virginia to know I'm leaving the state, so I don't know how I'm going to get Asia from Virginia because I'm not leaving this state without my daughter." We schemed up a plan. Ava was to wait until I got paid on Wednesday, and I was going to send the money to her by Western Union. I sent enough money for her and her daughter to take the bus home. Ava was going to get her daughter and tell Virginia she was going to take her shopping which is what she did.

Three days later, my sister and my niece were home. After Ava arrived, I still could not believe she was home with her children. We still had the problem of the living situation. My friend Taylor kept encouraging me to chant to reduce all my problems, no matter how impossible they seemed. I told him, "I am sure my sister's coming home was only a coincidence and had nothing to do with chanting."

Taylor told me, "Continue to chant for all your problems, and as they go away one by one; you'll be convinced it is not a coincidence. The more you chant, the faster your problems change. You'll see yourself developing a happier life condition." HA! Happy – me - I could never imagine my life filled with happiness. I thought it would only be achieved in my imaginary world, but I continued to chant because I wanted to see if it would change my life and make me happy.

One month later, out of the clear blue sky, I was evicted from my apartment. I did not understand because we were not late on the rent. I stopped by the real estate office to see if I could work something out with the landlord. He was rude and cold to me. He told me, "You have thirty days to move." I told him, "It's impossible for me to move then."

He then told me "If you can't move in thirty days move in thirty-one," and he offered to give me money to move with if I did not have enough. I was hurt they were willing to pay me to move. They wanted us out of the apartment. I left his office and cried all the way to work. I could not understand. We lived there for two years. It was odd they decided to put us out then.

I wanted to move into a place of my own with my daughter, but I could not throw my family out. I knew they would not be able to take care of themselves. So, I chanted about the situation as my friends kept encouraging me to do. I thought about moving out of Chicago, but where would I go? I could not dare quit my job because I feared I would never find another one. I was lucky the University of Illinois never checked my references because my employment application was full of lies. I had better hold on to the job I had.

I had to talk to Taylor because I was angry. I said, "If I chant, are not good things supposed to happen to me? I'm now facing a situation I'm not happy about." He told me, "Think about your happiness. If you want to be happy then you need to make some drastic changes in your life. Getting evicted is perhaps the greatest thing in your life. It is the means to your happiness." It made me hopeful; however, I did not see it the way he did because eviction was a big problem. He told me, "Don't worry, but do chant."

I called Michigan to talk to my sister, Gia. My grandfather answered the phone. "Hi, Arden. How are you doing?" I told him in tears what I was going through. "Granddaddy, I want to be on my own, but I still need to help my family." My grandfather told me, "Remember you always have a home here with me." I was shocked. He said, "I will talk to your aunt because she has a house you can rent in Battle Creek." My grandfather said he would help me to get myself together. I decided to move to Michigan.

My biggest fear was quitting my job and being able to survive. I still had the problem of not being a high school graduate. I was twenty years old and still did not know in what direction to take my life. Somehow, I felt I could get my life together in Michigan a lot easier than I could in Chicago. Still not knowing what to do, I put my faith into chanting to my Gohonzon, and I decided to not worry and make the move.

I told my family I was moving to Michigan. We had to move,

and I did not have much time. Ava and my mother would get drunk and start confusion. Many times, I found myself double-teamed by the two of them because I would never have a drink with them.

For my own peace and sanity, I wanted to move to Michigan by myself with my child. I wanted my family to be able to stand on their own two feet without me there to make sure they were okay. I could not move alone. My mother, Ava and her two children decided to move with me. I was angry about them moving with me though because I was taking some of my problems with me.

My father applied for and got disability. I did not have to worry too much about him because I knew he had a steady income and could afford to keep an apartment. Also, he had somewhat of a drug business making extra money.

I mentioned to one of my chanting friends, "I'm disappointed my mother and sister are moving to Michigan with me. I'm taking my problems with me." She told me, "You cannot run away from your problems. I want you to understand the concept of karma. You should not blame your misfortune in life on anyone but yourself. Whether you believe it or not, you asked to be born to your parents. Everything which happens to you is your own fault." I did not understand what she was talking about. However, I decided I would not be angry because Ava and my mother wanted to follow me. I could still live on my own with my daughter and search at the same time for my dream to be happy.

Within days of moving to Michigan, Ava swindled $800 from some horny old man and rented the house my grandfather said I could rent. I wanted to work, but I also wanted to go to school and get my high school diploma. My grandfather told me "Instead of working you can get on welfare and finish school." I told him, "I will not wait in a welfare line because they are too long. I would rather find a job."

My grandfather said, "I have a friend who works in the Kalamazoo Michigan Welfare office and I will call him to see if he can help you." I was amazed when my grandfather's friend helped me out quite a bit. He said, "I have a program I can put you in where they will pay you to go to school." I enrolled in school and was working towards what I considered a meaningful life. I was only going to stay on welfare until I had enough education to get a decent job.

After applying for welfare, my caseworker came to my grandfather's place where I was staying to issue me two checks for $352 each as an incentive because I had enrolled in school. In this case the welfare office came to me. I canceled an insurance policy I bought for my daughter when she was born. I received a check for $1600. I also received a check from the retirement pension plan I accumulated working for the University of Illinois Hospital for $2700. I had $5004; enough to get me started and on the right track. Ron Davis, my caseworker at the welfare office, told me, "As long as you stay in school; I will make sure you get enough money to live on."

Since I did not get the house my aunt had, I wanted to get the house on my grandfather's property, which I could rent for $50 a month. Happiness was on the way because I found hope for my future. Life was not long enough for me to accomplish all I wanted to achieve. I still had several problems to work out. My grandparents had read Gia's diary and were angry to learn she wrote she hated my grandmother. They felt since she hated them, then she could leave. My mother still could not take care of herself, and the same was true of her children. My mother and Ava were staying in the house Ava rented from our aunt.

Gia, Clayton and I were still staying with my grandparents because the house I was going to move into was a big mess. Yet I was not worried too much about the situation. Somehow, from the way I felt inside, I knew chanting Nam Myoho Renge Kyo had turned my life into a positive direction. I knew all my sorrows would turn into joy.

Before I left Chicago, Taylor said to me, "The road to happiness is tough. Life is extremely hard when you want to accomplish something of great value." I did not know much about chanting and Buddhism. I was encouraged to study as much as I could since I was secluded from other members. There were no Buddhist members in Battle Creek, Michigan. I had to practice alone. I was told to practice True Buddhism is difficult; however, when you do it correctly, you will be rewarded in your daily life.

I was told to study the Gosho writings of Nichiren Daishonin (February 16, 1222-- October 13, 1282,) -- he was the first person who chanted Nam Myoho Renge Kyo (on April 28, 1253.) While Nichiren Daishonin was in exile on Sado Island in Japan due to his strong conviction to teach others about Buddhism, he wrote letters to his disciples to encourage us to have steadfast faith.

I started reading one of the letters titled "Letter to Niike." Part of the Gosho reads: "The journey from Kamakura to Kyoto takes twelve days. If you travel for eleven but stop on the twelfth, how can you admire the moon over the capital (Kyoto?) No matter what, be close to the priest who knows the heart of the Lotus Sutra. Keep learning from him the truth of Buddhism and continue your journey of faith."

The Moon Over Kyoto stands for what we want to achieve in our lifetime. It means never give up, no matter how hard a situation may seem, or how long it takes. Never give up until a goal is achieved. I started writing my goals down and learning how to make them happen. I knew school and getting a place to live were my priorities. I felt obligated to help my younger brother and sister because they were really suffering. Clayton was in the twelfth grade. He also worked at my uncle's restaurant since he was nine years old and he supported Gia who was in the eleventh grade. I felt sorry for what they were going through because, like me, they had to support themselves.

The biggest lesson I needed to learn was self-discipline. Chanting was not easy, but I knew if I stopped, I would be giving up. And eventually, my life would be harder than ever before. I was determined to continue pursuing my goals and to challenge every obstacle in my way. It was physically impossible to continue living with my grandparents. The place was not big enough; we were not little kids anymore. The house where I had been planning to move was also small, but I would let Gia and Clayton stay with me until they finished school.

The house had been vacant for years. When I went to check what condition it was in, I saw it would need a lot of work before it was livable again. It needed a new roof; the one it had would not survive the next snowstorm. I found Acorn nuts left by squirrels in the house, which is worse than having rats.

I could not live in the house. Now I did not know what to do. On the one hand, I did not want to move too far from Climax because my school was already twenty miles away; if I moved to Battle Creek, school would be forty miles away. On the other hand, Battle Creek is where all the action was. Nothing happened in Climax. I believe it is named Climax because it means the end; it is where you end up living out your days. It is a hick town with a population of less than a thousand people. My grandfather was the only black man who lived in the town. My sister and brother were the only two blacks in their school. My school was in Comstock, where I was the sole black person. The town was even smaller than Climax.

Although the white people would never admit it, they were prejudiced against black people. A white man once told me, "I could never like you." I said, "How unfortunate you can dislike me when you don't know me." He said, "My father taught me to hate black people like you." A woman once said to me, "How do you know when you're dirty? Because your skin looks dirty all the time to me." Good thing I was mature. In my math class, the instructor said, "We are going to deviate from our lecture and watch a movie." It was about the south when blacks were not allowed into downtown stores and restaurants. The movie started out with a black man asking for a hamburger in a restaurant and being told, "Am surrey wees not allowed to serve niggers." It showed violence against blacks. I wanted to get up and leave. They sure seemed like they were letting me know I was not welcome there.

I made up my mind to transfer to a school in Battle Creek the following semester. I had to stick out the rest of the class to earn the credits. I had to deal with it until I completed it. I stayed to myself. I started looking for a place to live in Battle Creek. The house my sister rented was a small and nice place and perfect for her and our mother. Since my grandparents had read Gia's diary, they refused to talk to her. They would lock the refrigerator so she could not eat. Everything she ate was from what my brother brought home from the restaurant after he got off work.

I felt sorry for my brother. He had to work all night and go to school during the day. The restaurant closed at three in the morning and after cleaning up the filthy restaurant, he did not get home until five-thirty in the morning and had to be at school at seven-thirty. My grandparents were not helping them. They only provided them with a place to live. I tried to solve the problem while I was there. I made the mistake by telling my grandfather, "If you hadn't read Gia's diary, this problem would never have occurred."

My grandfather raised his voice and said, "If I find a book in this house – I don't care what kind of book it is -- I have the right to read it." There was no reasoning with him. My grandfather said, "Since you want to take Gia's side and not mine, you can leave this house right now." I found it hard to communicate with him because of his adamant attitude.

Gia was fifteen when I moved to Michigan, and Clayton was seventeen. I was twenty. They were both doing very well in school. Gia was a cheerleader and was getting "A's" in all her classes. Clayton was on the football team and the basketball team. He was a good player, but he was limited because of the lack of sight in one of his eyes. Clayton was also an honor student.

We came home late from visiting Ava and my mom, and my grandmother was on the warpath. We do not know why. Probably because she was mad at Gia for saying what she said in her diary. She said, "All of you can move out because I don't have to put up with you guys anymore." Usually, my grandfather would stop her and calm her down, but this time he agreed with her. He told us, "Get out all of you." It was snowing and very cold and it was after eleven at night. We had to go fifteen miles all the way back to Battle Creek.

We went to Ava's place and I told her we would only stay there until I found a place of my own. Every morning I would use my brother's car and take them to school. Then, I would go to school myself and then I would go and pick them up. I needed my own car because it was difficult trying to get everywhere in one car. I had $800 to spend on a car and found a good one for only $600. I bought a 1966 Buick LeSabre from an old lady whose husband had recently died. It was his car and she did not need it any longer.

I planned to finish the school semester in Comstock. Then I could transfer to Battle Creek school and would be closer to where we were staying. Also, Clayton was graduating from high school and Gia was going to transfer to Battle Creek High School for her senior year. When all this took place, life would be easier because we would not have to drive so far. Many times, I found myself ditched off the side of the road because I was driving in slippery icy patches. Driving in icy and snowy conditions simply terrified me. I once slid off the road and hit a tree which prevented me from hitting a house.

CHAPTER 19

MOVING UP TO BETTER PLACES AND POSITIONS

The situation at Ava's place was very chaotic. I was hoping to find my own apartment very soon. My mother was drinking quite a bit. Also, it did not take her long to find the bum hangout because she started dating one of the town drunks. My mother's boyfriend would fight her from time to time. One day my brother, my cousin and I jumped on him and beat him up. I said to him, "Hit my mother again and you will be dead."

I knew it was impossible for me to live in the same house as my mother and Ava. They were always starting trouble of some kind. Once, Ava and Gia got into a big fight. Every time a fight would start, Ava would run and get a knife, so Ava and Gia were fighting with a knife.

I told my brother, "Stop them from fighting." The next thing I knew, he was fighting too, and then a few minutes later, my mother started fighting. They were all on the floor, fighting. I saw blood and thought Ava had stabbed someone. The children were all screaming and crying. We did not have a telephone, or I would have called the police. Instead, we had a gun in the house. I went to get the gun, and I pointed it at them fighting on the floor and said, "Stop fighting right now or I will shoot." They all looked at me and said, "Oh it's Arden with a gun," and they kept fighting.

They knew I did not have the nerve to shoot. I then got upset and ran outside in my bare feet in the snow and started screaming in the middle of the street.

I was on my knees and I would raise my arms high and scream, "Help, please somebody help." Then, I would go down to the ground and come back up again screaming the same thing. I thought one of the neighbors would call the police. Instead, when my family saw me outside having a fit in my bare feet in the snow, they stopped fighting and started laughing at me. I was furious. Every day, a similar fight would break out.

It was hard to live with Ava because of all the fights. I had started looking for a place for Clayton, Gia, Chelle and me. I heard on the news about a mass killing in a house not too far from Ava. The house was big and nice. I called the newspaper to find out the owner's name and telephone number. To my surprise, the newspaper gave me the information. I called the owner and said, "I really need a house to rent and was wondering if I could rent your house." He said, "I could rent it cheap if you are willing to clean up the big mess. There's blood everywhere because three people were killed there." The people were killed because of some gambling or dope deal. I did not care. I was willing to clean the place and was not afraid to live there. The house was perfect for us, and it was an easy and cheap deal, so I decided to take it. We moved in and I was temporarily happy. Barbara Lee came to Battle Creek to help me clean up the mess.

At the end of the spring semester, Clayton graduated from high school and I passed my class with an 'A.' Also, I enrolled in a course with the CETA Program. It was a program training me to be a secretary and paid me during the training. I was happy with the program. I learned a lot and I enjoyed going. After about four months in, a CETA staff member called me into the office. "I have to kick you out because it has come to our attention you are not a high school graduate. This program is for high school graduates only." I said with tears, "When I filled out my application, I told the truth. I didn't graduate and I am going to adult high school in pursuit of my diploma."

I went in tears to the president of the program. "This program is my only hope for my future. I'm attending classes and working to receive my diploma." The president happened to have the same last name as mine, so he did me a special favor and said, "I'll let you stay, providing you have your diploma by December." It was July; I had five months to make up three years of high school. I was devastated because I was not sure if I could do it. I knew about the G.E.D. exam because I had taken it before I moved from Chicago, and then again after I arrived in Michigan. I did not pass either time.

Also, I had stopped chanting. It had become too difficult. Whenever I would chant, everyone laughed at me, and I was not into being made fun of. It was hard to chant without going to meetings. Chicago had many members, but in Battle Creek, I was the only member. I knew chanting worked and made me feel much better about myself, but I could not do it. It seemed my life was happy, and I did not need to chant anymore.

For fun and excitement, we went to the club down on the Corner. I met and fell in love with Keith -- a real lady's man with a lot of girlfriends. His main girlfriend was the one he lived with. Great -- I would have to fall for a man with a lot of girlfriends. The men who liked me were old, drunks, ugly, had no teeth or was shorter than me, none of which interested me. I wanted Keith, and I put all my energy into getting him.

Keith knew I liked him because I told him. On several occasions when I would see him in the club, he would say, "How about I come to see you tonight?" I would go home and get myself ready to receive him, but he would never show up. I know not getting with Keith was for my protection because he could only offer me the kind of relationship, I promised myself I would never go through.

After a few months of my siblings living with me, I was miserable. They both had friends, some of whom were there when I left for work, and others would be there when I came home. I was angry and wanted to throw everybody out so I could relax. Gia was still in high school and had only one more year to go. I made sure she went to school every day. My brother babysat at our house for my friend's four small children. Those kids tore my house apart. When I got home from work, my life was a disaster.

I evaluated my life and saw it was pretty much the same as it was before I left Chicago. I needed to start chanting again. I needed it because I needed my high school diploma. Plus, I had started on-the-job training at the VA Medical Center as secretary to the speech therapist. Between work and school I was gone from eight in the morning until six, and was about to start GED Preparedness from six-thirty until nine-thirty. I was not looking forward to being gone all day, and when I got home, I was not ready to deal with the life there.

My brother and sister and their friends would always complain and say, "Arden, you're too mean and anxious. You need to find a man." I never understood why I could not find anyone. Both of my sisters had boyfriends. My mother even had a boyfriend. My brother had a girlfriend. I had no one. I wanted Keith and I knew I could not have him. No matter how much I liked a man, he would never like me. I wanted to reserve myself for Smokey because I was afraid the lyrics in the song -- "It's sad to belong to someone else when the right one comes along" -- would come true for me. Sometimes, I was confident I would find Smokey and we would live happy ever after -- and at times, I was afraid I would never find anyone because I would waste my life waiting forever for Smokey. I went out to the club a lot, but no one ever seemed interested in me. The men would flirt and wanted to come home with me at night, but no one wanted a meaningful relationship. I could never be interested in a casual affair.

Soon my life started turning more upside down because Gia became pregnant. I did not know what I was going to do with a baby in the house. I told my cousin, Paul, "I'm going to start chanting again." I chanted for fifteen minutes. I felt a little better. I was looking forward to the next day so I could chant again. When I got home from work, Keith came by to see me. It was the first time he came by. I knew then it was because I chanted. After he left, I went into my bedroom so I could chant for the appreciation of finding Buddhism.

When I opened my Butsudan, which is a box I keep my Gohonzon in – it was gone! I went through the house screaming, "What happened to my Gohonzon?" One of the kids my brother baby-sat for pointed to his little brother and said, "He had it walking around with it in his hand today." I was so angry because I was ready to start chanting and my Gohonzon was gone. I did not know what to do. I looked everywhere in the house and the scroll was nowhere to be found. I would have been so embarrassed to tell my friends I lost it. I was told, "When you receive a Gohonzon to protect it with your life. And if you find someday you do not want to chant any more, turn the Gohonzon back to the Temple. Please do not destroy or lose it."

If you keep it, you have made a commitment to chant daily for the rest of your life. Even if you are sick you chant. If your favorite movie is on you chant." I would chant before I went to work, and I would chant again in the evening around seven. I felt irresponsible because I could not find it. Finally, when I was going to bed, as I pulled the covers back, I saw my Gohonzon safe under the covers. I knew it was true about the protection of the Gohonzon. When you protect the Gohonzon it will protect you.

I realized I needed to go back to Chicago to a meeting and get rejuvenated. I packed my bags and my friend Callum drove me to Chicago for the weekend. I always stayed with Barbara Lee whenever I visited Chicago. Barbara Lee liked Callum because when she came to Battle Creek to visit me, he put a hundred-dollar bill in her hand to flirt with her.

While I was in Chicago, I went to a Buddhist meeting. They were also having a party after the meeting. I had a good time. I had a problem reaching my father because he was moving. His telephone was disconnected, and his neighbors did not know where he had moved. I wanted to see my father. At the meeting, my friends told me, "Chant and you'll find your father." I thought, right, I am going to run into my father in big 'O' Chicago. Even though it was useless, I still chanted about the matter because I wanted to see my dad.

Barbara Lee and Callum had gone out for the afternoon, and I was at her place waiting for them to return. I was invited to another meeting being held later, so I waited for Callum and Barbara Lee to give me a ride and attend the meeting with me. However, it took them too long to get back, so I had to take the bus. I had waited so long for Callum and Barbara Lee until I was pressed for time in getting to the meeting on time. As I was waiting for the bus, I became impatient and I walked to the other corner because I could have the opportunity to catch either bus because where I was standing at first, I only had one bus I could catch.

I started thinking; if Callum and Barbara Lee come home soon, they will not see me from this corner. So, I was about to walk back to the other corner when I heard someone call my name. I looked up and it was my father in the car with his friend G-Man. My dad said he said to G-Man as he pointed, "Doesn't she look like my daughter waiting for the bus." G-Man said, "She is your daughter." I was totally shocked to see my father. I knew then chanting was what I should do forever.

I told my father, "Daddy, I chanted to find you." I had taught my dad how to chant and I told him "Please chant to get your life together." My father was so amazed. He said, "Here I'm in a neighborhood I'm never in, and who do I see but my daughter standing on the corner waiting on the bus and I thought you were in Michigan." My dad then said, "Baby this chanting is the right thing to do. I like it and you look happy."

My father was in a hurry and did not have much time, but he did drive me to the meeting. I wanted him to come with me because I was leaving to go back to Michigan after the meeting. My dad could not go with me because he said, "I have some business to take care of." I knew it was drugs. However, I kissed my father and said, "Daddy please take care of yourself. Don't forget to chant and please stay in touch."

I went to the meeting; it was great and inspiring. I was ready to get my life together. The first thing I had to do was get my high school diploma so I could remain in the CETA Program. I did not want to take the G.E.D. class because I did not have the time. I was afraid of the test because I had already failed it twice. I was not good at passing tests, but in a classroom environment, I could get an "A" in any class I took.

I wanted to go to a regular high school, so I could walk across a stage in my graduation gown to "Pomp and Circumstance" and get my diploma. However, to go to school and do it course by course would take me three years. So, I decided to attend the G.E.D. prep class to prepare me for the exam. The class was for six weeks. I could handle it. When I enrolled in the class, they offered the exam prior to the class so we could see where we needed more help and then we could concentrate on the subjects we needed help with. The exam was taken over two days. I went Friday night to begin the test.

The G.E.D. is a series of five examinations. Each exam is two hours long and five different subjects. I took two exams. I passed both as they were graded on the spot. I had to come back the next day to take three more subjects. I went home and chanted two hours with the strong determination of passing the other exams as well. Then I would not have to go to the class for the next six weeks. I took two more exams and I passed them both. Then it was time for me to take the last exam. I needed a thirty-nine to pass. Thirty-nine might sound easy, but I was averaging thirty-five to thirty-seven on each exam. Thirty-nine was a passing grade. I also needed an overall average of thirty-five to pass.

I asked for the last test and she said, "It is not enough time left to take the last exam." I begged, "Please let me take it today. I passed four exams already and I can take it in forty-five minutes." The instructor said, "By Law you must have two hours to complete each test." I looked at the instructor and started crying. I said, "You have to let me take it. I chanted two hours last night."

They were not going to offer the exam again for six more months. I was sure to get terminated from the CETA program if I did not get my diploma in one month. I was angry because I chanted two hours. As I was thinking I asked the instructor, "Can I use the score on the exam I took a year ago?"

The instructor said, "Sure you can. Follow me and I will look up those records." As I was following him down the hall, I chanted under my breath, if I had at least a thirty-nine on the test then I would pass the entire exam. (Nam Myoho Renge Kyo.) Math was my best subject, so I was confident. The instructor took out my file and said, "On the math you got thirty-nine." I started shouting and said, "I passed, I passed!" The instructor said, "Wait let me figure it out first."

I knew I passed, but he still had to officially figure it out. He came back and said, "Congratulations, you have an overall average of thirty-five, and you passed." I was happy. I finally did it, and I did not have to attend the G.E.D. class. They gave me a paper to verify I did pass the exam. I took it to the CETA Program President and showed him the paper. He said, "I'm so proud of you. You can now stay in the program until you graduate." I felt so secure. I knew I would find a decent job when I completed the program.

One of my leaders

My altar where I pray

CHAPTER 20

THE PASSING OF MY MOTHER

I started attending Buddhist meetings fifty miles away in Jackson, Michigan. Attending meetings made it easier for me to chant. When I stayed away from meetings, I found myself missing a day or two of chanting. I was working an on-the-job-training program because I had finally completed my course in secretarial training. The person I worked for was a speech therapist. He told me my resume should be written as if I am the best person in the world. He helped me by suggesting questions I should and should not ask on interviews.

I was learning so much about my life. My mother was not getting any better. She was being beat up by her old bum of a boyfriend. My siblings and their friends were at my house all the time. My life was still a big mess. I had a lot to chant about and I was determined to change all my problems.

I wanted so much for Keith and me to get together and have a relationship. However, whenever I saw him at the club, he would never ask me to dance or talk to me. I asked him to dance once, he turned me down – and then asked another woman to dance with him. I felt so bad. I really wanted to get to know him. I knew Keith had lots of girlfriends, but I did not care because I felt he was looking for a woman like me. I am the answer to any man's dream. I needed to get the message to him somehow. Once we got together, he would lose the desire he had for other women and marry me, and we would live happy ever after. Is not love what everyone wants?

My friend Cynthia -- the mother of the children my brother babysat for -- knew Keith because her father lived across the street from him. Cynthia knew Keith's girlfriend, so she told me a lot of things about them. She said, "All I don't know about him, I will find out and let you know as much as I find out." Everyone knew everyone in Battle Creek. There is only one high school, so they all grew up together.

Cynthia was free with her sex life. She was seeing many men. She came to my house and seduced my brother. She was thirty-five years old and my brother was seventeen. She came to pick her kids up and the next thing I knew she and my brother were in the bed together. You could hear them screaming from the sex feeling good while her kids were running around the house playing.

I went to visit Cynthia when she had one man in her bedroom while she was entertaining another man in her living room. Still, she and I were friends because she was a person I could talk to about Keith. Everyone else would say, "Stop talking about him because it's obvious he doesn't care anything about you."

I did not believe everyone because Keith gave me the impression, he did care about me. He did not want to make me the person he only goes to bed with because he had plenty of opportunities to ask me and I am sure he knew I would have said, "Yes," but he never tried. He would come to visit me from time to time. One time he took me for a ride in his new car. I knew then he liked me.

I was driving when Keith passed me and flagged me to stop. He said, "Where are you going?" I said, "I'm on my way to see Cynthia." He said, "I have something to tell you and I will meet you there." In my imagination, I thought he was going to tell me he was tired of fooling around and he was ready to settle down with me. When I got to Cynthia's, Keith drove up right behind me. Cynthia came outside, and we were talking. Keith had his friend Lamar with him. I noticed Keith and Cynthia were isolated on the side of the house together for a few minutes. However, I did not give it much thought. When they came from around the house, Keith hugged me and said, "I'm leaving." I said, "I thought you had something to tell me." He said, "I'll come by your house later and tell you." He and his friend got into his car and drove off.

I said to Cynthia, "I wonder what Keith wanted to tell me?" She responded, "I don't know, but I'll find out for you because Keith and I are going to see a movie together tonight. In fact, I better let you go because I have to get ready." I felt betrayed because I had told her about how much I liked Keith. I did not get angry with her because he and I did not date. I did like him. I knew Cynthia and Keith would have sex because she did it with every man in her environment.

I was foolish thinking Keith was going to come by my place later to tell me what he was going to tell me. When he did not show up, I felt awful. The next day, Cynthia called me early telling me all about their date. She said, "Girl, we didn't go to the movies. We went to a park and we were drinking in the car."

She then said, "A cop pulled up on us. He found out there was a warrant for my arrest for unpaid tickets and they took me to jail." She said, "Keith paid $100 to get me out. After he got me out, we went to Lamar's place and had sex." She said, "My legs are sore because he had them pulled so far apart while we were having sex." I was not surprised, but I did feel disgusted. I wanted to throw up. I wanted to be the person who had sex with Keith. I was twenty years old, and had not had sex in three years. I wanted to meet someone I liked but I could not. Keith was the only man in the whole town I wanted. A lot of men liked me, but I wanted to wait and be ready for Keith.

I could not understand why Keith wanted Cynthia more than he wanted me. She was a nice-looking woman, but she had sex with so many men, and she had been married twice and had four children. I was fresher. I could not understand. The next day, I saw Keith at the club. He was trying to be nice to me. I told him, "I'm disappointed because you would rather have a woman like Cynthia than me." He said, "I wanted to have some fun with her. I like you." I was so confused. I told him, "I have not had sex in three years. I want someone who is going to care about me and my feelings." The last man I had sex with was Steven two years before I moved out of Chicago and it was going on two years living in Michigan.

Keith and I went to his friend's house. He said, "I don't believe you haven't had sex in three years. You mean a person as nice and good-looking as you don't have a man?" I told him, "I want you and I'm willing to wait for you. I want you to see I'm the best woman you could possibly have." I told him all about my past and what I had been through. He hugged me and said, "You really do deserve a nice person. I am your man. Can I show you?" He kissed me and talked me into having sex with him. I gave in to him because I knew he was being as sincere with me as I was with him.

The next day, I thought he would call me and say hello. I felt good about us. I felt someone is in love with me. My body tingled all over. When I realized he was not going to call, I cried a little. I could not believe he did not call me. He tricked me into having sex with him. I was angry. The next day, I did not see him, but I found out he was with Cynthia again. I was not going to get in the middle of some crazy relationship. A lot of women in Battle Creek shared men. A woman told me her man would bring another woman home and she would sleep in the living room and the other woman would be in the bed with him. The women would fight each other, and the men would sit back and enjoy the women fighting over them. I tried to relieve myself of the feelings I felt for Keith.

A few days later Cynthia called me. "Can you give me a ride?" When I picked her up and she said, "I need to find Keith because I have something to give to him." She could not find him, but we found his car. She left a note on his windshield asking him to come by to see her later because she had some money for him. I felt silly. I never told her Keith and I were together because I was embarrassed. I then started dreaming about Smokey again. I thought if I cannot have a man in my life whom I wanted and who wanted me, then I could have the man I wanted in my imagination.

I chanted about all my problems and I found something to be hopeful for. Paul, my cousin and I were driving around when we saw a construction site with a big sign saying "New apartments coming soon. Fill out your application now." We stopped, and I filled out an application. They asked me for a deposit of $100 and my apartment would be ready in about six months. They told me the money would assure me an apartment. I could not wait to move into my new place with my daughter; only the two of us.

Clayton got arrested. He was in jail in Kalamazoo, Michigan. It seemed like they were never going to let my brother go to trial or let him out of jail. The only crime he committed was disturbing the peace by laughing and playing in a small town called Augusta, Michigan. It was smaller than Climax. All these towns were full of prejudiced white people. When they saw my brother, a black man in their town, they assumed he was a criminal.

Clayton happened to be dating a white girl who lived in Augusta. They were standing around laughing and having fun when the police pulled up and threw my brother in the police car and took him to jail. They did not give him a bond. They treated him as if he had killed someone. I had talked to several attorneys, but they all talked as if there was no hope for my brother for disturbing the peace by laughing loudly at two o'clock in the afternoon on a public street. They were telling me the judge may send him to prison. I became so angry because it was only prejudice. I do not know why white people hate black people so much.

Not too many black men who lived in Battle Creek were employed. A lot were dope dealers, gamblers or pimps. Most of the black men had women taking care of them. I was beginning to hate living in Battle Creek, but I did not dare go back to Chicago.

I was getting a lot of opposition from my family. They blamed me for Gia getting pregnant and Clayton for going to jail. I told them, "No one wanted to help me take care of them, but you criticize me when things go bad." I was especially angry with my mother. I tried to take her to Alcoholics Anonymous, but she would not let me. My sister Ava was drinking heavily also.

However, she always took good care of her children. She did not leave her responsibility on someone else, like my mother did.

Every time my mom came around, a big argument would occur. My life was as hellish as it was in Chicago. I had no control in my own house. I told my mother, "Gia and Clayton need you because when I move into my new apartment, no one is moving in with Chelle and me." I even told Gia she was going to have to do something because I was moving soon. Gia was a senior in high school. Even though she was pregnant, she was determined to graduate.

I went to a party and met Marvin Simmons. Marvin was about five years younger than me, but he looked good enough to make any woman drool. Marvin really liked me. He reminded me of Smokey because he had a fair complexion and had those mysterious looking green eyes and was good looking.

Marvin and I because friends. He would always buy me gifts. He knew I was crazy about Smokey, so he told me, "I'm your Smokey." He came to see me every day, but he was too young for me. Not only was he too young but he was too immature. However, he was a sweet person. He would come over and bring a poem he wrote for me. He wanted to have sex with me and always asked. I gave him a hard time because a lot of times when he came over, I would not let him in. I did not want to hear him beg me for sex. If I wanted to have sex with him, it would not be in my house. It is hard for me to have sex with someone when everyone in the house knows what I am doing. I would put him off and told him, "When my apartment is ready, we can then have privacy."

I got notice my apartment would be ready in two months. I went to my mother and said, "Mom you have two months to get yourself together because I'm moving." All she could do was cry and say, "I want to go visit my son." I took her to the jail to see my brother, and all she could do was tell Clayton, "I'm never going to kiss you again." We had to visit him through a glass window while talking to him on a telephone. She said to the guard, "I beg of you to please let my son out." My mother was too far gone in her mind to take care of Gia and Clayton.

I wanted Clayton and Gia to be well taken care of, but I could not do it any longer. Everyone thought I was cold and uncaring about my family. I wanted to live with my daughter and myself. I could not understand why I was the only person they could live with; and because I did not want them to live with me, I was inconsiderate, yet they were not. I could never get them to understand. Ava and her boyfriend broke up. She suggested Gia come to live with her. Ava was the type of person who could not live alone. Also, my uncle said Clayton could stay with him when he gets out.

My apartment was finally ready, and everything was all set for me to move. I was starting to pack my things when I discovered I had some things belonging to my mother. I went to her place and she was not home. I tried to find her to tell her to get her things.

When I found my mother at someone's house, I was very mean to her. I said, "I am moving tomorrow, and you need to come and get your things, or I will throw them away." My mother was stoned out of her mind drunk. I do not think she understood one word of what I was saying to her. When I walked in my mother got a big smile on her face, walked over to me, and said, "I love you." She started to kiss me and tell everyone in the house, "Hey everybody, this is my daughter. Isn't she beautiful?" I could tell she was proud of me.

I was brushing her off and telling her, "Don't touch me." I said, "I want you to get all your things out of the house, so I can move into my new apartment." The only way my mother responded was, "Can you take me to go and see my son?" I told her what time I would pick her up. The next day came, and I moved into my new apartment. After I got settled, I went to pick my mother up to take her to the jail, and she was not there. Gia, Ava and I went to the jail to see my brother. He was disappointed because my mother did not make it. I told him, "I went to pick momma up, but she wasn't there. I will find her and bring her tomorrow."

While at home enjoying my first evening in my new apartment, a knock came to my door. It was a white lady with a child who was mixed with black. She introduced herself, "My name is Patricia

Ford, and this is my daughter, Lisa. I moved in the same building as you and your cousin Celeste told me you were moving into this complex too and since we have a lot in common, we should get to know each other." Pat and I did have a lot in common, and our children liked each other. I was glad I had found a friend. I lived a little distance from town, and it would probably get lonely.

Ava called me at nine o'clock the next morning and said, "Arden, get over here right now because Momma is dead." I jumped up and left the apartment at once. When I got in my car, it was stuck in the snow. I tried hard as I could to get the car unstuck by rocking it back and forth. Finally, a man helped me get my car out of the snow.

I chanted all the way to my sisters hoping my mother was not dead. I wanted to hold her and tell her I loved her. I was mean to her the day before and I wanted to apologize and beg her to get help. However, when I got to Ava's place, it was true. My mother died the night before, and I felt awful.

We did not know what to do. The funeral director said, "The cheapest funeral will cost $1200. How will you be paying for it?" We had no idea where we were going to get the money from. My grandfather, her father, had money but he refused to give us any money on the burial. He said, "I don't have any money." It was hard to believe my mother was his only child. He did not care about her final resting place.

Fortunately, her mother, said, "I have a life insurance policy on my daughter." It paid the funeral cost. We still needed $400. My grandmother was angry and demanded, "I want my daughter's body shipped to Chicago to be buried." "Grandma, it will cost more to ship her body and we already didn't have enough money." Her response was, "I hope they have singing at the funeral in Michigan." We got a payment arranged to pay the $400 balance in monthly installments.

Ava and I wanted Clayton to attend our mother's funeral. We went to the jail and pleaded with them to let my brother out. My brother said to the officer, "Can I go to see my mother before she goes to her final resting place?" They told us to go to the court and explain our situation. We brought a court order back for them to release my brother for three-days to attend the funeral. However, the guard at the jail refused to release my brother.

I got angry and yelled at the top of my lungs "You didn't put President Nixon in jail, and my brother didn't do anything wrong. He was having a good time. He didn't have any malicious intent." The officer came out to calm me down and said, "Don't worry, I will personally bring him." I was still upset because we had an order from the courts to release my brother for three days. The judge who gave us the court order release was black and the white officers did not want to adhere to the judge's orders. I pleaded and pleaded but they would not change their minds.

I could not even cry about my mother's death. I loved her, but I was not sure if I was sad or happy, she passed away. My mother had not been dead twenty-four hours before her sisters and Grandma Ruby were talking about her. They told Ava, "Geo is not sure if Clayton is your father or not." My sister got angry and went to see my father. "Daddy, is the rumor true? Are you my daddy?" My father said, "Ava, you are my daughter." We could not understand why they were saying those things about my mother. One of my mom's sisters said, "Ava's real father was one of my old boyfriends." She was implying my mother had a baby by her sister's boyfriend.

The tears came from my eyes. My mother was a good person. She gave money and things freely to others. She was especially good to her sisters. If I could turn back the hands of time, I would force my mother to get help for herself. I was so angry, but I found the strength to keep my mouth shut. I realized I still had my father. Somehow, I had a mission to save my father because I did not want the same thing to happen to him as what happened to my mother.

At the funeral, it was funny because the same sisters who were talking about my mother as if she were some indecent human being, were now falling on the floor crying at the funeral. I wanted to slap one of my aunts. I could not take it anymore. I said, "Get up off the floor and stop acting so phony." She tore into me wanting to fight. This was in the middle of the funeral. We struggled but everyone pulled us apart before a fight could break out. I could not believe the way they were all carrying on.

Ava and I had to restrain ourselves from laughing. When we got to the burial site, we wanted to watch our mother lowered safely into the ground, but the funeral director had to stop the ceremony because my aunts were screaming and hollering. They should all have won Academy Awards. The guards did bring my brother to the funeral. They kept him far away and in handcuffs. I could not believe they would not let him join the family seating. My brother was no animal or a criminal.

A group of my chanting friends came from Jackson to the funeral to support me. I was so depressed. I mentioned to my friend, "I am sorry for everything bad which has happened to my mother." The friend said, "As long as you are alive - then your mother is still alive because you're a part of her. It's never too late, and please don't let your mother down." I promised myself and my mother I will make her better through me.

My mommy and me

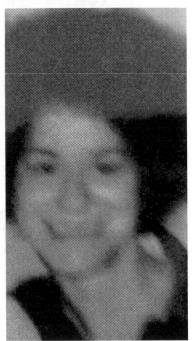

My beautiful mother

CHAPTER 21

I'LL HELP YOU DADDY

Shortly after my mother died, the CETA Program I was working in ended. However, I graduated with high scores and was recommended for a job working with the Community Action Agency. I was interviewed and hired to be the secretary for the media department. It was a fun job. I typed press releases I would read in the newspaper the next day. The position was temporary for six months, but I was not worried because I knew I would find a job. I was going to learn as much as I could and practice my secretarial skills.

Things were going well. I was chanting every day. I was going to Buddhist meetings at least twice a week in Jackson. I absolutely loved going to meetings because it was the only place I could go and feel hope, a sense of accomplishment and peace. I would get inspired to try harder and to put one hundred twenty percent effort into whatever I did. My family was doing better also. My brother had finally gotten out of jail and was dating Renee, his childhood sweetheart.

Renee, who is white, ran away from home to be with my brother. Renee's mother then put her into a juvenile home, and my brother broke her out. Renee's mother was very prejudiced and, despite her best efforts to keep them apart, Clayton and Renee were married. They both had restaurant jobs.

Gia had a beautiful boy -- my beautiful nephew. They were living with Ava, and all was well as could be expected for two sisters who often did not see eye to eye. Ava's place was too small for all of them. It was not long before Ava found a man who fell in love with her and rented a house for her and her kids. Ava moved into the house and Gia kept the apartment. Though Gia had a few problems with her son's father, I did not worry about her too much because she is one strong person and seems to win all her battles. I was proud of her; she stayed in school and took care of her baby. She was doing an excellent job.

I was content living in my comfortable apartment and finally being able to be a mother to my child. I looked forward to coming home and cooking her a good dinner. I would perhaps prepare fried pork chops or chicken with fried potatoes, with a tossed salad -- lettuce, tomatoes, and cucumber with Thousand Island dressing -- and we would have Kool-Aid. If I wanted something to last for a couple of days, I might make a pot of spaghetti or chili.

While I was in the kitchen preparing the meal, Chelle might be walking around playing in my clothes and high heel shoes or hiding under my dress. If I had company, she demanded my attention. If my company were a male, she would cut up. She would always say with a whining voice, "Arden, I'm hungry." She would say it as if I had never fed her. Many times, she would start yelling at my male company and tell them she hated them.

It was hard to control Chelle, but I did the best I knew how. I tried with all my might to encourage her to do well in school, but it seemed impossible for her. I started getting more into my chanting. I noticed the more I chanted, the better my life was and the less I chanted, the worse my situation was. I was happy with my job. I did not make much money, but I got a supplement check from the welfare. I was not rich, but I did have what my child and I needed. The only thing I needed was a man to share my love with. Patricia and I became good friends and went out clubbing together. I was hopeful I would soon meet someone nice.

The first time Pat and I went out together, she knocked on my door the next day with a big bruise and cut on her nose. I asked her, "What happened to you?" "CG beat me up for going out with you." CG was her boyfriend. She said he told her, "Arden is out looking for a man, she's a slut. If you hang out with her, she'll give you a bad reputation." I said, "Pat, you're a fool to have a man like CG. If I were you, I would walk away while you still can. No man should have the right to hit you." But Pat was in love and had to see this for herself.

Pat was a hard-working woman and raising her child as I was doing. She was unfortunate to have a man like CG in her life. Marvin was still trying to have a relationship with me. He was sweet, but he was wild in the streets. He always found it necessary to have his gun by his side, ready to kill anyone who moved wrong. I would rather be alone than be with a man who treated me badly and made me unhappy. I knew if I succumbed to Marvin and agreed to let him live with me, he would eventually treat me the way some men in Battle Creek treated their women -- I would get beat up and he would let me know I'm sharing him with other women.

Enjoying an evening at home, I got a telephone call from Ava's husband in California. Dexter said. "I'm out of jail and on my way to Battle Creek to see Ava and my children." Ava did not have a telephone and lived quite a distance from me, and my car was broken. I was desperate to get to my sister and tell her Dexter was on his way.

I regretted giving her address to him without consulting her first. I asked one of my neighbors, "Can you please take me to my sister's? I have an emergency." When I got to Ava's, I said "Please don't be angry with me, but Dexter's coming, and I gave him your address." She said with excitement, "Don't worry. I still love my husband. Maybe our marriage can work this time." I was doubtful; Dexter was always crazy, and I did not think he had changed much.

When he arrived, Ava was happy because her family was together. But she and Dexter would often get drunk. They both liked it when they were drunk. They felt they were having a good time. I did not trust Dexter. He was unstable, and I feared his being there with my sister and the kids. After a week passed, things still seemed okay. I went on a camping trip with my chanting friends. I left on Friday and came back on Sunday. Ava kept Chelle while I was away. When I returned and went to my sister's house to pick up Chelle, there was a note on the door for me to pick her up at Gia's place. When I got to Gia's place, there was a note on her door telling me to go to Climax where my grandfather lived.

Afraid something must be wrong with Chelle, I hurried to Climax, vigorously chanting everything was okay. When I arrived, I was relieved to see Chelle in the front yard playing, but my relief did not last more than a minute; Dexter had savagely beaten Ava. I did not recognize her because her face was so disfigured. In tears, I hugged Ava and said, "I'm sorry Ava. I feel horrible giving Dexter your address." Chelle said, "Arden, I tried to help when he hurt Ava, but Dexter yelled at me and said he would hurt me, too." Chelle was eight years old. I was so sorry she saw him beat her as well as Asia and Bear.

Ava said, "I'm terrified. Dexter is on the run; no one knows where he is, and I cannot go back home. The last thing he said to me was he was coming back to kill me." I felt bad for my sister because she thought her family was getting back together and maybe some good new memories could erase the bad old memories. We later found out Dexter shot a woman in California, which is why he left there in such a hurry – and this happened not even a month after he had been released from prison. He was a habitual criminal. Our fears were over. Dexter was found in Detroit and admitted into the psychiatric ward of the V.A. Medical Center. They were holding him to extradite him back to California to face charges for the shooting. We were so relieved. Ava could go back home.

I was feeling happy about my life. My friend Pat and I went everywhere together and had a ball – and each time we would go out; CG would beat her up. I could not understand. I asked Pat, "Would you go to a Buddhist meeting with me in Jackson, because if you chant, it could make you stronger and have a happier life?" She said, "No thank you." "All I can do Pat is continue to encourage you to try it for yourself. It will prove to you through your life if it works. Is that not worth trying?"

I went to New York to a convention my Buddhist organization put on celebrating the country's bicentennial. It was one of the highlights of my life. I had never been around so many happy and positive people. We put on a fantastic talent show at the Louis Armstrong Theatre. I also proudly marched in a parade on Sixth Avenue.

There were fifteen thousand members from all over the world. I was proud to be a member of the group. At the convention, I started to think about looking for another job because the program I was working in is ending and soon I would be unemployed. I needed a job so I could pay my rent on time every month. When I returned from my trip, I applied for a dental assistant position and got the job. They would train me to be a chair side dental assistant. I could not believe I went through secretarial training and was now starting a career as a dental assistant.

However, it was not long until I figured out the medical field was not right for me because the second day on the job, I fainted. The dentist had cut a patient's gum down the middle and removed a cyst. I was aspirating the blood. I felt sweaty all over. I asked my trainer, "Can you give me a wet towel?" I was trying to be cool because I did not want the patient or the doctor to realize I was having a hard time.

When I got the wet towel, they thought I was going to wipe the patient's head, but I put the towel up to my face so fast. The dentist realized I was having a tough time, so he motioned with his head for me to leave the room. All I could do was lie on the floor for a while before I could get myself together and stand again.

I did not have what it takes to be a dental assistant. However, I was not ready to look for another job right away. So, I decided to work there until I figured out exactly what I wanted to do. In a month, I was doing better, but I still did not like the idea of being in someone's mouth every day. I needed to find another job. The dentist fired the woman who trained me and hired another woman, whom I had to train. I taught her everything I had learned.

My boss said, "Arden, you did a fine job on training the new employee." A week later, he called me in his office and said, "Things did not work out for you, so you are fired." I was so upset. I had never been fired before. Getting fired was my biggest fear. I thought I would never find another job. I really needed a job. I had left another job to work there. I chanted many hours about the situation. The next day, I found a job at Sears working part-time as a cashier. I did not like it either. I wanted to work in an office. I had secretarial training and I wanted to pursue it.

I went to an employment agency named Snelling and Snelling. "There is a fee of $380 for our services." I paid the fee and they sent me to a savings and loan bank. In the interview I said, "If you hire me, I promise I will be the best employee you ever had." He said, "I like what you said, and you're hired." It was not exactly an office position, but it was a teller position. It was a prestigious atmosphere, and I would have a chance to dress, act and be a professional.

I learned a lot about professionalism working for First Federal Savings & Loan. In a year's time, I became the only teller hired since 1939 who had balanced my cash drawer every day. They started making me an example for the new tellers. I would speak to them and give them tips on ways to balance their cash drawer. I was my dad's banker when I was ten years old. I knew how to count money.

My boss was strict with me. They would check up on me when I was not at work. They would call the house to make sure I was home if I called in sick. If I did not answer, they would ask for a doctor's slip. They even had a spy who would park outside my house and would follow me to see where I was going. Many of the white employees and customers were prejudiced against blacks. Some customers refused to let me wait on them and would wait for a white teller. I eventually found the work situation at the bank to be intolerable and began to concentrate on finding another job.

My father was having some problems in Chicago. My father called me and asked, "Can I borrow twenty-five dollars from you?" I knew when my father asked me for money he was in bad shape. My father had never asked me for money before. My father was the type of person who would always make me believe he had a lot of money.

If I asked my father for money and he only had ten dollars, he would give it to me and pretend he had more. I knew something was wrong with him asking me for money, so I begged my father, "Please come to Michigan so you can get your life in order, because I refuse to see you kill yourself like momma did." I told him "If you don't seek help from your drug problem, then you are slowly killing yourself."

My father promised me, "If you send me the money, I will come to live with you in Michigan." I knew he was lying, but I sent him the money anyway. To my surprise, my father came to Michigan. He said, "I want to kick this drug habit and become a better person." My father was fifty-eight years old. I told him, "I'll help you, dad, as much as I can." My father said, "You know it will be hard. I'm not sure if I'm strong enough to deal with the pain I have to go through to kick this habit." He was crying to me as he was expressing his fear.

The day after my father came, my income tax check came in the mail for $500. My father's eyes got big when I showed him my check and he said, "Can you buy me a little dope?" At that moment, I realized not only was my father not strong enough to kick his habit, but I was not strong enough to see my father suffer. I said, "You know, dad, the V.A. Hospital where I did my secretarial training has a drug abuse program. Would you want to go through a program to help you get off drugs?"

I knew they had a program. When I was working there, I once talked to a man about twenty-five years old. He was there to kick his heroin habit. I asked him, "Are you through taking drugs now?" He told me, "I only want to clean my system out. I'm going to start using again as soon as I get it out of my system." I got firm with him and asked, "Do you have any children?" He said, "Yes

I have a little daughter." I said, "Think of what you're doing to your little girl's life." I told him about me and what I went through with my parents on drugs. I said, "One day, your daughter will be suffering like me, trying to get her life together. She'll have to work extra hard to establish a decent life for herself because of your failure to provide a strong foundation for her."

This man said to me, "I've talked to special drug counselors, psychiatrists, analysts and social workers and none of them told me what you told me." He said, "With your honesty, you've encouraged me to quit drugs for good." The speech therapist heard me tell him the information. He said, "Have you ever thought about taking some college classes in counseling? You could possibly be hired as a drug counselor here at the hospital." He said, "Not too many people had the experience of living in a drug situation. Most counselors only have the theory and not the actual experience. People look up more to those who had the experience as opposed to the knowledge." I never want to counsel drug abusers. I was only interested in helping my father.

When I wanted my father to go through the V.A. Program, I had not worked there in quite a while. However, the director remembered me. They admitted my father and told me, "Don't worry we'll take good care of him." My father stayed in the hospital for sixty days. He kicked his habit and was a significant role model for the younger guys. The hospital even had write-ups about my father in the hospital newspaper. I was so proud of my dad. The young men there called him 'Pops.' He helped them quite a bit.

My dad even went around the city talking to outreach programs and was helping alcohol and drug abusers. My father's next problem was to find a steady income. I did not want him to start selling drugs again because I knew he would start using. When he was released from the hospital, he felt great. He was proud of himself and what he did, and we were proud of him, too.

CHAPTER 22

SECURITY WITH
SOCIAL SECURITY

My father did not know what he wanted to do with his
life, so I went to see the man in charge of the CETA
Program. He and I had the same last name, so we called
each other cousins. I asked him if he could get my father a job.
They accepted my father in the CETA Program and paid him to
attend school. My father enjoyed going to school. He learned a
lot and felt worthy.

My dad was sitting in the living room on the couch. I got on
my knees in front of him and asked him, "Daddy, what started
you to selling drugs?" He told me, "I wanted to have the absolute
best for my family. I did not want to send you to school in the
projects. Many people who must live in filth and poverty lose
their hopes and dreams and give up on accomplishing anything
of value. I didn't want that for my children." My father wanted
us to have more than a regular job would have allowed him to
do. He said, "Arden, selling drugs was fast money and for a while
it seemed it was the right thing to do. But I'm sorry I caused so
much suffering in this family."

I truly understood my father. I said, "I'm happy you did it for
the family. I'm glad I was able to live the life I lived." With a big
smile I said, "It's worth writing about." We did go to good schools
and got a good education." I appreciated my father and gave him

a big hug and a kiss. I told him, "Daddy I love you." However, I resented him a little because I had just gotten my own apartment and I knew I was going to find a man soon. But what man would put up with a woman whose father lived with her (or so I felt at the time.) I would never let my father know how I felt. I was willing to help him, so I had to suffer a little longer.

I was having some problems at the bank where I worked because my boss accused me of prostitution. As I was working one day, a man had come to my teller window and asked me, "Do you know anyone interested in buying a bed?" I said "Me, I'm interested." He said, "I own the hotel across the street and they're tearing it down, so there's a lot of furniture for sale." He told me the price of the bed was $50, which was in my price range. I told him, "I will meet you there when I get off."

My father's school was down the street from where I worked. He would ride with me. My father met me, and we went to the hotel. I saw the bed and I told the man, "I'll take it." I gave him the cash and said, "I'll have someone pick it up tomorrow." And we left. The next day at work, my boss came to me first thing as if he were waiting for me to arrive and said, "I need to talk to you." He took me back in the vault the one we never use and asked me, "Why did you meet one of our customers at a hotel last night?" When I told him why, he was surprised because he was certain I had met the man for sex. He said, "If you ever have any financial problems, you can consult me, and I'll help you." He was soliciting me for prostitution. I was so angry, I wanted to quit at once, but I could not. I had a vacation coming soon and will chant to find another job while on vacation.

My friend Patricia had been hired by the government for a decent job with the Department of Defense (DOD.) I applied and was invited to take the test. I took my grandfather's manual typewriter as I had to bring my own. I looked around and everyone had an electric one. I even heard snickers, but I passed the typing test and was qualified to be a Federal Government Employee. I chanted I would be called during my vacation. I was happier having faith everything was going to work out.

My father finally graduated from his training program, and they got him a job doing office work at a vocational high school. He liked the job, but he could not see bringing home two hundred dollars a week when he could make more in one-day selling drugs. My father moved back to Chicago, which worried me. I was afraid he was going to get involved with drugs again. I taught my father how to chant, and he did chant. I knew he would be protected if he chanted. I chanted for him and I did not worry. I was starting to become bored with my life. Patricia and I went out to the club all the time. The same people were there every week. I still liked Keith, but he was no good. I was so confused about what to do and what man to see.

I found out about these government homes for low-income people who wanted to own property. I applied and was told there is a two-year waiting list. I chanted it would be sooner, and within two weeks, I found a nice red brick house with a big back yard and a big basement. I moved in and enjoyed living there. After I lived in the house for twenty-five years, I would own it. My rent was cheap -- only $50 a month – but I had to take care of all the repairs. My dad had come to visit but I could not get him to stay. I was still worried about him, though I felt reassured he was through with drugs because he did not take any during the two-weeks he was there visiting me.

While my father was visiting, I took my vacation. I wanted so much to find another job. I did not want to work for the bank any longer. To my surprise, I got a letter in the mail from the Social Security Office in Kalamazoo asking me to come for an interview for a data entry position.

I went to the interview and got hired. I was ecstatic I could go back to work and give the bank a two-weeks-notice informing them I was leaving. I chanted to find a new job while on vacation and I did. I got exactly what I chanted for again. I was getting paid two dollars more an hour and I would have better benefits. It was a long drive, but I had a new job with a raise, and I had a new place to live for hundreds of dollars a month cheaper.

The welfare office offered to pay for after school care for

Chelle. I had to have a paper signed and bring it to the welfare office by five, which I could not do because I worked until four-thirty and could not get to the office until after five because of the distance I worked from them. My worker decided to wait for me. I got there at five-fifteen and gave her the paper. The welfare office stayed open fifteen-minutes later to help me. Usually at five they will shut the door in your face. This is further proof chanting was working for me.

This was all good – great – but I was still dejected I could not find a decent man to share my life with. Every man I met only wanted a one-night stand. Jolanda gave me advice on how to handle a man. She was a college student and had a boyfriend. Before I met her, some girls who worked in the office were talking bad about her: "Wait until you meet her, she is a snob who thinks she's better than everyone else."

Jolanda alternated terms between college and work. She was at school when I first came, so everyone was preparing me for her arrival. I have always been the type of person who liked people more when others tried to turn me against them before we even met. I was looking forward to meeting Jolanda, but I did not tell my co-workers. When I first met her, I walked up to her and introduced myself. She shook my hand and said, "My friends call me JoJo."

JoJo and I went to lunch. All the other girls in the office were worried I was going to tell her what they said about her, but it never came up during our conversation. She started telling me about her boyfriend. I told her, "I don't have a boyfriend and I don't know why." She said, "It's your fault. Women make the problem for themselves. We care too much. If a woman did not let herself get so excited when a man was around, he would like her better." I said, "I don't understand what you mean." "I'm saying, do not expect too much from any man. If you are strong inside no man can hurt you. Be too busy sometimes. Don't be at his beck and call." JoJo and I became good friends. We had a lot in common and we got along well. We went to lunch together every day. We even went to clubs on weekends. At least her boyfriend did not beat her up when she went out with me, like Pat's boyfriend did.

After JoJo and her boyfriend broke up, she was hurt but assured me she would find someone else soon. We went out together, and when she met a guy who was crazy about her, she told me, "I'm going to experiment with him." When he came to her place, JoJo called me and said, "Call me at eleven tonight and I'm going to pretend you're a man." She wanted him to think she had several men in her life, and she was not depending on him. She told me, "When he calls, I tell him I'm watching my favorite TV program or I'm washing my hair. Make him think you are not too busy but too busy to talk to him."

I wanted to be forthright and honest in a relationship. I did not think a real love relationship could develop from such deceit, lies and misconceptions. However, he did ask her to marry him, and she accepted, and I was in their wedding. She told me she had played the game well. Then I felt lost. I knew I could not play the 'get a man game' and I thought I would never find one.

I got a phone call from Mars. I was surprised to hear from him as I had not talked to him since my mother died. He called to tell me my father had been stabbed and was in the hospital. I called the hospital and talked to my father. "Daddy, what happened?" "Some nigger stabbed me, but I'll be okay." I told him, "I will be there on Friday." It was Tuesday. Thursday, I called the hospital again. The nurse would not let me talk to my father. She said, "He is in intensive care and can't speak." I told her, "Tell my father I'll be there early Saturday."

I took the train to Chicago and arrived about eleven Friday night. Something told me to go straight to the hospital and not wait until the next day. When I got there, my father was in a coma. He did not even know I was there. I asked the nurse, "What happened to him?" The nurse said, "Oh honey he is going to die tonight." I could not believe what I was seeing and hearing. I left the hospital and went to chant with a friend for about two hours. At about three in the morning, the hospital called to tell me my father had died.

I felt cheated. My father was trying to get his life together. It had been about a year since he had done heroin. There was absolutely no way we could pay for another funeral. We still had payments left on my mother's funeral. We were never close to any of my father's relatives. He had two sisters and a brother. We talked to them from time to time, but we never met them. I called them to tell them about my father's death, and they came to Chicago. They lived in Houma, Louisiana. They had not seen my father in thirty-five years. We had to go and pick them up at Grand Central Train Station. There were hundreds of people there. It was hard picking up someone I had never met. However, we found each other.

When they arrived, they went to the funeral home with us and gave us $500 on the funeral cost. I went to the Veterans Administration Building, and they gave me a $400 check as my father was a veteran. The total price of the funeral was $1100. All we had to come up with was $200. Fortunately, we paid for the funeral with no problems. It ended well because had Mars not called me, I may have never known he had been stabbed and he could have died without me knowing. He would have had a state burial and he deserved more. We had a Buddhist funeral for my father. We all chanted he changed his negative destiny and will rest in peace eternally. What else can one say about death?

My dad and me
I'll take the money

CHAPTER 23

WHERE DID MY FREEDOM GO?

My boss at the Social Security office showed me how to get an additional $200 for the funeral expenses. We sent the money to my father's sister. She sent it back and told us to split it. I missed my daddy so much. We had him cremated because it was cheaper. About one month after the funeral, we received an iron urn in the mail which had his ashes. "Ava, do you want to keep the Urn?" "No." "Arden?" "No." "Clayton?" "No." "Gia?" "No." None of us siblings wanted to keep the urn, so we had it buried at the foot of our mother's grave. One of my sister's boyfriends gave us the remaining $98 balance we owed on our mother's cemetery plot, and they charged us an additional $15 to bury my father. I think my parents would have been proud to see how we took care of everything.

I was starting to get calls from Chelle's school telling me about her argumentative attitude. I tried to talk to her about it. Ava always told me how terrible a mother I was. She said, "Chelle is out of control, and you need to beat her butt." I did not think it was right to beat anyone. My parents never beat me, so why should I beat my kid? But the calls from Chelle's school were getting worse. She was disruptive and rude. I went to the school to question her teacher because he tore up some pictures she had. I was fussing at him and said, "I will report you to the Board of Education."

The teacher said, "She left out the part where she threw a book at me and told me to shove it up my ass." She was in the sixth grade then. I could not reason with Chelle without nearly going crazy because of the way she talked to me. I would ask, "Can we talk about what's bothering you?" she would say, "I don't want to discuss it." If I became firm and demanded her to talk, the situation would get worse. She would start hysterically crying. I felt helpless because I realized I had no control over her. I could not be as strong as I needed to be to address the situation. I did not let the problem get me down. I chanted about the problem and hoped I would find the wisdom to change it.

Pat was having some challenging times with her boyfriend CG. It was Christmastime, and Pat was sick in the hospital. She had been evicted from her apartment and CG was fighting her all the time. Her father gave her a car and CG would not let her drive it. He soon wrecked it.

Pat kept everything from her parents because they were highly opposed to her being with black men. They did not even want to acknowledge their granddaughter Lisa because she was half black. For these reasons, when Pat got out of the hospital, she had nowhere to go. I could not believe the courts were going to make a woman and her child move on December twenty-third. It was very cold outside. They expected her to sleep in the streets or something. Were they Ebenezer Scrooge? I felt bad for Pat and even though it was against what I promised myself, I told her, "Your daughter and you can move in with me." I knew I was setting myself up for an invasion of my privacy, but I thought I was her only hope.

The only people I wanted to live with me was my daughter and my man – except I still could not find one. I told Pat, "You can move in under two conditions: one) You pay half of all expenses and two) CG cannot spend the night or eat our food." She gave me her word, "Oh no, I'm through with him." She said she could never see him again because of what he did to her. He destroyed everything she had; all her and her child's clothes. He put them all in a tub and poured bleach all over them. He then sold everything of hers having any value.

Pat moved in and we had lots of fun, at first. Chelle and Lisa got along well, and Pat and I did, too. Pat's ex-husband -- Lisa's father -- would pick Lisa up and take her to the zoo, the movies, or visit. Sometimes he would bring her a toy or something, and when he was not taking her somewhere or buying her something, one of his sisters or his mother would.

Chelle started to resent the attention Lisa was getting. They started to fight and argue all the time. Once, we were having fried chicken for dinner. Pat put a piece of chicken on Chelle's plate and then she put a piece on Lisa's plate. Lisa said, "I wanted the piece you put on Chelle's plate" and started crying. Pat took the chicken and switched them. Chelle started crying and said, "Give it back to me!" Lisa quickly took a big bite out of the chicken, and Chelle went crazy. She started hysterically crying and throwing pieces of chicken across the room. I grabbed and shook her. "Chelle! stop it right now!" I tried to reason with her. "The chicken is all the same." She said, "Lisa gets whatever she wants, and I never get anything I want." Chelle was hurt. I tried to comfort her but could not make her feel better.

At school, Chelle had her teachers afraid of me. She would tell them, "My mother will come up to this school and she will be very angry with you, and I don't know what she'll do to you." Her teachers were very shocked to find out how cooperative I was. I explained to them I was only fourteen years old when Chelle was born and I did not have much guidance on how to raise her properly. I assumed it was the problem. After I explained my situation to her teachers, they understood and tried to work with her.

Chelle was hard to deal with. There was no compromise when it came to her. However, I understood Chelle's problem when she showed me a letter she had written to her father and asked me to mail it to him. In the letter, she said how much she wanted to get to know him and how she wanted him to know her. She gave him a big list of things she wanted for Xmas, and at the end of her letter she said, "If you don't answer this letter, I'll never write you again." I mailed the letter for her. I was hoping Bob would return her letter because it meant a lot to Chelle. However, he never did return a letter and it was hard for Chelle to deal with such rejection. She could not understand why her father hated her so much.

It never bothered her until Lisa moved in and her father paid attention to her. I wanted to help Chelle, but I did not know how. Some days were better than others, but there were still problems. I was trying to understand her, but I was starting to get angry. Every day by nine, my phone at work would ring and it would be Chelle's school, "We are sending her home because we cannot tolerate her behavior." I would have to take off work and get her. Chelle had no cause to be so disruptive. I could not understand. I explained to Chelle, "Your father's irresponsibility does not mean you are a bad person. Your dad will be sorry because of how he treats you. He is the bad person."

She would say, "I'm ugly and no one likes me." Whenever I shared these problems with my friends, they all responded the same: "Beat her now while she is young." Chelle got spanked from time to time, but I never hurt her or hit her with a belt. She would get a couple of slaps on her arms or her legs, and someone would swear I was killing her because she would scream her head off. I often avoided hitting her.

I throw myself a party for my twenty-third birthday. Chelle and Lisa were about to go to the babysitter's when Chelle went hysterical. She was kicking and screaming on the floor. Her strength was tremendous. One of my cousins was over and said, "I would never put up with my child acting up on me because I would beat her." I broke down and started crying. I could not beat her because she had an emotional problem. I knew she needed help I or a beating could not give her.

Chelle ended up at the sitter's and I had my party, but I worried about her all night. The next day, I called everyone I knew seeking how to help her. I was guided to the Adult and Child Mental Health Clinic. We went there for sessions every week. I did not think the program was helping. They never could find anything wrong with Chelle. They told me she was a sweet and even-tempered child. According to them there was not anything mental about her case and she does not belong in mental health. They then asked, "Do you feed her hot merals." as if I am the problem. However, I was still getting daily calls from her school because they could not put up with her conduct.

I could not believe the mental clinic would not correspond with her school. They said, "Chelle is ok. The five percent of the times she acts up is not considered a mental issue." I could not get them to see her problem was ongoing and daily. There was something wrong, and I knew it. All I could do was chant about the situation and hope things would get better. All I had was hope. I was so worried. Not only was I worried about Chelle, but also Pat had started seeing CG again. His mother was sick and dying from cancer. Pat felt sorry for him and took the bum back. I hated the way he treated her. I knew it was not his fault because he had no gun on her and she had no chains.

I was incredibly angry when I woke up early in the morning to go to work and CG would be asleep in the bed with her. I sternly said, "I don't want CG to spend the night!" I did not even have a man of my own I would allow to spend the night with me. I was angry because he was there, and I let her know. Pat ignored my request and would not tell CG I did not want him to sleep there. She was afraid to tell him because he would beat her. I told her, "I'll tell him myself, if you can't do it." I would leave for work before Pat did, and I found out she routinely left CG asleep in bed while we were at work. CG never worked. He would sleep all day and party all night. I went into Pat's bedroom, (which was Chelle's bedroom,) "CG, you can't spend the night here anymore." He said, "Okay." Later CG was in the bedroom fighting Pat.

I busted into the bedroom and said, "There will be no fighting in my house, and you have to leave now." He started getting angry with me and said, "You are meddling into our business." Pat started saying, "We're playing and not fighting." But I knew he was really fighting her, and he soon left.

One day, CG's friend Donaldo came over to my place with CG. I knew Donaldo and he would talk to me every time he saw me. I was not interested in him; he had just gotten out of prison and I did not trust him. CG told him I was crabby because I did not have a man. He said if I had a man in my life, I wouldn't treat him so badly when he came around to see Pat. Pat said, "CG said you're jealous of our relationship and do not want to see us happy; and you would do anything to break us up."

When Donaldo came by, we played a chess game. I beat him. I then went to the grocery store and Don went with me. He paid for my food. I was shocked because the men in Battle Creek had a reputation; women are supposed to take care of them. They did not believe in contributing. Although his paying did not impress me, I started dating Don because I did not want CG and Pat to think I was jealous.

Don talked all the time. He never stopped running his mouth. He always said, "I praise myself and I'm so great." He told everyone loudly and many time how fantastic he was. He did tell me, "I'm tired of running the streets. I'm ready to settle down." He was working so it was a plus. Don had a big house his father left to him. I would stay at his place from time to time. Another reason I started dating Donaldo was not because I liked him, but because I thought five years from now, he would be cute. It was a stupid reason, I know. Don was well groomed and was not a bad looking man, but he was not as handsome as I liked.

Pat and I got our income tax check on the same day. CG knew Pat had gotten hers and he knew I got mine. He mentioned to Don I had gotten my check. Don asked, "Can I borrow $60 from you because I need to get my car fixed? If I do not have a car to go back and forth to work, I'll lose my job and end up back in prison because I will have to rob people." I loaned him the money. He said, "I promise I will pay you back in a few days." A few days passed and he did not pay me. He had some sob story for an excuse. He then started telling me about an ex-girlfriend whose father owned a liquor store in Albion MI, a small town about thirty minutes east of Battle Creek. He said, "She gives me money all the time and she never expected it back."

I was angry and told him, "Don't compare me with anyone else because I'm different. I need my money and I'm not going to fight about it." He told me he would pay me the next day. I did not hear from him until late that night. He came over to tell me, "Don't come by my place tonight because my old girlfriend stopped by and is going to spend the night." He then asked me to please stop by the next day.

I said, "Where is my money? If you cannot pay me my money, then get the hell out of my house right now." He then balled his fist up and placed it on my face as if he were going to hit me. He knew better than to hit me because he would have either been dead or back in prison. He did not trust me or know me. He did not know what I would have done. I am so glad he changed his mind and did not hit me.

I had taken my chess set over to Don's place because we would play all the time. The set was special to me because my dad had given it to me before he died. I went to Don's house. He was not there but his girlfriend answered the door in her robe. She also had a black eye. "Is Don here?" I asked. "No." "Can you please give me my chess set." She said, "I can't give it to you because he will get mad at me."

I told her, "You're pitiful." I was glad she was the one getting abused and not me. I demanded her to give me my chess set. I told her, "All he is going to do is beat you up again." She still did not give me my set, but she told me Don was at the park. I was not going to rest until I got my chess set. I went to the park where all the non-working "niggers" hung out. I saw Don when I drove up, and I was walking towards him.

He was flirting saying, "I'm happy to see you," as he held his arms out like I was going to hug him. I said, "I want my chess set, and I will meet you at your place in one hour to get it." He could tell by the look in my eyes I meant what I said. About forty-five minutes later, I went to his place. I brought a man I worked with to make sure he was not going to try anything violent. I got my chess set and I never saw Don again.

CG was angry with Don because he had messed things up for him. When I was with Don, I would spend the night at his place and CG would be at my place with Pat. Don and I dated about one month. The night Don and I broke up, I ran into Marvin and went to visit him. I told him about Don and me. Marvin said, "I'm your friend and I'm here for you." I thought Marvin was the right person for me. He had matured some and he looked good as ever.

Since CG could not spend the night at my place anymore, Pat started staying stay places with him. She would leave Lisa home with me. Pat never would buy food. If it were not for me, sometimes Lisa would not eat. CG's mother had died. When his mother was living, CG really did not have a problem sleeping and eating, so with his mother gone, there was no one else except Pat, and her problem was she did not have her own place.

Pat came to me in tears and told me, "CG's stepfather told him he couldn't sleep at his place nor eat there for free." Pat then went to the grocery store and bought $100 worth of food. I was mad about it because she bought the food so I would not complain about CG eating food I had bought. I could not believe she would buy food for her no-good ass man and not for her own child.

We had a bad snowstorm one night. Pat was away from home somewhere with CG. Everything was covered with snow. There were all types of warnings to stay off the streets. The emergency crew was trying to help people stranded in their cars and homes from snow cave-ins. All businesses and schools were closed. I was stuck with Lisa because Pat could not get home. She did not even call until the next day. I was low on money and food and I was angry. Pat was somewhere having the time of her life and I was home being bothered with Chelle and Lisa crying and fighting all day.

Just because I was home and not doing anything does not mean I wanted to take care of someone's child while they get their cheap thrills. However, I loved Lisa and I did what I thought was necessary to help. I could not wait until I talked to Pat to tell her how much she disrespected me by disappearing.

A couple of days later, Pat came home. We had a long talk and decided she should move out and find her own place. But no matter what happened between Pat and me, we remained good friends. We still went out together and we still had fun together. A few times, I took Pat to Chicago with me to visit my friend Barbara Lee, who is hilarious.

When we went to Chicago, we partied all the time we were there. From Battle Creek to Chicago was one hundred-fifty miles. It took about two and a half hours. Many times, we took off on a Friday after work and did not return until Monday morning only in time to go to work. When we did not want to drive, we would take the train.

Pat finally found a place and moved out. I had my place to myself again. Another wonderful thing happened to me; I transferred my job to the Federal Center and was happy to be closer to home. I lived walking distance from the job. I did not have to drive twenty miles to Kalamazoo in snow and ice. On the mornings when the weather was bad, I had goose bumps on my face from the adventurous drive.

CHAPTER 24
CRAZY RELATIONSHIPS

Chelle and I were still having problems, but I was working at them and was not going to let them get the best of me. I can say for once I had a normal life. I spent my days at work and Chelle had her days at school. In the evenings, I was cooking dinner and helping her with her homework. It was hard to control Chelle, but I did the best I knew how. I tried with all my might to encourage her to do well in school. I know she was lonely because I worked all the time.

My aunt's dog had puppies and she suggested one would be company for Chelle. She gave one to us. It was a beautiful German Shepherd. We named her Tocki. When we got her, she was only one month old. Right away, I housebroke her very quickly. It was as if she understood everything I said. The first time she messed in the house, I talked to her. Most people say rub their noses in it and beat them and throw them outside. However, all I did was talk to her. Within days, she would run to the door and bark to go out.

At night, I would let her out and she would stay outside. Usually, I would get up and let her back in around three in the morning. One night, at about the same time, my doorbell rang. I got out of my bed and looked out the peephole and no one was there. I could not understand who was ringing my doorbell. I got back in bed and I heard the doorbell ring again. I got up to look again and no one was there. I thought it was the ghost who lived with me.

When Pat stayed with me, we returned home after a night out and soon realized neither of us had the key. We were locked out. I told Chelle to check the front door to see if by chance it was open. She checked the door and it was locked. Later, we decided we would break the window and get it fixed the next day. I returned to the front where Chelle had just checked. I was about to break the window when I looked, and the front door was ajar. There was no logical explanation, so we called it our ghost. There were a lot of things which would come up missing and would appear from nowhere.

However, at three in the morning the doorbell was ringing. I finally peeped out the window and Tocki was sitting on the porch; the dog had been ringing the doorbell by jumping up and her paw would hit the bell. From then on, whenever she wanted to come into the house, she would ring the doorbell. Another time, at about three in the morning, I got up because I heard some noises in my living room.

I was so surprised to see about five dogs in my house. My dog was having a party! My front door was wide open. I was not sure if my dog opened the door and let her friends in, or if I went to bed with my front door open, or if my ghost was on the loose again. I could not figure it out. Soon, I had to keep Tocki tied up because she had started attacking people. I had a big back yard, and I kept her chained to the side of the house. One day, it was cold outside. It was turning fall. It was five-forty-five in the morning and I wanted to be at work by six.

When I saw Tocki outside, I felt sorry for her and decided to let her stay in the basement out of the cold while I was at work. When I let her off the chain, she took off running and I could not catch her. I thought, "Forget her, I'm going to work." I knew she was not going to run away; I did not want her to attack anyone. As I was pulling out of my parking space, I noticed Tocki in my neighbor's garbage. She had knocked the can over. I stopped the car and went to get her and picked up the mess she made.

I grabbed her by her collar and started leading her home. She was soon leading me. I fell while I was still holding on to her collar. She was dragging me in the dirt across my neighbor's yard. Imagine, six in the morning, late for work, and being dragged through the mud by a dog who I felt sorry for and wanted to protect from the cold weather. I was angry. I had to change my clothes.

Tocki was a good dog. She was like part of the family. My daughter and I loved her so much, and she really loved us. Getting home again at three in the morning, Tocki was tied up outside as usual. I let her off her chain, so she could spend the night in the house. I had seen a weird movie and I was scared. As soon as I let Tocki off her chain, she leaped towards a man who was walking quietly towards me in my back yard. I did not even see the man. She attacked him and bit the blood out of him through his pants. He jumped up onto the top of my car and shouted, "Get your dog! Get your dog!" I asked him, "What are you doing in my back yard?" He told me, "I'm just passing by." Somehow, my dog saved me because he was up to no good. I do not know what he was planning, but thanks to my dog, he got a big surprise.

I was twenty five years old and still looking for a man in Battle Creek. I had a lot of one-night stands. I always thought the men cared about me. However, whenever I gave in, he would never come back. If I saw them out, they would ignore me. I could not understand. If I saw a man I liked, and I had sex with him, suddenly he did not like me anymore. A woman said to me, "You are too easy, and men don't like easy women. Make him wait for the sex and then he will come back for more." However, I knew it was not true because I tried not giving in, and they would become angry and would not come back. They did not want to get to know me.

First, there was Steven. We had a three-night affair. Then there was Freddie; he was so good-looking. We had a two-night affair. Those were about four months apart. Then there was Robert, a young college man. I thought he would be the right man for me.

We had a one-night affair, and he did not give me the correct telephone number.

Then there was Finley. He was the big gambling and numbers man of the town. We had a two-night affair. And let's not forget Dennis, who was married. We were together a couple of months. For my birthday, he bought me an expensive bottle of perfume. I did not like seeing a married man, though he was the nicest of all the guys I had seen. We mutually ended our affair. I needed to see him when I needed to, not when it was convenient for him.

There was a man who invited me to his house and came to pick me up. He got drunk and said, "You have to spend the night." He was trying to force me to sleep with him. I became furious and hid from him in his own house. When he fell asleep, I took his car and left a note saying I would bring it to him the next day and I did.

Another guy was Phillip. He was good-looking and could have been a great man for me. He took me to his house to meet his grandmother. We had not had sex yet, but we kissed. When he dropped me off, we told each other we were looking forward to seeing each other again. However, a couple of days later, he was killed in a car accident. I felt bad because we were getting to know each other. I also could not believe two days before he was killed, we were riding together in the same car and on the same street where he would die.

There was also a guy, Michael -- the best-looking man I had ever laid eyes on. He was after me, but I did not want any part of him because he had been to prison many times. Also, he was a women-beater. There were other men, but none worth mentioning.

I believe one reason none of these relationships worked out is because I am protected against any man who would make me unhappy. I did a lot of chanting and studying, and one thing I read from the Gosho "On Prayer" by Nichiren Daishonin was, "...should the tides cease to ebb and flow; or should the sun rise in the west, it could never happen that the prayers of devotees of the Lotus Sutra would go unanswered. Even if the devotees are not sincere, have insufficient wisdom, have impure bodies or do not observe precepts, they will be protected as long as they chant Nam Myoho Renge Kyo."

I was fed up with men, but because of my chanting and studying, I tried not to let it bother me. I always tried to keep the positive attitude the right man would come along soon. Smokey finally made a new album, *Where There's Smoke*. My favorite song on the album is "Cruising." The lyrics says, "And if you want it, you've got it forever, this is not a one-night stand." Prior to that album, I would tell my friends how I wanted a man to come into my life who would tell me we can make love and I did not have to worry because it was not a one-night affair. He would be coming back.

Through his music, Smokey has always encouraged me to feel better about myself. It was like his songs were my friends. They were little signs telling me to never give up my dream: to meet Smokey and personally thank him for being my best friend through his music. I felt as though he grew up with me and helped me find my way out of some tough situations. After I heard the song "Cruisin," I did find the hope -- and was trying to find the confidence -- I would find the right man.

CHAPTER 25

THE BURNING OF MY FRIEND

Barbara Lee started selling cocaine. She brought it to Battle Creek and she cleaned up by making a lot of money. It was easy to sell there because it was hard to come by. I did not like cocaine at all. The only drug I could tolerate was marijuana. I could not drink or take pills. I have tried heroin, acid, mescaline, and alcohol, and each one made me sick. Marijuana was the only drug I consumed without side effects and did not make me sick.

My financial situation started changing for the worse. I would receive a supplement check from the welfare program. It helped a little, but I did not want them to help me any longer. I hated turning in all my receipts and pay stubs to them. I took myself off the welfare program and got a part-time job, which I worked in the evenings and on weekends. All I did was work. I had to work two jobs because if I only worked one, I could not pay all my bills.

The Federal Center was my full-time job. I was on flextime. I could go to work anytime between six and ten in the morning. I had to put eight hours in from the time I started. I always tried to start at six because I could go home at two-thirty and it would be plenty of time to fix Chelle's dinner and spend some time with her before I had to be at my part time job at six.

I would average fifty hours hours per week on my full-time job and I would work twenty-five hours on my part time job. On average, I worked seventy-five hours a week. I was so tired. It is awful how I had to work hard to earn a decent living. I had a friend who said "You need a sugar daddy. I have this old man you can entertain for an hour about two days out of the week and he will give you the money you need. You ain't got to work all those hours." She set up an appointment for me to meet him. I agreed to meet him. He came to my house. When I saw him walking from his car to my door, working seventy-five hours a week suddenly appealed to me more than being with some old dried-up fool.

One weekend when Barbara Lee came to visit, I had to work all weekend. I worked from six in the morning until ten at night on a Saturday. When I got off, I was so tired. I wanted to relax and go to sleep, but Barbara Lee and everyone else wanted to go out to a club. Barbara Lee told me, "Girl Toot some coke and it will perk you up." I tried it, and by the time we got to where we were going, they had to wake me up in the car. I felt tired all night. I did not enjoy myself at all. I never wanted to do coke and have never done it since.

My sister Gia was pregnant again. Right after she got pregnant, her boyfriend's family moved to California. Gia was planning to move to California when her baby became six weeks old. Her first son was two years old. I was so proud of Gia because she finished high school and got a good job working for an insurance company. Gia was still living in her own apartment. When Gia was seven months pregnant, I was worried about her being alone, so I encouraged her to move in with me. I knew she was going to be leaving shortly after the baby was born, so I could deal with her staying there. We lived there together, and all was well.

When Barbara Lee would visit, we had a lot of fun. She gave me a nickname, Ugmoe. My nickname for her was Ugmore Turd. We would even address letters to each other with those names. We would get together, act silly, and laugh as if we were children. Barbara Lee and I would get together and sing our old grammar school alma mater. Gia was a very funny person also. When Barbara Lee and Gia got together, I spent the whole time laughing hysterically and rolling on the floor. As to what made them so funny, all I can say is you had to be there.

My friend Steven from Chicago called. He wanted to come

to Battle Creek to visit me. I had been living in Michigan for five years, and all those years, I had never heard from him. Sometimes, I would visit him when I went to Chicago, but his girlfriend would act crazy and start a fight with him. Eventually, I stopped calling or trying to see him when I went to Chicago. His girlfriend did not know we had seen each other when I worked at the hospital, but after she found out we had been together, she thought when I came it was for more than a friendly visit.

Steven came to see me one weekend and of course I had to work. The little time I spend with him was relaxing. He went back to Chicago and I never saw or talked to him again. I wanted to find a steady relationship. Marvin and I still saw each other from time to time. Usually when I saw him out at the club, he would say, "Hey Arden want to come over." or "Can I see you after the club." When we were together, it was always spontaneous, never planned. Marvin was still very immature.

When he came to visit me, he would always bring his gun. I hated guns and told him, "Don't visit me if you have to bring your gun." He told me, "My gun is my best friend and I take it wherever I go." Also, since Marvin was so handsome, he dated several women and they were immature also. Some of them carried guns too.

Each of his women was ready to fight any other woman if she thought they wanted Marvin. I tried not to see Marvin so much, but he was a very romantic man and would say to me as he romantically whispered in my ear, "Arden I really care about you. Would you marry me?" I ask, "Will I, or would I?" "Which do you mean Marvin?" Even though I knew he did not mean what he was saying, it was nice to have someone hug me and tell me they cared. Marvin also reminded me of Smokey, and I always pretended he was.

One day when Marvin came over, he was playing with his gun. He pointed it at his head and said, "I'm getting ready to blow my head off." We were sitting on my bed. He then cocked the hammer back and held it with his thumb while his finger would pull the trigger. I was yelling, "Marvin stop!" If he were to make the slightest mistake of letting his thumb slip from the hammer, he would have blown his head off right there in my bed in front of me. Marvin had gone crazy. I decided then I would not see him again.

Soon the news spread through the town Marvin had shot and killed a man in cold blood in a bar one night. Rumors had it he shot the man because he was sitting in the seat, he wanted to sit in. While in jail, he wrote me poetry and would say he missed me and wanted me to visit him. I never went to visit, nor did I write him back. I did not want any part of him.

Gia finally had her baby, a beautiful boy. She now had two boys. She also moved to California as she had planned. I wished I could have gone with her. I could not bear living in Battle Creek any longer, and there was no way I was going back to Chicago. I stayed in Battle Creek and would soon figure a way out.

Chelle and I were alone again. It was so peaceful when it was the two of us. Tocki was very ferocious. She broke off her chain and attacked the little boy who lived next door. He was only three years old. My dog almost killed the boy. I felt horrible. The mother was so nice about the situation. She could have called the police and I could have gotten in trouble, but she decided not to. She said, "You had her locked on a chain so it's not your fault." Tocki was getting to be too much trouble. However, she was a good watchdog for me. I did not want to get rid of her, but I did not want to be charged with murder or attempted murder because of my dog. I was glad the woman decided not to press charges against me. I started keeping the dog inside in the basement. I hated to keep her in the basement in a dark and ugly place, but I had no choice. They did not make a chain she could not break.

I met a guy at the Federal Center named Raymond. He liked me. We had established a good relationship with each other. He was new in Battle Creek and on a work study program from Ohio State College. He was on a summer program at the Federal Center, but he had one more semester in college, and after graduating, he would be moving to Battle Creek for his job at the Federal Center.

Raymond would buy marijuana, and since he was new in

town, he did not know where to get it. My cousin Celeste was one of the biggest marijuana dealers in Battle Creek. I would take him to her place. Raymond and I eventually became good friends and lovers. I knew I had found the right man. He was about three years younger than me, but I figured it did not matter. He was a working educated man, which was rare in Battle Creek.

Raymond would take me out to dinner, and we would go to the movies. We had good times together. Even though Raymond was nice to me, he still never communicated with me. He never told me anything about himself. He was always quiet. I would urge him, "Talk to me and tell me about your life." He would get angry and say, "I don't have anything to say." I was totally confused, because he would call me every day. I assumed he liked being with me because I like being with him.

When the summer was over, Raymond left to go back to Ohio to complete his studies and was coming back in February after he graduated. He never contacted me the semester he was away. I still decided to wait for him. My grandfather had started helping me financially. He loaned me money when I was low. He would say "Here is $100 to help you. You can pay it back next week." I was glad I could depend on him. My grandfather once said, "When I die, I'm not leaving anything to anybody. I worked hard for mine and am not giving it to anyone." He also said, "Don't predict anyone's death because you might go before them."

He also helped me keep my house up. He came over and fixed my plumbing and fixed the wiring. My grandfather and I had a conversation one day. He said, "I will always be here when you need me. You lost your parents and you need help." I was so pleased because my grandfather could care less about any of his grandchildren. We all had to depend on each other, which was hard because none of us had anything. We all struggled to make our own ends meet.

The day after my grandfather and I talked, he got sick and was in a coma in the hospital. I could not believe it because he was such a strong and healthy man. He had never been sick before. He was seventy-five years old. I was so happy he was better in two weeks. We were at my grandfather's side when he woke up from his coma and he looked directly at me. He could hardly talk, yet he asked me, "Where is the money I loaned you?" I felt angry, not because my grandfather owed me but because I was struggling and working two jobs trying to make ends meet. It was not because he needed the money. He was quite wealthy. What would be wrong with helping me, but he quickly wanted it back? I believe My grandfather did not want to die with me owing him money.

I gave my grandmother the money. My grandfather got well, but he kept getting sick. He was unable to help me with my house. I found myself needing too many things done to the house. Also, my dog broke the window in the basement and a mouse had gotten in the house, plus, I was starting to see roaches. There was no way I was going to live in a house with mice and roaches.

It would have cost more than the house was worth to fix everything and call for an exterminator. I need to find an apartment so I can call the landlord when there are problems. I could not handle watering the grass and keeping the yard clean from falling leaves or shoveling snow.

I did not want to get rid of my dog, but I knew it would be impossible to have her in an apartment. I saw an ad at work where the military was recruiting dogs for training. I called, and they were interested in buying my dog. I was extremely interested in selling her to the military because I felt she would get good treatment. I sold her, and she was shipped to Texas.

The military paid me $300 for Tocki and paid for shipping her to Texas. I had to take her to the airport in a cage. She was sad to leave, and Chelle and I were sad to see her go. However, I needed to move, and I wanted her to have the best life possible.

After weeks of looking, I finally found the perfect apartment. I enjoyed living there. It was a nice big two-bedroom luxury apartment with a dishwasher, air conditioning, intercom system, and a balcony. It was wonderful living there.

After I got settled in my new apartment, I decided to give a housewarming party. Raymond came and had an enjoyable time. I thought for sure we were going to have a long-lasting relationship. I was having a great time at my party until Raymond wanted to leave.

I asked, "Why are you leaving? What do you have to go home to?" He would not answer. I said, "That's right, run away. I do not understand why you are leaving" He got angry and said, "I'm not going to argue with you," and he stormed away. I was not going to let the situation bother me. I continued to enjoy myself.

All my friends came. Pat and CG were there, and although they claimed to be broken up, CG would not let her be. She wanted to dance and have fun, but she could do neither because CG would not dance with her nor would he let her dance with anyone else.

Pat and a friend said, "We're going to the club to get more people to come to the party." It was a lot of people coming and going but we wanted more people. It was one in the morning when Pat and Sandra left. CG had left before Pat. CG returned at two and Pat had not returned yet. The party was still going on. There were about seven people at my party. CG stayed until three. Pat never returned, and CG seemed angry.

At three-thirty everyone left, and I was tired and went to bed. At four-thirty my phone rang, and it was CG, "Did Pat ever come back?" I told him, "No, she never came back." I hung up the phone and went back to sleep. At five-thirty, it was CG calling looking for Pat. I told him, "I never heard from her." I was worried about Pat. I thought she would come back. She only left to go to get more people.

The next day it was raining, and I did not go anywhere. I did not see Pat or talk to her. She did not have a telephone. We worked in the same building, so I knew I would see her at work. I wanted to find out why she never came back to the party. However, Pat did not come to work on Monday. I had to work my evening job. I got off at ten. I drove to Pat's and she was not home, and her front window was broken out. I feared something terrible had happened to her.

Tuesday, I decided not to go to work. I called Pat's office and they said she was not in. I went over to her place. She was there, and she was limping across the floor. I was happy she was alive. I asked her, "What happened to you?" and she told me, "CG broke my window because he was angry, I wouldn't let him in." Then she said, "Ouch I have a cut on my leg from a piece of glass."

She showed me the cut. It looked really bad and I said, "You need to go to the doctor. You probably have glass stuck in your leg." I did not think she was telling me the truth. She had a terrified look on her face. I thought she could at least talk to the doctor if she could not talk to me. I offered to take her as she did not have transportation.

Pat was in the doctor's office about fifteen minutes. She came out and said, "I have to stay for a few days." I had to drive her to get her daughter and gather her things she needed for her hospital stay. I questioned her in the car. I asked, "Why would the doctor put you in the hospital for a little cut on your leg? I mean it's bad but not bad enough to be hospitalized." She then told me the truth.

She said, "I spent the night with a guy I saw at the club. CG was hiding in the bushes and saw the guy drop me off. I went into the house. A few minutes later CG knocked on my door and I refused to answer it. The next thing I knew, he broke the window and was inside."

She said CG walked in and did not say one word to her. He walked over and turned the iron on. She said, "I thought he was going to iron something, but when the iron got hot, he held it close to my face." He then said, "You can't go out with another man, whether we are broken up or not, or you'll wear an iron print on your face."

She said, "He then took the iron and pressed it to my stomach burning it. I was in the nude. After he pressed the iron on my stomach, I rolled over and he then pressed the iron on my side. I was screaming and trying to get away. Then he grabbed an umbrella and tried to put it up inside my vagina. I was desperately trying to get away from him. I started kicking him and he grabbed my leg and started biting it. He bit a plug of skin out of my leg."

She then said, "My skin was in his mouth and he spit the skin covered with blood onto me as he was standing over me." She said he then shook his head from side to side as if he was coming back to normal. Pat said he started crying and hugging her and saying, "I'm sorry. Pat, I love you very much and did not want to hurt you. Pat please I love you."

She kept emphasizing how many times he told her he loved her. She said, "He wants me to himself and he does not want another man to share me, and so we made love." She said, "As we were having sex, there was blood all over me because my leg as well as my burns were bleeding." All I could do was cry. She said she had to go home and pack some things for the hospital. First, she had to find a babysitter for her daughter. Lisa's father agreed to take her in, so we dropped her off.

We then went by Pat's place where she left a note for CG. The note read, "Had to go to the hospital for a couple of days, nothing to worry about, Love, Pat." I told her, "Pat, you're crazy! You need to call the police and have him arrested." She did not comment or say anything except, "I have to go to the bank to leave him some money, so he can pay for the window." I took her everywhere she had to go. I then took her to the hospital.

After she got settled in her room, I asked her again, "Pat, do you want to call the police?" She told me, "I don't want CG to go to jail." I asked her, "Why don't you stop seeing CG?" She said, "I'm afraid and I did stop seeing him. That's why I'm here in the hospital." I picked up the telephone, called the police, and asked them if I could do something about what he did to her. I told the police how he brutalized her, and she will not press charges. I told them she was afraid of him and she needed professional help. The officer I spoke to said there was not a thing I could do without her permission. He said, "Some women like to be beaten by their men." I realized when Pat described CG beating her, she kept emphasizing how he was telling her he loved her. The only time he told her he loved her was when he was beating her. In a sense, she looked forward to her beatings to be told she was loved.

Even though I went through some hard and similar times

with Bob, I could not relate to a person enjoying being beaten. I did notice when we were talking about CG and her, she would convince herself during the conversation she did something stupid and deserved what he was doing to her. I hope never to deal with such a relationship. I wanted Pat to realize she should have more self-respect; wake up and get the hell out. I thought she was through with him until she left him a note. I could not believe it.

The next day, when I went to the hospital to visit her, Pat was on the telephone in tears, calling the police on her daughter's father because he was running into a problem keeping Lisa. He was remarried, and his wife was expecting a baby any day. She did not want to keep Lisa, so he was telling Pat she had to find another babysitter. Pat was telling the police about an incident when her ex-husband was carrying a gun which happened about five year ago. Of course, there was not a thing the police could do. I then asked Pat, "Why would you call the police on your daughter's father because his wife doesn't want to babysit but you won't call the police on the man who put you here?" She hunched her shoulders as if to say, "I don't know."

I then told her, "If you cannot tell CG to get the hell out of your life, then you should buy a forty-five automatic and blow his head off." Pat looked at me and said, "I know, I'm going to ask CG to get me a gun." I told Pat, "You are sick and crazy." Every ounce of respect I had for her (which was not much) left my body. I walked out of the hospital room and did not want to see her again. It was time for me to find another friend. I would feel awful if CG killed Pat because she and I went out together. I did not want to see her again for my safety. Somehow though, Pat was like a sister I could not turn my back on her. I figured I would not hang out with her.

CHAPTER 26

PARTY TIME

I wanted to develop my relationship with Raymond, however I noticed he was starting to take breaks with this woman who worked at the Federal Center. I thought she was unattractive. She would grow hair on her face, and she would shave. She also had little black spots all over her face like she had chicken pox scars. I could not understand how he could be with her in front of me. I wondered if they were dating.

I noticed they were having lunch together in the cafeteria in front of everyone. Raymond never wanted anything from me but sex. He would call me at night and wanted to be with me, but he never would take a break nor have lunch with me. I started complaining to him about being with her so much. I told him, "I thought we were together, and people think you are dating her and Raymond it's embarrassing to me." He assured me nothing was going on between them. I believed him, so I continued to see him.

Ray's car broke down, so I offered to pick him up for work. He told me he would walk. I could not understand why he would not let me pick him up. I soon found out Spots – my nickname for her -- was picking him up every morning. He never told me she was picking him up, but I found out. Every time Raymond and Sharon (AKA Spots) did anything together, I would receive a telephone call from someone who had saw them together. A couple of times, Pat saw her drop him off, so I knew they were riding together.

When I confronted Ray, I said, "You want to come over to satisfy yourself. You do not care anything about me. I am no sex machine and I refuse to be treated like one. You absolutely humiliate me in front of my friends." I was so angry with Raymond. I did not want to see him anymore or talk to him. I wanted to forget about him.

I met another friend named Brenda who also worked at the Federal Center. Like Pat, Brenda is white and has a half-black daughter. Brenda would visit my desk or call me all the time. We started becoming close friends – eventually, even closer than Pat because I was having problems being Pat's friend.

I first met Brenda at Christmastime. She was a new employee. She mailed me a Christmas card saying she was hoping we would become good friends for a long time. We had a lot in common. We shared secrets, hung out together, and made plans for a great Christmas together with our daughters.

I got Chelle a big sister from the Big Brother/Big Sister Organization. Because I was working two jobs, I could not spend as much time with Chelle. Her big sister, Cherri, was incredibly good to Chelle. She came over and picked her up almost every weekend and was a major help to us. Cherri would buy Chelle clothes and tried to help her with her disciplinary problem at school – and Chelle started to improve.

On Christmas Eve morning, Chelle wanted to go shopping to buy a gift for her big sister's mother. I told her, "Wait until I get off and I will take you shopping." I was working from nine to two. I told Chelle, "Don't leave the apartment." She was eleven years old. I would leave her home alone while I was working evenings and weekends. I did not want her out while I was not home because she was safe at home.

My part time job was at K-Mart. Because of the time of year, the store was busy. While I was working, I looked up and saw Raymond standing in line buying something, though he was there to see me. He had been trying to find a way to get on my good side, but I remained angry with him and refused to see him. I told him, "You have to stop seeing her before I will see you again because you are disrespecting me." I am sure he was planning to say something sweet to me so I would melt and say, "Okay, you can come over." But I was determined to show him he was not going to treat me any way and still be with me sexually.

The moment I saw Raymond, my supervisor said, "Arden you have a phone call from a hospital saying it's an emergency." I grabbed the phone, "Hello." "Are you Ms. Arden?" "Yes." "We have your daughter Chelle here in the emergency room. She was hit by a car." I said, "You must be mistaken. I left the house half an hour ago. My daughter is at home. There has not even been enough time for her to be hit by a car and already taken to the hospital. Plus, I told her not to leave the apartment. My daughter would never disobey me."

Nevertheless, the nurse said, "Get here immediately because she has to have surgery." I told Raymond where I was going and left for the emergency room. When I arrived, Chelle was in shock. She had a broken leg and a minor concussion. They needed to operate on her leg, but they were having a hard time giving her the anesthetic to put her to sleep because she would not let them stick the needle in her arm.

Every doctor and nurse on staff were in Chelle's room trying to comfort her and hold her down. People stood at the door trying to see what all the screaming was for. I was so nervous, I soon felt faint myself, and one nurse had to attend to me. When they finally had Chelle pinned down and were ready to administer the shot, she said, "Please, please, please let me say one more thing." The nurse said, "What is it, honey?" Chelle said, "Let me get the hell out of here." Chuckles filled the room. They finally got her sedated, set the bone in her leg, and put a cast on it. I felt bad Chelle had to spend Christmas in the hospital. I had some extra cash and made sure Chelle had the best Christmas ever.

When she woke up from surgery, I was there with all her gifts. Cherri came and had lots of gifts for Chelle too. Brenda also came and we spent the day playing with Chelle's new toys. Visiting hours were over. We stayed until security made us leave. Chelle started crying and said, "Please don't leave me here." I assured her I would be back the first thing in the morning, which would be Christmas Day.

Brenda, Pat and I went out to the club to party for Christmas Eve. I truly could not enjoy myself. All I could think about was Chelle. We should have been home together on Christmas Eve. A friend of mine named Percy was at the club, and we started dancing and talking. We had a "one-night stand" some time ago. He called me and tried to get back with me, but I had been mean to him, and told him not to call me anymore. I told him about Chelle's accident, and I was feeling lonely and depressed.

Percy said, "Do you want some company? You should not wake up Christmas morning all alone." Under a normal situation, I would have told him, "Go to hell" but this time, I told him it was okay for him to come by. I could not be with whom I wanted to be with because he was too busy spending time with another woman, and I did not want to be alone. The next morning Raymond was knocking on my door. I do not know how he got into the building because the entrance was locked. A person would have to ring the doorbell to get to my door and I had a choice to let them in or not. Raymond said, "I want to spend Christmas Day with you." I let him in. He said, "I called Chelle and talked to her and wished her a Merry Christmas."

I told Raymond, "I have company in my bed, asleep. I'm also going to spend the day with Chelle." Raymond got angry and called me a slut. "You're probably glad Chelle is gone so you can screw around." At first, I was upset because I did not want the man in my bed. Then, I thought it serves Raymond right. He only called Chelle to make sure she was indeed in the hospital and I was alone, and he could come over and talk me into having sex with him. I would never let him, or any man spend the night with me if my child were home and Ray knew it.

He was probably going to trick me and leave after sex. I hated he only wanted me for sexual purposes. Later at work, Raymond started changing. He stopped spending lunchtime and breaks with Spots, and it was not long before he and I started to see each other again. Brenda, Pat and I would go out together and terrorize the town. All the women hated us, and all the men loved us. Most of the women especially hated me because I was the new girl in town. Brenda and Pat were both from there, but all the women hated them too because they were white and only dated black men. I saw too with my own eyes how a 'black man will pass up two naked beautiful black women to get to a fat ugly white woman.' Black men would run me over to get to Pat or Brenda to flirt with them and try to get something going on with them.

Most of the time, Brenda and Pat were the only two whites in the club. Also, because I never did hang out with any of the black women, they thought I thought I was better than they were, but I did not know any of them. I had a few black girlfriends, but we were casual acquaintances. I was afraid they were like Cynthia who ended up sleeping with the man I confided in her about. I did not trust many women.

Brenda and Pat both had cars, but CG would never let Pat drive hers and neither would he give her a ride anywhere. Pat did not even have a telephone, so it was hard to communicate with her outside of work. So sometimes, Brenda and I would go out together and Pat would stay at home. Once, Pat, Brenda, and I, and each of our daughters went to Lansing, Michigan to visit my sister Ava, who had moved there. We went out to a club and had a heck of a good time. I entered a leg contest and came in second place. There was no second-place prize though, but it was fun. (We met Earvin "Magic" Johnson. He was in the club.)

Three in the morning, we were on our way back to Battle Creek. From Lansing to Battle Creek was a forty-five minute drive. About fifteen minutes after we started back, my car broke down. Chelle had a big cast on her leg from her ankle to her thigh. We were stranded on a very dark highway. There was not a light in sight. It was snowing heavily, and boy, was it cold. Brenda had a gun with her and pulled it out of her purse, thinking someone may try to harm us. I said "We don't need a gun. All we need to do is chant." Of course, Pat and Brenda looked at me as if I were crazy. I then started chanting. I said "Nam Myoho Renge Kyo" about four times and out of nowhere came a big truck and it stopped to help us.

It was a huge Meijer's Department store semi-truck - on its way to Battle Creek. It was nice and a miracle the trucker stopped. He could not see us as he pulled up, and he did not know our intentions. When he saw it was three women and three children stranded in a blizzard, he offered to take us to Battle Creek. However, there was not enough room for all of us in the truck. Another Meijer's truck was following him, and he radioed for him to stop. He did, and we all piled into the two trucks. It was funny seeing Chelle climb in the truck with a big cast on her leg. It was such a huge truck, we had to climb a ladder to get inside.

The truck drivers were nice to us. On the way to Battle Creek, we were talking to each other on the CB radio. They bought us coffee, plus, they bought great big suckers for our kids at the truck stop in Battle Creek. We called a cab from the truck stop and went to Pat's place.

Pat was afraid because it was about five-thirty in the morning when we finally got to Battle Creek. She did not know how CG was going to act toward her for coming in so late. She knew she was going to get beat up. So, Brenda and I went to her place to explain to CG why we were back so late/early. I did not know what was wrong with my car. I did not worry much, though because the car was old, and I had it for about three years already and only paid $150 for it when I bought it. Luckily though, there was a minor problem with my car. It only cost $15 to fix.

CHAPTER 27
NO USE, IT'S NOT WORKING

My relationship with Raymond started going bad because he was starting to see Spots again. Brenda called me at work and said, "If you go by the credit union right now, you'll see them together." I walked down the hallway and sure enough, there they were talking. Raymond walked away from Spots when he saw me walking towards them. I did not stop. I kept walking and pretended I was going to the credit union.

On my way back to my office, I saw them again in another place as if they were hiding from me. I walked over to Raymond and asked, "Can I talk to you?" He said, "I don't have time." I became angry and said, "You better not call me tonight because I never, ever, ever, ever want to see you again!" I walked away angry and Raymond and Spots watched me walk off.

A few minutes later, Raymond called me at work and asked, "Why did you act so silly? We're only friends." I told him, "If you talked to me as much and as many times as you talked to her, I would feel like I was your friend too. You treat me as if you're embarrassed to be seen with me."

I was so angry, I said, "I can't believe you want a spotted man-faced woman who has to shave instead of a beautiful woman like me, and my beauty is more than looks because I'm a good caring person, too." I asked him, "Do y'all use the same razor to shave in the mornings? I bet you guys fight over the razor and the mirror." He said, "You are crazy" and he then hung up the phone on me.

A few minutes after our phone call, Spots came to my office and asked if we could talk. I said "OK." She said, "Did you tell Raymond I had a man looking face, and do you call me Spots?" I immediately started laughing. I told her, "I was truly angry with Raymond and it was personal between him and me. I do not dislike you and I did not mean it derogatorily towards you and, if I did, I would have told you to your face."

She said, "Raymond and I are friends and you should understand." I told her, "I don't understand. Why does he want to be with me sexually and does not want to be with me around other people?" She said, "You want what I get, and I want what you get, because I want to have sex with Raymond."

We did have a good talk. "Hold out on the sex part as long as you can. I would much rather have him as a friend than a sex partner. If you hold out on the sex, maybe he'll marry you." I apologized for being so silly and immature as was sorry for some of the things I said about her. With some of the animosity between us now gone, we left each other feeling better.

When I told Pat and Brenda what happened, they tried to persuade me to beat up Spots. I never wanted to fight. I told them, "I am going to back away from the situation and find someone else." However, Raymond would not leave me alone. He always called, and sometimes I would agree to see him. I did not love him as much as I was lonely for love.

I knew I was getting the wrong kind of love. I wanted someone who would treat me like I was special in his life. I did not want a man to make love to me and then tell me he really cared about me, or I was the only woman in his life, when, in fact, he was a lying dog. They do not call the next day because they will be doing and saying the same things they said and did to me but with a different woman.

More than ever, Pat seemed to be under a spell with CG. Brenda and I could not believe the changes she was going through. Pat, Brenda and I would have lunch together every day, but Brenda wanted to stop Pat from going to lunch with us. She was sort of a mooch. She never had money, and one of us would end up sharing our food with her or buying her food. Plus, sometimes we would smoke marijuana and Pat never had any. She always smoked ours. Brenda and I had made plans for lunch. It was easy to do because we worked in the same office. As Brenda and I was leaving, Pat called.

"I want to go with you." I did not tell Brenda Pat was meeting us. When Brenda and I arrived at the car, Pat was already waiting. Brenda looked at me and asked, "Does she have to come with us?" I said, "Let's go to my place for lunch." I only worked a few blocks from home. Brenda said, "If she's coming, then I'm not." It was uncomfortable because Brenda had said all of this in front of Pat.

Brenda and Pat were rivals because they were both white women with black daughters. They both liked black men only, and they both liked men who treated them like dogs by taking their money and beating them up and having other women. When I first met Brenda, she was recovering from her ex-husband beating her with a table leg. All her men beat her too.

Brenda claimed CG had been making eyes at her and had driven past her place several times. Pat claimed CG said Brenda made eyes at him. Pat, Brenda and I were such good friends, but I suddenly found myself in the middle of a war between them. They would each badmouth the other to me. Sometimes when they were drunk it was worse. I do not know how I got mixed up with these people because I was not like them at all.

Brenda and I were on a break together when Pat walked up to Brenda and said, "I heard CG was trying to date you." Brenda laughed and said, "I would never have a man who treated me like an ironing board." I was sitting in the middle between them. Pat told Brenda, "At least my man didn't beat me with a table leg." It was back and forth. They started calling each other fat and ugly. Finally, I said, "Please stop acting like children." They were even talking about fighting each other. I said, "If you fight, you can lose your jobs." I then pleaded for them to come to their senses. Finally, Pat left.

Brenda started taking advantage of me. I offered to watch her daughter while she went out. She had started hanging out with these women who were not at all my cup of tea. One woman was a prostitute, the other was a gangster who participated in shoot outs. I refused to go out with them. It was on a weeknight when I offered to babysit for Brenda's daughter. The next morning came and Brenda had not come home all night. I could not even go to work because I could not leave her child alone. I was so mad. I was sure I would never babysit for her again.

Battle Creek was making me live the kind of life I did not want to live. I was desperately trying to find the right way to live and be happy. None of my relationships worked -- neither the relationships I had with men nor my friendships with women. I still had chanting. I did it every day, which gave me hope and I would find the right man and a respectable friend or two.

I kept close communications with Gia in California. She found a good job and a nice babysitter right away. Now and then she would call me and say, "You would like it here in Los Angeles." I agreed, because when I went to get Bear, I liked the way the air felt when it hit my face. I was not ready to move to California without first having a job and a place to live lined up. I had to know I would be able to support my child and myself. From time to time, I thought about moving, but I was in Battle Creek for now and had to survive until I could find a way to move.

CHAPTER 28

TRYING TO FIND A
DECENT PLACE

I t was February again, the year I turned twenty-six. I asked
Raymond if we could spend my birthday together. We had
been talking from time to time, but we hardly saw each other
anymore. He said, "I have something to tell you. I have a fiancée
in Ohio. She is getting ready to move here with me. We've been
dating for years." All I could do was be sarcastic. As my jaw
dropped, I said, "So, now you share something personal with
me. Too bad the news did not come with a gift receipt because I
would have exchanged it for an iron and taken a few lessons from
CG and burned your butt. Why weren't you honest with me?"
He said, "I couldn't tell you." "Raymond, you took advantage of
me." He said, "If you thought I was seeing other women, then you
should have left me alone." Hmmm I thought "If that iron is too
expensive, I'll get a Louisville Slugger." I could not understand,
but I did not let the situation bother me. I started dreaming about
Smokey again, and moving to California was sounding good.

What convinced me to move to Los Angeles was when my
sister sent me Smokey Robinson's address. I wrote him a fan
letter to thank him for being who he was and for existing in my
lifetime. I am sure he did not read the letter, and if he did, he
probably got a good laugh. But I did not care how he felt because
I was in total ecstasy to write a letter to my lifelong dream date.

Chelle and I were getting along better, but she would make me so angry when I had to take her to the doctor for a checkup on her leg. At one point, they wanted to change her cast. All they had to do was cut the old one off and put another one on. Chelle screamed and yelled like a fool, and I screamed and yelled back at her like a fool. She was afraid of the cast saw. The nurse said, "Look, honey," and rolled the cast cutter across her hand to show Chelle it was not going to cut her or hurt. Chelle still would not let her cut it off.

I was so angry, I said, "Chelle, I'm going to kill you if you don't let them take it off." I then hit her in her nose right in front of the doctor. Her nose started bleeding. The doctor said, "Now mother, don't get upset with her. We'll put her in the hospital and cut if off while she is asleep." I was so angry with Chelle because I had wasted my time. I had to leave work early at least three times a week to take her to the doctor. I wanted her to at least cooperate. Finally, Chelle's leg was healed and the final cast was ready to come off. I thought she would be happy to finally get her cast off. However, we still had to go through the same issues. This time I said, "Please, Chelle, be brave and let them cut it off."

When we got to the doctor's office, she was brave to a point. They partially cut it off and she started having fits as they were almost finished. Finally, the doctor came in and said, "She'll have to be hospitalized again so we can do it while she's asleep." Mustering all the anger and strength in my body, I tore the cast off with my bare hands. I was glad she did not have to be hospitalized again.

Now she needed physical therapy to regain the strength in her leg. She absolutely hated therapy and cussed at the therapist every time I took her. There was no reasoning with Chelle. However, we got through it somehow. It was turning summer, and it was a horrible winter we had been through! Not only was it wintertime outside, but I felt as if I was in the winter of my life. Nichiren Daishonin says in his Gosho," "Winter always turns into spring."

I could not wait until I was in the springtime of my life. I wanted things to get better. As summer approached, I was very tired of working two jobs. I wanted to quit K-Mart, but I really needed the money. My job title was evening and weekend supervisor. Many people resented me because some employees had worked there for over ten years and could not handle the supervisory position. They were always lying to me and making my job difficult. Most of the time, they refused to do what I asked of them. One day, I could not take any more. In the middle of a busy day, I handed in my keys, told them, "I quit" and walked out.

I started taking a new approach in my Buddhism practice. Most people think Buddha is a little fat man whom people thought of as God. But he was a man who reached enlightenment and spent the rest of his life helping others do the same. As a Buddhist, I was striving to reach "Buddhahood: the state of an enlightened being who has found the path to the end of suffering." But I was still suffering. I was not living up to my true aspirations. I knew chanting Nam Myoho Renge Kyo to the Gohonzon was the greatest of all joys. It was not working for me. I then decided to elevate my life condition; chanting more will do it.

I took a new approach towards my friends. I started encouraging them to chant. I started attending more meetings. I was wholeheartedly ready to put my practice first so I could change my dreadful situation. With a new determination, I started chanting at least one hour each day. As a result, within one month, I received a promotion at work and was now making what I made working two jobs. I was now starting to feel the springtime entering my life.

There was this little voice in my head saying, "Don't give up. Fight hard to overcome." It is like climbing to experience *The Moon Over Kyoto*. I told Brenda, "I'm moving to California because I have got to get out of Battle Creek." Brenda said, "Yeah, Arden, okay." She thought I was crazy.

Somehow, even though I was feeling better and overcoming some of my hardships and making more money, I found myself with the biggest problem ever: I had fallen behind with my rent. I had never paid my rent late before and considered it a catastrophe when I could not pay on time. I thought the promotion would make a difference. My apartment was too expensive for my budget and I was falling behind. If I worked two jobs, I could afford it. But I was tired and could not stand having a second job any longer. I had been doing it for two years. I needed a break.

I called one of my chanting friends and told her I was having hard times. I thought she could encourage me because she had been chanting for ten years, plus she was a big leader in my chanting group. I asked her, "If I'm chanting like I'm supposed to, then why am I facing such difficulties?"

She said, "Chant until the problem is gone." She explained in Buddhism, there are two types of benefits. One is conspicuous, and the other is inconspicuous." She said, "What you are experiencing is called inconspicuous benefits. Something is changing in your life. You will soon see the benefit if you continue to chant. When you give up is when you'll lose." Easy for her to say. However, I was encouraged to continue. She said, "Find a dream. If you do not have dreams, then you will not experience the true meaning of being a true Buddhist. One must have goals and dreams. Do not flow with society. Make some noise. Make some waves."

I was encouraged but totally confused because I knew the one dream, I already had was impossible to achieve: getting Smokey. What a stupid dream for me to have. Waiting for a man who do not know I exist. Also, he was married for years to the same woman. They were once featured in a magazine talking about how much in love they were. I still chanted for it because I did not know what else to do.

The last thing my friend said to me was, "Remember, Buddhism is commonsense." The next commonsense thing to do about my situation was to find a cheaper apartment. My rent was $250 a month. I thought I could afford something between $180 and $200. I started looking, but I was getting depressed because I was so comfortable in my luxury apartment. Cheaper apartments were not as nice, and I found it hard to step down even a little. One apartment I looked at had mice running across the floor. I could not bear the thought of moving out of my luxury apartment for a place having mice and roaches.

I thought about applying for a loan at my credit union, so I could pay the rest of my rent and go back to my part-time job. I had a choice: either work myself night and day and never be home to enjoy the apartment I was working so hard to keep or stay home and spend my evenings in surroundings I truly hated.

I chose the first because I needed to be happy in my living situation. I went to my credit union and put in for a $300 loan. They turned me down. I asked, "Why did you turn me down when I have an excellent work history and a good pay history with you? I had a loan before and paid it back never missing a payment." They told me, "We have to follow the Federal Reserve Bank and they have forbidden credit unions to issue loans." I told them, "They are destroying my life? What's the telephone number to the Federal Reserve Bank?"

I got the number to an office in Detroit. When I called the number, I spoke to someone who gave me another number to call in Chicago. I called the number and they told me, "The reason we can't give loans is because we are following orders from the President of the United States."

I hung up the telephone and called information to get the number to the White House. I was so angry, I wanted Jimmy Carter to tell me personally why my credit union could not give me a loan. "Hello, May I speak to President Carter please." I was encouraged to call my senator, so I called his office. The person I spoke with said, "I understand your frustrations. I suggest you write the President and gather all your friends and family and have them write letters too." I said, "I tried to call him. I don't understand why he won't talk to me." He suggested I might want to become a politician. He said I had the fighting spirit. I was flattered, but I still had a problem. My credit union would not give me a loan. I went home, and I wrote the President a letter and I chanted about it.

I thought it would be exciting to have Secret Service men come to my home and investigate me, so I made a few sarcastic remarks to the President. I wrote he was stupid and did not know how to run a country. I wrote my child could do a better job than he was doing. I told him I wanted him, personally, to call my credit union and tell them to issue me a $300 loan. I only wanted to pay my rent with it.

My salary was low, only $1000 a month before taxes. My rent was only $250. I could not understand how come out of $1000 a month; I could not afford to pay $250 for rent. I was not extravagant. I did not have furniture, nor did I have many clothes. I did not buy cigarettes, alcohol or drugs. All I did was tried to exist from day to day. I did not have credit cards. However, despite all my problems, I was never without a smile on my face. I never treated people badly and would go out of my way to help a friend. I never even had an attitude or was cranky. People complimented the way I carried myself and many times I was called a saint.

One day, I got a telephone call from a man named Willis who lived in California. He told me he was a friend of my sister and her boyfriend. He saw a picture of me and liked what he saw. We talked a long time -- about two hours. I told him I wanted to move to California. He told me, "Los Angeles is a bad place to live. You wouldn't be happy here." He did not discourage me, though. I still wanted to move there. Willis started calling me at least twice a month to say hello. In less than a week, I got a response to the letter I sent the President. It read:

"Dear Arden: Thank you for your message to President Carter. The President is pleased that you took the time to share your views. Although we would like to respond in detail to the many comments, suggestions and questions which are received at the White House each day, the volume of mail on hand now makes it impossible for us to do so in a timely fashion. You may be sure, nonetheless, that the content of your correspondence has been reported to the President. The enclosed material has been prepared in response to interests expressed by a great number of people. Topics are alphabetized for convenience, and we hope you will find helpful information, which addressed your concerns as well as other matters of importance to our Nation.

With appreciation for your letting us have the benefit of your thoughts and with our best wishes.

Sincerely,
Daniel M. Chew Director of
Presidential Correspondence"

He did not even answer my question. As for the booklet they sent, I did not even understand the questions let alone the answers. I wanted to know why my credit union could not give me a loan. I asked the President to call my credit union and tell them to approve my loan. Did he not read my letter? I thought I would be visited by the Secret Service, but they will not come unless I threatened the President.

The President did not care about me. I guess when it was said, "All men are created equal," they did not mean they would be treated equally. I was angry at society because I have worked extremely hard all my life and I could not even afford a decent place to live. Even though I felt defeated, I was not going to give up trying.

CHAPTER 29

MOVING TO CALIFORNIA

I went back to my credit union and reapplied for another loan. They turned me down again. I went back and applied again one week later. I was going to apply every week. I needed the loan, and I was going to get it. Finally, they approved the $300 loan. When I got the loan, it was in June. The apartment I looked at with the mice and roaches, called the same day I got the loan to tell me he wanted to rent me the apartment. The rent was $125 a month.

While I was trying to decide what to do, Pat called me at work. I said, "I'm so torn. I want to take the cheaper apartment, but I do not want those living conditions. I want to keep my luxury apartment, but I cannot afford it. And I do not want to work two jobs any longer. It's hard for me to decide."

Patricia said jokingly, "Girl, you should use the money and move to California." I said, "I might. Let me call you back." I quickly ended the call and phoned Gia in California to tell her I wanted to move there, and I wanted to check if I was welcomed. She was excited and assured me I should move there. I still had the problem of not having a job or a car when I got there. My old car could never make it. I needed to know I could support my child and myself.

I thought about moving to California all day. Finally, I called United Airlines and they had a $99 sale on tickets to LAX, one way non-stop. It was the last day of the sale. The next thing I knew, I was at the ticket agent and left with airline tickets to California for Chelle and me. Chelle's ticket was only, $79. Had I waited another day, instead of it costing me $178 for the both of us, it would have cost $700. It was June, and I was leaving on September seventh. I had three months to find a job in California and prepare for my big move. I started packing boxes and sent some of my things to California.

I ran into a little problem with my record albums. There was no way I was going to leave my records behind. They were my friends and I could not part without them. The boxes were too heavy for UPS and the Post Office, and if I had split them up, I would have had too much work to do, and it would have been too much money. Finally, I went to the Greyhound Bus Co. and they accepted my box. It weighed seventy-five pounds. In my head, I was well on my way to California once I knew my records could go.

Since I worked for the United States Government, I thought I could easily transfer my position to California. I did not know how I was going to do it. I needed to be available for interviews before I could be hired. I did not want to quit my job and I had no vacation time; even if I did, I would not be able to go to California for an interview, come back, and then go again. I thought I could set up some interviews for the first week I got there. I put in for a leave of absence so once I got to California, I could interview and be transferred, but if I quit then I would not be able to be transferred with my seniority. I had worked there for three years.

I could not believe my request for a leave of absence was rejected. When I found out I had been turned down, I marched right into the Commander's office and said to him, "It is unfair to deny my leave of absence. Why can't you help me find a job in Los Angeles? There are government positions I qualify for." The Commander said, "I'll help you. Come, follow me." He walked me to the personnel office and told the personnel manager, "Find her a job in California." The personnel manager had a friend who worked in Los Angeles and asked her to send a list of job postings. When my new friend Willis called, I told him I was moving there. He said, "Don't worry, I'll help you with whatever you need for a smooth move to California. I'll look out for you."

"I need a job more than anything else." Gia found a job very quickly. I thought I would, also. Willis worked for the government, too, and told me to send my application to where he worked. Meanwhile, I had sent my application to over twenty government agencies in Los Angeles long before I knew I was moving there. I only got one response, from the V.A. Medical Center in Brentwood, California, but there were no positions available. I had received the notice some months ago. I called to find out if they happened to have an opening in my field, which was data entry.

I spoke with someone in personnel. She said, "I was looking over your application a few days ago, but I wasn't sure when you wanted to move to California, so I put it back in the file. However, we do have a position available in the data entry field in our pharmacy department." She described the position and asked if I was interested.

"Of course, I'm interested," She said, "The supervisor will call you for an interview in a day or so." About thirty minutes later, I received a phone call from a Mr. Mittler, the pharmacy supervisor. He interviewed me and said, "No one had ever worked the computer because no one knows how. We input everything manually, but we want everything on the computer." I told him, "If you hire me, I'll get it working. I'll read every manual and figure it out." He said he would check my references and let me know within a week or so if I was hired. I went home and chanted two hours I would get the job.

The next morning when I got to work there was a message Mr. Mittler had called and would call back later. He called about ten minutes later. I thought he forgot to ask me a question or two, but he said, "I have decided to give you the job. When would you like to start?" I was scheduled to leave on September seventh, and I told him, I will report to work on on September eight at eight o'clock in the morning sharp." I was hoping it was okay because I still had two months to go. Mr. Mittler said, "I'm looking forward to you starting and getting our computer going. See you in September."

I was so happy. I went through the halls of the Federal Center screaming, "I got the job, I got the job! I'm moving to California with a job to go to." I was crying because I was so happy. I do not think I had ever been so happy. I had a whole two months left and I felt I only had a day. I had so much to do.

I went to Brenda and said, "Look, I got my plane ticket. I told you at the beginning of the summer I was moving to California and getting the hell out of Battle Creek." I chanted for all this and I got it." Brenda said, "I don't see how chanting did it." I told her, "I chanted for it and got what I chanted for. Who knows, maybe I will meet Smokey Robinson too." She said, "Girl you're crazy." I felt so special. How many people find a job over two-thousand miles away via the telephone? I was convinced it was the power of chanting Nam Myoho Renge Kyo. I was on top of the world. I decided to move to California, got a job, and I was proud of myself. I was looking forward to moving.

Willis was happy I was moving to L.A. He said, "I will help you as much as possible." A few days later, I received a bankbook in the mail from Home Savings and Loan. Willis had opened a bank account for me. He only put $10.00 in it, but he told me by having an account, it would be easy for me to cash my paychecks. So, I was moving to California; got a job, a bank account, and still another month to go before I leave.

I bought a lottery ticket and instantly won $700. Now I knew what my chanting friend meant when she told me my benefits were inconspicuous and would soon be conspicuous. All it took was a little more effort and determination. I did it and I have no doubt I am the happiest person in the world. The only problem I felt coming on was I had never met Willis and I was hoping he was not expecting me to be his girlfriend as soon as I got there. I did not worry about it much though because I knew I would be able to handle the situation.

I called a Buddhist member in California. I got her number

from a woman who was visiting Battle Creek and lived in California. I introduced myself. I said, "I'm a member and I'm moving to California." She was excited and told me, "I can't wait until you get here and share your experiences with all the other members." Already I had friends in California and was not even there yet. Finally -- my last days in Battle Creek. I decided to party. I knew I was leaving, and I did not care what anyone had to say about me, so I let myself go. I did not do anything to embarrass myself; I had fun.

When it came time to leave, because my flight left from Chicago, I decided to spend my last week there, so I could say goodbye to my grandmother and to Barbara Lee. Before I left Battle Creek, I went to Climax to visit my grandfather and said bye to him. It was hard to leave him because he had taken sick again. He was not looking so good. I hated leaving him so sick.

Since I was going to Chicago, and Chelle was eleven years old and had only seen her father once when she was seven, I decided to take her by his house so they could see each other. At first, he said, "It is so nice to see her" as he hugged her. He then said, "Maybe you guys can come back for dinner tonight. Call me later and I will ask Sherry if it's OK."

When I called back later, I put Chelle on the phone to talk to him. He asked her to put me on the phone. When I took the phone, he said, "I don't think it's a good idea for you guys to come by. I wish you would have told her you did not know who her father was. I don't know her, and she doesn't know me, and we should not change it." Chelle was asking me, "What is he saying? What is he saying? Can we have dinner with him?" He said, "I can't be the full-time father you want me to be." I knew then he was as crazy as he always was. I told him, "She's not asking you to be a full-time dad. She wants you to acknowledge her. We are moving to California. All you have to do is send her a birthday card once a year and maybe a Christmas card, and if that is your idea of a full-time father, then I'm glad you disappeared from her life."

I told Chelle the truth of what he was saying. She did not seem to be too upset. I explained to her how foolish and out of his mind he was. She agreed, and it did not bother her. I admired Chelle because she is strong when she needs to be. We enjoyed the rest of our stay in Chicago, although it was hard to say goodbye to my grandmother. She was crying and said, "You should move back to Chicago, so you can see about me. Your old grandma will not live much longer."

She said, "You remind me of your mother and having you near is like having my daughter back." I told my grandmother, "Don't worry because I will be back to visit." She said, "I will be dead by the time you come back." It was hard to leave her. There I was, leaving my grandfather and my grandmother. My grandmother was not sick; she was only thinking about getting sick. But my grandfather was sick. I felt bad about leaving but I did not think it was right to sit around and wait for someone to die. Life must go on. I had to do what I had to do, and I needed a new life in a new place.

Finally, it was time for "California, here I come." We got to the airport about three hours early. I was excited and anxious to leave and start my new life. When I arrived at LAX, Gia, my two beautiful nephews, her boyfriend, and Willis picked us up. I was so happy to see everyone. I asked Willis to take me by where I will be working so I can see where it is and how it looks. Everything was so perfect. My job was a fifteen-minute drive and a thirty-minute bus ride from my sister's place where I was staying. I was all prepared to take the bus to work until Willis told me, "I will pick you up every morning until you are able to get a car." Willis lived in Santa Monica and my sister lived in Venice and it was not far. Willis worked across the street from where I was working. Was this all a coincidence or what? It was because I was chanting and protected.

I did not want Willis to go out of his way for me. But Willis convinced me to not take the bus. He said, "All kinds of weird things happen to people who take the bus. I don't mind picking you up." I was so grateful to him. The day I got there we drove around sightseeing. Since my sister lived in Venice, we were near the beach, and Venice Beach is one of the most famous places in Los Angeles. I was so excited to see so much happening at one time. There were people dancing and singing with crowds of people around them looking and throwing money at them.

I saw real live bums. Not like the bums in Chicago and Michigan. We have drunks who hang on the corners, but they had a place to sleep at night. They did not have to carry their blankets around and sleep on benches and in the streets. We then went to Hollywood. I was so excited. I thought I would see a movie star or something. While we were driving down Hollywood Boulevard, my head was turning from right to left trying to see all the action. I loved it. People of all walks of life were walking the boulevard. I noticed a little old white couple about sixty years old walking hand in hand. I saw prostitutes and gays standing on every corner. All kinds of different people all cluttered together to make it "Hollyweird" as, so many people called it. I was absolutely fascinated.

Then Gia's boyfriend Daren said he had a surprise for me. We drove to what looked like a ritzy neighborhood. Turns out it was Beverly Hills. He parked in front of a beautiful gorgeous home with a strip of colorful lights shining and could be seen from a block away. Daren said, "Smokey Robinson lives here." I could not believe I was sitting outside of Smokey Robinson's house. I knew I could not intrude. I told Gia, "This is the neighborhood we are taking the kids in for Halloween next month."

I wanted to let him know I was his number one fan. I could never tell him I loved him, or I wanted to be his wife because he was married. Somehow, I never thought I would get so close to Smokey. Even though I was in front of his house and not in front of him, it was still as close as I had ever been, and I was excited about making his house one of the houses we take the kids to for Trick or Treating.

I then felt depressed because I realized I might never fulfill my fantasy of becoming Smokey's wife. Since I was nine years old, he was all I had dreamed about. I could not face the reality he was happily married. However, I thought I would meet someone real, and soon I would no longer depend on my imagination to make me happy.

CHAPTER 30

LOOKING FOR LOVE IN ALL THE WRONG PLACES

Monday morning came, and it was time for me to report to work. I walked into the supervisor's office and we were both happy to meet each other. The V. A. Hospital I worked for was the psychiatric hospital. It was one gloomy and depressing place. I had orientation with a group, and we were warned to be careful because all the patients had mental problems.

They said, "The patients can get violent and, in the past, have killed employees." Also, they stressed how important their medicine was. They were all on antidepressants, and they walked around in a daze. I called them the living dead. I noticed some of the patients did not have clean clothing or take baths. Some of the patients wore suits and looked very neat. They all walked around freely. Some were inpatients, and some were outpatients. One thing I found out right away is it was hard to distinguish the patients from the workers --and even worse-- someone pointed to a person and asked me, "Do you think he is a doctor or a patient?" I said, "A doctor" and I was wrong. You could not tell the doctors from the patients.

I was a new face. Everyone started talking to me and was nice to me, even the patients. I had the bright smile no one else seemed to have. When I told everyone, it was my first day in L.A., they understood why my smile was so bright. Most people were telling me, "You have a nice smile." I was saying thank you to so many people on my first day. My first day was interesting.

On my second day, it was the same except I was having lunch on the patio when I saw a man walking towards the canteen. He was gorgeous. I knew he worked there because he had a uniform on, navy blue pants and a white shirt. I had seen several guys walking around with the same uniform. I sat there starring at him while holding my hamburger in my two hands about to take a bite. I noticed he noticed me. I saw him look my way. He did not speak, and he acted as if he did not see me. I knew I had to get to know him. He went and sat with some women sitting on the opposite side of the canteen. I went back to the pharmacy and told the two women I worked with how I saw this guy who was gorgeous. I described and asked if they knew him. They had to see him first before they could tell me if they knew him or not.

I would see him all the time. He never would acknowledge me though. I was not going to make a fool out of myself, so I started ignoring him also. There was a man who came to clean the pharmacy every morning. He was an attractive man, but he did not turn me on. However, we would talk all the time. He asked, "Would you like to go out with me, so I can show you more of Los Angeles."

I went with him because he seemed to be a nice person. He took me to Malibu Beach to see the sun set. It was so beautiful. He pestered me trying to get me to go to his house and spend the night. I told him, "I don't know you, I'm new in LA and I want to take it slow." He became angry and said, "I thought you were mature." The next time I saw him, he had several hickeys on his neck. He was showing them off to me, which was silly. If he thought he was making me jealous, then he was crazy. Also, he was a lot older than me; I was twenty-six and he was in his forties.

I later discovered the man I was attracted to was named, Pierre. My coworkers told me he was the hospital playboy. Of course, those are the types of men I was attracted to. Willis -- who would have married me if I suggested it -- was not the right man for me. To me he was not attractive. He was nice to me and did whatever I asked him to. Those were the types of men who turned me off. I could never understand why. It is the "Good girl – bad boy syndrome."

I did make it clear to Willis I was not ready to have a steady relationship. I wanted to be careful because I did not want to make any of the same mistakes I had made in the past. I was lying to Willis because I was looking for a steady man. It is like the lines from Smokey's song "Choosy Beggar:"

> "But though my heart is begging for love, I've turned some love away. Maybe one was true love – I'll never know which – Cause your love is the only love to make this beggar rich. I'm a choosy beggar and you're my choice."

I wanted who I wanted, not who was best for me. If I choose the wrong person, then I will "Suffer what there is to Suffer" and then get out of it. And, if I choose the right person, then I will "Enjoy what there is to Enjoy." I got this saying from one of Nichiren Daishonin's Writings/(Gosho.)

I soon met another man. He was very nice-looking, and he was a doctor. I liked him, and we went out a couple of times. I thought to write all my friends and tell them I was dating a doctor would have been a great honor. His name was Ray. Great — another Ray. We went out and he told me, "I beat my former wife almost to death with my bare hands. If it were not for my little daughter, I would have killed her. After I realized I hurt her and she was near death, I rushed her to the hospital."

I knew then he was crazy, and there was no way I wanted to get involved any deeper with him. When I saw him, I would be cordial, but I would not go anywhere with him. I still liked Pierre. He still ignored me. My chanting friends really helped me chant about all my problems. During the six years I lived in Battle Creek; I was a Buddhist who was far away from other Buddhists. It is difficult to chant without other members to encourage me, so I was glad to meet some friends who really cared about me. I knew practicing Buddhism was the right thing to do.

I found one of my major problems was going to be saving enough money to have my own apartment and get a car. Little did I know a two-bedroom apartment in Los Angeles was at least $450 a month. I was so disappointed because my job transfer did not come with a raise. I still made the exact amount of money I made in Battle Creek and if I could not afford to pay $250 a month, how was I going to pay $450? I could not go on living with my sister. She and her boyfriend argued every night. I needed my own place for peace and serenity. I believed they were having problems because Chelle and I were there. Their place was small, and Gia had two small boys. It was only a two-bedroom apartment. I found myself so depressed.

Willis said, "We can get an apartment together." I told him, "I don't want to use you and I can't live with you because I'm not ready for a committed relationship." I had to know I was with a man I would not cheat on. If I was dating Willis and do not love him, then I would still look for the right man who turned me on. If I found him and he loved me then I would drop Willis like a hot potato. I did not want to hurt anyone. I do not know why he did not turn me on, and I could not pretend he did.

Ray called and asked if I would go out with him. He told me a doctor friend of his had won the baseball pool for two-hundred dollars and he wanted to take some people out to celebrate. I figured no harm since others were going. He had called me several times prior and I always turned him down. This time, I decided to go. It was six of us. We went to a quaint little bar in Westwood. I had one drink. We left and went to a club. It was not in a good neighborhood. I had a drink there which meant I had two drinks.

Everyone was having a good time. Soon everyone in the club started fading away. Suddenly, I could hardly see, and I was dizzy. I told Ray, "I am getting ill and I need to go home right now." I could hardly walk. Ray helped me out of the club, and everyone was looking at me. When we got to his van, he put me inside and said, "Wait here while I get the rest of the people" because he drove. He was gone for a long time. I felt myself getting sick. I had to throw up. I opened the van door and I was leaning halfway out of it throwing up. I heard a voice, "Miss are you okay?" I looked up and it was four guys standing around looking at me.

I was lucky they did not take advantage of me. I was very helpless. I had never been so sick before. I knew I could not be drunk because I only had two drinks and they were Pina Coladas. No way could I get drunk on drinks they do not put a lot of alcohol in. Somehow, I found the strength and walked back into the club. There Ray and his friends were dancing and having a good time. I walked onto the dance floor and grabbed one woman by her arm and told her, "I'm sick and I need to go home." Ray saw I was serious, and he then decided to take me home. I fell asleep and the next thing I knew; we were at his house. I looked up and said, "I want to go home." I was so angry with him. I started screaming at the top of my lungs, "You better take me home right now or I will destroy your career." I knew he put something in my drink. He finally gave in and took me home. I did not want to see Ray again. I hated him.

When Chelle was hit by the car, I talked to an attorney about the incident. He did not believe we could sue anyone, but I received a telephone call at work from the attorney. He did not even know I had moved to California. He called my old job at the Federal Center and they told him I no longer worked there. He called the personnel office and they told him where I moved to and where I was working. Under a normal situation, there is no way the personnel manager would have given him information over the telephone. I did have a secret clearance. But, because all the Buddhist Gods protect me because I chant, she gave him the information. The attorney told me, "I made a $7000 settlement with the bus company and the driver of the car who hit your daughter."

He said, "I will send you the check for your signature and please immediately return it back to me." I was so happy because with the attorney's fee, I was still getting over $5000. The same day I found out about the settlement, we got a telephone call from my brother, He said, "Granddaddy passed away." I was sad because I was not by his side. I wanted to go to the funeral, but I was not going to have my money before the funeral. My aunt, one of my grandfather's sisters and his brothers decided to send Gia and me the money to come because they said we should be there. I was going back to Battle Creek after only being in L.A. for one month. I was sad it was for my grandfather's funeral. He lived a long fulfilling life, so I was happy he at least died old instead of young like my mother and father. He was seventy-eight when he passed.

I explained to my boss I had to take off for my grandfather's funeral. They understood. I was leaving work early because my flight was leaving in a few hours. I had gone over to the canteen and I ran into Pierre. I walked up to him and introduced myself and we ended up having a one-hour conversation. I told him, "My grandfather passed and I'm leaving tonight to go to the funeral in Michigan." Pierre said, "I'm sorry about your grandfather. When are you coming back, because perhaps I can take you out?" I said, "Sure." I could not wait to get back.

Gia and I went to Michigan. We left the kids behind because the trip was $1000 for the two of us, and with the kids, it would have been $1000 more. We were only going to be gone for three days anyway. When we arrived in Battle Creek, everyone was glad to see Gia because she had been gone for over a year. I had not been gone for a full month, so they had not missed me yet. Besides, Gia was raised there, and she was closer to the family members and she had lots of friends.

I was glad she got to see Grandma Ruby again. She had raised Gia, and though they had their differences because it is hard being raised by someone who is not your mother, they had a chance to renew the love they felt for each other. The trip was rather enlightening, but I was glad to get back to see if Pierre and I could pick up where we left off. One week later after I returned, I received my check. I knew I could buy a car and get an apartment.

Those were my priorities. Upon my return to work, Pierre did not say anything to me. I would see him pass the pharmacy, but he would not speak. I tried to not let it bother me though. My main concern was my priorities.

Willis was helping me look for an apartment to make sure the neighborhood was good. I did not want to live near drunks or gangs. I wanted to have everything in my own name. However, I owed so much money on bills and did not make enough money, so I was not getting any of the apartments I applied for.

Willis told me, "Money in the hand talks, so I applied for one apartment and gave the manager $1000 cash. She called me later and said, "Come and pick up your money because I don't want to rent the apartment to you. I checked your credit and it is bad and I can't take a chance." Cash in the hand did not do it for me. I saw Ray in the hall at work. I told him I was looking for a car. He told me, "I have a friend who has a car for sell. I will call you on Sunday and take you to see it." I did not want to go with him because I was afraid of him. I thought if my sister and my daughter go with me then it should be okay.

I later ran into Pierre. He asked me, "Do you want to go out with me on Saturday night?" I told him "Of course." We went out and had fun. I was so excited to go out with him. We went to his friend's place and played cards. I met a woman who chanted. She lived in the same building as Pierre's friend. We talked, and we had a lot in common. She invited me to attend her Buddhist meetings. I had a good time. Pierre and I left his friend's place and went to a disco club. Pierre treated me so special. He bought me flowers. After we left the disco, we went to get something to eat. After we ate, he asked, "Do you want to go to a motel?" He really turned me on, so I went. We went to the Snooty Fox on Western. I did enjoy him.

When we woke up, I wanted to hurry home because I was supposed to go with Ray to look at a car. However, Pierre wanted to take me to breakfast, and I wanted to go. I got home Sunday afternoon. I had missed Ray's call. I called him back, but he did not answer. I went about my day. Ray called back. He was yelling at me saying, "We had an appointment to look at a car and you were not home when I called you." I got angry with him and told him, "You're crazy. All you had to do was call me back, and I would have gone then to look at the car." I did not care because I did not need him to look at the car.

Ray came to the pharmacy and asked, "Will you come to my office because I have something to tell you?" When I walked into his office, he slapped me in my face and started yelling! "I fought in Viet Nam and went to medical school! Do you think it was easy? I don't have time to put up with your mess." I was so angry with him I wanted to turn him in to the authorities; however, I decided I would handle the situation myself. I will not pay any attention to him because he was nuts.

Pierre and I became good friends. We saw each other about three to four times a week. I would see him every day at work, but when we got together, we stayed in motels. Pierre was living with his girlfriend and she had his baby, just my luck. Of course, he said, "The relationship between us is not good, we don't sleep together, and we are not on good terms." He then said, "How about you and I get an apartment together since I am looking too?" I could not have been happier. I made appointments to look at apartments, but he would never go. I always had to call Willis to take me. Willis was always there when I needed him, and I kept him at a distance. I did not want him to think I was interested in him.

I finally got my car. It was a 1972 Datsun 2000. It was a good car. The previous owner took good care of it. It cost $1200. Willis took me to get it. I was happy because then I did not have to depend on Willis and have the responsibility of his car. Now all I had to do was get an apartment. Willis suggested, "You can use my name to get an apartment because I have good credit. If it looked as if we are going to live together then they may be more apt to rent because there would be two sources of income." I really did not want to use Willis' name because I knew I was going to let Pierre move in with me and I did not want Willis to be angry with me or feel as if I was pulling something over on him.

I told Willis, "I will only use your name if I have to." I thought to try a few more apartments. I told him, "There will be no obligations for me using your name." He said, "That's fine, I want to help you Arden." Meanwhile, Pierre and I slacked off a little seeing each other. It was Christmastime. I was very depressed because Pierre had not called me. He called me about one week before Christmas and told me he had bought Chelle and me Christmas presents, but when Christmas came, he did not come by or call. When I saw him at work, he would be nice to me, but he would not call. I was hurt because Willis bought Chelle and me nice gifts.

Willis was trying hard as he could to get me by buying me nice things and being there when I needed something. I never did ask Willis for anything, he always volunteered to do it himself. I thought he was trying to buy me. However, I was not for sale. Most people called me a fool but deep in my heart, I believe if I were to submit myself to being his girlfriend he would change and would not do anything for me. I am sure I would have been miserable with him. He was still my friend, but I knew he wanted more. He always made me feel so uncomfortable.

Since Pierre did not call, I decided not to bother him. I thought I will find someone else. On New Year's Eve, Gia, Daren and I went to a party. I could not enjoy myself. Other guys were talking to me, but I was not interested because I wanted to be with Pierre. I was in a state of melancholy. I could not believe I was going through these changes. I should be strong, but I felt weak. I thought a man could never send me through such changes. The next day, New Year's Day, I felt worse. I started to chant but I stopped in the middle. All I could do was cry. I was making a big thing out of nothing. My sister was trying to comfort me, and I went off on her.

I was telling her, "I will leave and go stay in a hotel if you don't want me here." She said, "I'm not telling you to leave." I was also going off on Chelle because she was telling me she did not want Pierre to live with us when we move. I was defending Pierre and he was not even calling me. Finally, I got a hold of one of my chanting friends, and I complained to her about my problems. She said to me, "Don't complain — change it." I told her, "Easy for you to say because you have a boyfriend and a place to live." She said, "A man is not the answer to any of your problems. You should have more faith in yourself."

I felt much better after I talked to her. I then went to my altar to chant to become stronger in my area of weakness. I knew I would see Pierre at work, and I was determined not to show him I was angry. The next time I saw Pierre, he was explaining how sorry he was he missed spending the holidays with us. He started explaining his problem about how broke he was. He said he could not come over empty-handed. I told him, "I understand." We spent the night together.

I had an enjoyable time with him, but I was aware of my weakness and I did not want to upset myself because of his fickleness. I asked him, "Can you help me look for an apartment since you're intending to live with me?" He said in his drunken voice, "I don't have time to help you. You should forget about me because I will never fall in love again." I felt bad but still could not understand him wanting to make love to me but could not fall in love. I did not believe him.

I tried to be strong and go about my business because I was not going to be his plaything. Willis took me to look for more apartments. No one would rent an apartment to me. I even applied for an apartment which was a dump and they still would not rent it to me. I would not have taken the dump. I wanted to see if they would rent it to me. I wanted the apartment I wanted, and I could not see myself settling for anything else.

In Buddhism, there is no compromise. When you sincerely chant you can get exactly what you want. The apartment I wanted had to have new drapes, new carpet, two bedrooms, two bathrooms, a new stove and refrigerator and no roaches. It had to be clean with no cracks in the walls, and the rent had to be no more than $450. If I looked at an apartment not having everything I wanted, I would not apply for it.

I started getting disappointed because I was turned down for all the apartments I applied for. I wanted my place in my name, but I finally decided to use Willis' name. I was in a bind. As I always do when I am in a bind, I chant more and called a chanting friend for guidance. The person I called told me I was doubting the power of the Gohonzon and chanting Nam-Myoho-Renge-Kyo. She said, "Try harder. Exert yourself in shakubuku ('telling others about the Buddhist practice and how it can change their lives for the better') and you will be protected. Whether the people you tell about chanting accept it or not does not matter. The act of telling them is sufficient as you are planting a seed."

I followed her guidance and I told every man, woman and child about the practice of chanting and how it can help them. Most people thought I was crazy, but a few tried it and they soon saw the practice worked. I loved telling people about chanting. I would want them to say the chant. I would say repeat after me. A quote from Nichiren Daishonin Gosho, which encouraged me was: "...when once we chant Myoho Renge Kyo, with just that single sound we summon forth and manifest the Buddha nature of all Buddhas; all existences; all Bodhisattvas; all voice-hearers; all the deities such as Brahma, Shakra, and King Yama; the sun and moon, and the myriad stars; the heavenly gods and earthly deities on down to hell-dwellers, hungry spirits, animals, asuras, human and heavenly beings, and all other living beings. This blessing is immeasurable and boundless..." They did not know by saying the chant they are protected. They did not know what I gave them.

I finally found an apartment. I got the apartment with no problems using Willis' name. In fact, the first time I used his name, they rented the apartment to me. The apartment was in his name and mine. I was planning to drop his name after I lived there for a while and showed the landlord, I am reliable in paying my rent. The apartment had all the features I chanted for. There were people who lived in the building who chanted. I was happy. I moved into my apartment on my birthday. It was the best present I had ever received from me. I was feeling very lonely when I moved into my apartment. I called Pierre, "I got a new apartment and I want you to come over."

I had everything I needed. Before I moved, I went to a beautiful house in Playa Del Rey near the ocean where they were advertising furniture for sale. The furniture they were selling was beautiful and expensive. I got a king size bed for me, a queen size bed for my daughter, a love seat and sofa and a twenty-four-inch floor model color TV all for $800. All the furniture was expensive. I had everything I needed except for a dining room table, and one of Willis' friends gave me hers. I was set, ready and happy.

Pierre came by and said, "I am so proud of you Arden." He spent the night and he asked me, "Can I move in with you?" I said, "Will you help me pay the rent?" He said, "I will help you as much as I can." The next day, he moved his things in, and he had all the other stuff I needed like towels, dishes and silverware. We had a good time together. Even Chelle liked him when he moved in.

Willis and I were still friends, but he did mention, "I'm hurt because you moved Pierre into the apartment." However, I never lead Willis on. I was always truthful with him. I did not tell him I was planning to move a man in, but he did not need to know everything. The way he felt was because of his feelings and not mine so I did not feel bad.

The first month, Pierre and I had an okay relationship, but he was starting to get drunk every day. Most of the time he would not come home until after midnight. Pierre called and said, "I'm on my way home." He was drunk as a skunk. It was raining, and it was treacherous. I chanted for his safety. He never came home.

I was worried about him. I was hoping he did not get into an accident or get arrested for driving drunk. The next day, he showed up. I did not get angry because he stayed out all night. I figured he was too drunk to drive. A week later, Pierre did not come home again. It was a Friday. I did not see or hear from him until Monday morning at three and he had to be at work at six.

When he got into the bed, I asked him, "What happened to you? Where have you been?" He told me in an adamant voice, "I went to Las Vegas." I did not say anything else. I turned over and went back to sleep. For the next week or so, our relationship was the pits. Pierre would get drunk and fall asleep on the couch. I would try to wake him, and he would not budge. He was a pitiful sight. I felt so bad because I realized Pierre and I were not going to last much longer.

One morning Pierre did not get home until five. I hated him coming home to shower, put on his clothes and left for work. Somehow, I wished he had gone to work from where he spent the night instead of coming home to get ready. I was rubbed the wrong way. I told him, "I do not like the way you are doing me," but he ignored me. I did not want to argue. When I got to work, I could not stop thinking about how Pierre was treating me. I cared about him, but my feelings were fading because I do not like drunks. Drunken people reminded me of my mother and all the bad memories from her drinking. While gazing into space at work, I picked up the telephone to call Pierre to tell him how bad I felt because of the way he disrespected me. I then asked him, "Where did you spend the night?" His response was, "You are not my wife. When I did have a wife, I did not have to explain anything to her, and I am not about to explain anything to you." I said, "Okay."

I walked around trying to figure out what I should do. When I got home from work, I was still thinking about what to do. I chanted for a while and in the middle of my chanting, I decided he should move. I called him at his favorite bar, and he was there. "Pierre I'm on my way to a Buddhist meeting and I will return at nine tonight and I want everything of yours out of my apartment." Pierre said, "But Arden, baby, I don't have any place to stay tonight." "Stay where you stayed last night because I want you out by the time, I get home." He said, "Okay." When I returned home, most of his things were gone.

I broke down crying and called him at the bar. I was going to beg him to come back because I did not mean to put him out. I was glad he was not there. I needed to have more control of myself and be stronger. I was too good to be treated the way he was treating me. I then started resenting him for not taking all his stuff. I wanted everything of his out. I called Pierre and asked him kindly, "Please come get the rest of your things." He ignored me and refused to get his things. Finally, I told him, "I will bring all of your things to work and place them outside of your van." He then came to get his things.

I was hurt and felt empty inside. I wanted someone who would love me as I loved him and someone who would treat me as I treated them. I needed help, so I called a senior leader and she came to my place to give me guidance on my situation. I knew there had to be a man out there for me somewhere, but I could not understand why I could not find him. My leader told me, "If you want a man you have to accept a man for who he is. Forget about changing the man. The only person you can change is yourself and you should work on yourself." I did understand what she meant. I took on a new attitude. I decided to advance my education and improve my job. I needed to occupy my mind with something else besides a man.

Pierre

CHAPTER 31

BUILD A GOOD CAREER

I found myself having major financial problems, so I decided to get a part-time job. I also decided to go to school and try to find a higher-paying full-time job. I did end up taking a part-time job at K-Mart. It was what I had to do to pay my rent. I worked and worked. The class I was taking was an ABC steno course so I could find a good-paying secretarial position. I wanted to be financially secure. I was doing okay but hoping something better would come along. Finally, after five years of completing secretarial training, I was promoted to the personal secretary to the chief engineer at the hospital. It was not my dream job, but I would continue to look.

Ten months after I moved to California, my sister and I wanted to take a vacation together. We decided to drive across the country so we could see everyone in Battle Creek and Chicago. We made all the necessary preparations. Gia and I had everything all mapped and planned. Gia was taking her two children and I was taking my daughter. The night we left, neither of us had much sleep. We thought we would drive straight through without stopping. The first night was no problem. We drove all night. We started running into problems the next day sometime in the afternoon. I thought my car had a flat tire. We pulled off the highway into a gas station in some small town in Iowa.

I stopped at one gas station and asked the attendant, "Can you please check my tires?" He said, "I have nothing to check your tires with." As we pulled into another gas station, a vicious dust storm started to blow. Tumble weeds were rolling everywhere, Even over the top of the car. People were holding on to poles. We then said forget about the tires because I did not have a flat, and we decided to get something to eat. Upon leaving Burger King, my little nephew fell and hit his head on the sidewalk. His head became so swollen we got nervous and thought we should take him to a hospital to make sure everything was okay. We got directions to the hospital but got lost driving in this small hick town headed towards a small dirt road.

I told Gia, "Let's keep going on the highway and if we find a hospital on the way, we will stop." We figured he was okay unless he started sleeping a lot or vomiting. Soon Gia said, "We have come a thousand miles and we have a thousand miles to go." I freaked out. I could not stand another thousand miles.

I was ready to turn back and go home. Gia said, "Rather we turn around or go forward, we still have a thousand miles." I calmed down and Gia suggested we stop at a hotel to sleep. I was a basket case. I gave the desk clerk a long explanation, "You see, we have been traveling for a thousand miles. We are so tired. My back hurts and the kids are restless." The woman said, "Would you want to rent a room?" I said, "Oh yes, yes, a room is what we want." In the room, my nephew cried all night. We could not stop him from crying. The whole trip was turning out to be a horror story.

Three days later, we made it to Chicago. I was never so glad to see a sign saying, "Welcome to Chicago." We screamed and jumped for joy. I could not enjoy myself on the vacation. All I could think about was the drive back. I was not looking forward to driving back. We stayed one week, and it was time to go back. I tried to act as if I was okay but deep inside, I was dying of fear. We drove all night the first night and all was well. As soon as we saw a sign reading "Welcome to Blackwater Missouri," the hood blew up and smoke was everywhere. The car had stopped.

Blackwater is in the middle of nowhere. This town was smaller than Climax, Michigan and I did not think it was possible. We found a place who would fix the car for $180. I did not have the money, so I called Willis and he gave me his credit card number which is how I paid for the car repair.

While the man was fixing my car, there was no place for us to wait, so we rented a hotel room. It took all day and we were on our way only to breakdown again five miles away. I was so upset. We had to get back to where the car was repaired. No one would stop. A highway patrol car went by and he did not stop for three children and two women who were stranded.

Finally, the only person who stopped was a trucker. I told him while crying, "I need to get back to the next town. It's about five minutes away." Chelle and I got into the truck and Gia and her sons stayed in the car waiting for us to come back. The trucker was weird. He started telling me, "Sometimes I keep driving until I get to New York." I saw a stick I picked up and held in my hand. I thought if he does not stop, I would start hitting him with the stick.

He did drop us off, and the mechanic towed us back to his shop. He told us it was too late for him to fix it and we had to wait until the next day. We re-rented the hotel room and spent the night. I had a nightmare the KKK busted into our room and tried to kill us. I was so ready to be home.

The next day after the car was fixed, we started driving and got about fifteen miles away and the car broke down again. We stopped at another gas station. The mechanic's son was there and told me I needed a thermostat. He took the cover off the thermostat and the cover broke in half. I could not believe what kind of luck we were having.

Because foreign cars are not popular in the Midwest, I wanted to find a Datsun dealer. There was one thirty miles away. I was not sure if the car would make it. When we arrived, it was Friday evening at four-thirty and they were closing at five and would not be open until Monday. I was not staying there until Monday. I called Willis who paid for five bus tickets from Kansas City to Los Angeles. We all were so exhausted. I could not believe we had to spend the next three days on the bus.

When we arrived, Willis and Daren met us at the bus station. All I could do was cry. How was I going to get to my two jobs and to the class I was taking? There was no way I could do everything without a car. I could not find the nerve to ask Willis to transport me or to let me take his car again. However, Willis said, "I will loan you the money to buy another car."

I was hurt because I knew I was not going to be able to pay the money back, plus I did not want to seem like I was taking advantage of Willis. I explained my every thought to Willis. I told him, "I will not be able to pay you back anytime soon." He said, "Don't worry because I do not really need the money and you can pay me back a little at a time." Every day, Willis took me around to look for a car. I was looking for something cheap and in good condition. I found a Datsun B-210. The asking price was $1600. I told Willis, "Let us see if we can get it down to about $1400. Bring the cash so we can negotiate."

I suggested, "How about $1200 cash for the car." The seller said, "No." I then said, "$1300?" He said, "I wanted more for the car." I then said, "How about $1400?" He said, "Ok I agreed." However, Willis felt embarrassed because I was negotiating. Willis then said, "Let's give the man $1600, his asking price." He said it in front of the man. I could not believe Willis was so willing to pay more than he had to. I was angry with him and told him, "He would have taken $1400, and since I am paying you back then you should pay as little as possible." Willis told me, "Pay me $1400 and don't worry about the other $200." He said it as if he had money to throw away. I will never take a man car shopping with me again. I had wheels now and was "On the Road Again."

It was hard at work, because I was still in love with Pierre and I would either see him or his brother who also worked there. He was always on my mind. I missed him so much. After I got back from my vacation, I called Pierre to tell him the saga of driving across the country. Pierre asked if he could come over. He did, and we had a wonderful time. I knew I had to find another job to avoid seeing him because I was so weak for him. I seriously started looking for another job. I did not want to work two jobs anymore. I was so disappointed after looking for a job because I found out how hard the job market was. Many jobs did not want to pay my salary requirements. Jobs having good salaries were not hiring me. However, I did not give up because I knew I was destined to find something great and soon. My grandfather always told me good things are not easy to achieve. The Dotson Dealer called me and told me they sold my car and sent me the $300 for it. It helped.

Pierre started treating me like a sex machine. He wanted to drop in anytime he wanted to. I enjoyed him, but I did not like what our relationship had developed into. When he was living with me, he took part in paying the bills and buying food; however, with me being his sex machine, all he had to do was enjoy the sex and did not have to pay anything.

I started chanting to fall out of love with Pierre. If I felt love for him, then he could continue to use me. One day he came over and tried to do some freaky things to me while he was watching porn; he wanted to masturbate me with objects. He also suggested I have sex with one of his friends while he watched. I told him, "You really hurt me. I can clearly see you have no respect for me. Leave my apartment." As he left and closed the door, my love left with him. The next time he called and asked to come by, I told him, "I never wanted to see you again." He said, "I'm going to come over anyway." I told him, "I will not let you in." Forty-five minutes at one in the morning, he knocked on my door. "Pierre, please leave. I'm not going to let you in."

He started crying and said, "I'm drunk and can't drive any further." I told him, "Sleep it off in your van because I'm not going to let you in." I then added, "And get away from my door or I will call the police." Pierre asked, "Why are you treating me so bad?" I said, "Please leave." When he called, I would hang up. I finally was rid of the love I debased myself to have.

At my part-time job, I ran into Donna, an old co-worker from Battle Creek. She said, "I moved to Los Angeles and I am staying in a hotel." We exchanged telephone numbers. When she called a couple of days later, I mentioned Smokey. She said, "You know

Stevie Wonder is my good friend. I will take you to his studio to meet him. By the way, can I move in with you?" She then said, "I'm having a challenging time finding an apartment. I have enough money, but I need to be sure of the right neighborhoods and schools to put my children in." It was the end of August, and soon school would be starting.

I wanted to help her because I knew how hard it had been for me to find a place. She had three children. She had her own car and I thought she would soon get herself together. She could introduce me to Stevie Wonder, and he could introduce me to Smokey. There was a method to my madness.

She moved in. We both agreed if she did not find a place in thirty days, she would move back into a hotel. I told her she did not have to pay me any rent. "More than money, I want you to get a place as soon as you can." I did not especially like anyone living with me and I told her if she hurried and move it would be OK with me.

Two weeks after Donna moved in, she ran out of money and it was two weeks before she would get more. She did not have money to buy food for her and her kids. Her children were fifteen, thirteen and eight years old. I had to share my food with them. I did not have much money myself. I was working two jobs trying to make ends meet for my child and me. Also, I was looking for a better paying job.

One day when I had a job interview, I left work early. After my interview, instead of going back to work, I went home. When I walked in the door, Donna was sleeping on my couch. It was so hard for me to see this woman sleep while I was working so hard. All the money she had coming in was in welfare and Social Security checks. I knew Donna did not want to work because I tried to take her with me when I went job hunting. She always had an excuse of why she could not go.

She called Stevie Wonder on the telephone in front of me. I thought she might be lying about knowing him, but she did have pictures of them together. I could not understand why she would not ask him for a job. She never did intend for me to meet him.

She always had a reason she would not invite him over or take me to his studio.

When the beginning of the next month came, she had not found a place. I told her she had to move out as we agreed when she moved in. She became upset with me and begged me to take her whole check to let her stay a little longer. I told her, "I am not interested in the money. I want my place back to myself."

I met another man, and we were starting to see each other. I could not have privacy with him because she and her children were in the way. She finally moved, and I had my place back to Chelle and me again. My new boyfriend helped me get over Pierre as it was not hard because Pierre absolutely disgusted me. I also found a new job working at Litton Industries in the guided missiles division department. When I walked into the personnel office, they gave me a typing test. She came back and said, "Do you know you typed over one hundred words a minute accurately?" I was hired immediately. It was an excellent job and the pay allowed me to quit my part-time job.

It was not long before I broke up with my new boyfriend. We dated about four months. I could not put up with disrespect. He would never let me come to where he was staying. I knew he was not married and did not have a woman living with him. In fact, he had a male roommate. I still could not understand why he was so secretive about where he lived. I bugged him about it, and we fought every time he came around. Our relationship truly ended when I asked, "Are you gay? Why else would you be so embarrassed to let me come to where you live?" After we broke up, I did not want to see anyone else.

At my job, there were lots of professional and well-educated people. They encouraged me to go to school and get a college degree because my company would pay for my education. I enrolled in school and I was taking classes towards getting a degree in business administration. I had to take some remedial classes because when I tested to enter the college all my test scores were low. I was starting all over again. I learned so much and I really enjoyed going back to night school.

I knew it would take me a long time to get my degree, but I was not in a hurry. I wanted to learn all I missed by dropping out of high school after the ninth grade. I met a lot of friends at Litton. I was the only black woman who worked in the building. They had several buildings and they had other black women who worked in those buildings, but I was the only one in the building I worked in.

Everyone made a big deal out of me. My boss and all the people I worked for seemed to like me. They would take me out to their business lunches if they had a black client. I did not care if they were using me as their token because I did get free steak and lobster. Some of the people who worked there were very prejudice. I could tell by the way they ignored me. One woman tried to make me look bad in front of other people because I made the mistake of telling her I was only fourteen years old when my child was born. She would bring her visitors to my office and say, "This is the woman I was telling you about who had her child when she was only fourteen." It was like she was bringing her friends to see me as if I was a zoo creature.

One time she gave me some money because she felt sorry for me. She had a husband who made $200,000 a year and she made $75,000 a year. She dressed nicely every day, carried herself with arrogance and she would wear expensive perfume. She had a Louis Vuitton purse she said she paid $800 for. After she showed the price it looked and smelled like dodo to me. She always tried to make me feel bad because she knew I was a single mother living from paycheck to paycheck.

I was so proud of myself because working at Litton made me realize how much I had been through and how most people would not have survived as I did. I had problems, but I had a simple and happy life, although I was starting to have more and more problems with my daughter's behavior. I was twenty-seven years old and she was thirteen. Willis moved to Oklahoma to take care of his ailing mother and we remained friends.

CHAPTER 32

HARD TO HANDLE / OUT OF CONTROL

I thought moving to California would help Chelle change her disciplinary problem but after we had been in California for only a month, she was in trouble in school. In fact, by the time we were in LA for a year, she had been kicked out of two schools. Her teachers would give her a break, saying "Chelle if you mess up again, you will be kicked out of school. Do you want to be kicked out of school?" Chelle would say, "No," but she would still mess up again the next day. Their only recourse was to expel her from the school.

I was sure there was no end to Chelle's getting in trouble. She was very disruptive, and no one could tell her anything. While the teacher was trying to teach the class, Chelle would disrupt and start doing her own thing. When the teacher confronted her, she would cuss and say to the teacher, "You can't tell me what to do." When I talked to Chelle about the situation, she would become defensive and argue with me. I really did not know how to correct the situation. I was so confused. I thought she wanted to have a relationship with her father and was crying out for attention.

We had gone to Chicago when she was thirteen and she saw her father. She told him, "Please call me sometimes." Chelle built an imaginary relationship with her father. Whenever we got into an argument, she would call him hoping he would protect her and be on her side. He called a few times when we got back to Los Angeles, but he never wanted to talk to her. He would say, "Put your mother on the phone." I would refuse to talk to him. Chelle was totally depressed because her father would not respond to her. Chelle wanted me to cook some barbecued chicken and I was going to bake a cake. I was famous for my oven baked BBQ chicken. The dishes had not been washed in about a week. Every dish in the apartment was dirty. I told Chelle, "I'm going to the store to get the chicken and cake. You wash the dishes so I can cook when I return." She said, "Okay."

When I got back, the dishes were not done yet. I said, "Could you please do the dishes so I can start cooking?" Chelle told me, "I'm not washing anything." I said, "Why are you talking to me so rudely." I then angrily ordered her to wash the dishes. She still refused. She said, "They are your dishes, you want them cleaned. You wash them." I grabbed a tennis racquet and I was going to beat her with it.

She grabbed the racquet out of my hand and threw it across the room. When I ran to get it, she jumped up, ran out the door, and down the street. I chased her a bit, but she was running too fast. She came home about thirty minutes later. When she got back, I asked, "Are you ready to wash the dishes?" She still refused. I tried to talk to her and ask, "Why are you acting like this?"

She was yelling at me as she was sitting on the couch, "What are you going to do about it?" I stood up and walked over to her and started to slap her in the face when she took her foot and pushed me in my stomach. I fell back and was almost pushed out of the window. I fell on the couch and Chelle walked over and started fighting me. I was hurt and could not hit her back. I was horrified because she was hitting me. All I could do was cry.

My neighbor, Mia was watching us fight. Mia befriended Chelle because she would babysit for her daughter. I felt so embarrassed. I told Chelle, "Get out of my place and you need to find another place to stay because you can no longer stay here."

She was refusing to leave. She then called the police. When they arrived, they told Chelle, "You're unreasonable." I asked, "Can you please take her away from this home? I don't want her in my place. I hate her." I could not believe she hit me after I was so good to her.

The police said, "We can't take her away because she didn't commit a crime." "Her hitting me is not a crime? Then I'm kicking her out." The police said, "You can't put her out. You are responsible for her until she turns eighteen years old." I was depressed and hurt. I could not do anything with her. I told her, "Then on your eighteenth birthday you are getting the hell out of my house." She was not on drugs or alcohol nor did she hang with boys nor did she stay out late. It was her mouth. She had no respect for me or any adults whatsoever.

After a few years of living in Los Angeles, I felt secure in my job, but I was still trying to improve myself. Another black woman named Julie started working at Litton on the same floor with me. I was not the only black woman anymore. When I was their token, they liked me very much. Julie and I became friends. We were inseparable. We took breaks and lunches together.

I saw my boss resented us being friends. If I was taking breaks with them and talking to them, it was fine. I could go on a break with a white co-worker and be gone for an hour on a fifteen-minute break and nothing was said. But if Julie and I were gone for twenty-minutes, they would call us in the office and complain. I knew they were complaining because I was hanging out with Julie. It is crazy because when black people work together in an all-white company, they do not like us to congregate with each other. They are afraid we are plotting to get them back for slavery.

At work for some reason my co-workers held it against me because I was trying to get ahead. I got comments like, "Why are you going to school? Isn't it going to take you too long?" or "Why are you trying to get another position, don't you like your job?" I was there for three years. It was time to do something different. I wanted to stay with the same company, and I wanted a better position. I applied for every promotion. I never did get hired for any of them.

One position I thought I would get, my boss's daughter got. I was hurt but I got over it. One day, the office administrator came into my office and said, "Stop what you are doing! We have a new position and it is a good opportunity for you. Follow me as we want you to start right now." They exaggerated it up and I thought it was a great opportunity. However, it was really a demotion. I complained to no end. I also went to the Affirmative Action program at Litton Guidance Systems to file a complaint. They then moved me to another position. This position was difficult because the man who was training me said, "I'm angry because they do not pay me enough to train you." He had it out for me before I started.

I had such a challenging time there. It was about thirty whites and three black women. The other black woman they hired seemed to have something against me. She once mentioned to me, "Your complexion is light so white people like you." I hate it when people tell me that. She felt insecure because her complexion was dark and mine was light. It is like black people nor white people liked me.

Even my co-workers had it against me because I did not drink coffee. They had a coffee club and every Friday they had a donut party, which I could not belong to or take part in. They would throw a donut in the trash before they would offer it to me. I would drink milk at my desk, and they would complain. I could not understand why they could drink coffee at their desks, yet I could not drink milk. I was so unhappy.

I complained so much to everyone. Finally, my boss and I had a long talk. I was trying to understand what I was supposed to be doing. He said, "I see your potential and I'm going to make sure you get the right training." He was so nice to me. I knew I was going to go far. However, one week later, he had a heart attack and died. I then got a new supervisor, Cheryl. She was the woman who pointed me out to her associates and other people because of my age when my child was born.

She gave me a tough time by yelling at me in front of others. She would point to her watch and say, "I'm timing you every time you step away from your desk." She harassed me to no end. She even wrote me up for drinking milk at my desk and put it in my personnel file. I could not believe I had worked there four years and now I was having serious trouble.

One day Cheryl said to me as if we were friends, "Stop by my office on your break so you can look at my vacation pictures from Hawaii." I told her, "No," which I believed made her angry. A friend said, "You should have looked at her pictures and said, 'Oh Cheryl, these pictures are so lovely.' You know play the corporate game." I am not into playing games with anyone. If I had to play and pretend it was not the right job for me. She was only trying to make me feel less than her. Cheryl even said to me, "I am going to get the ghetto out of you."

Cheryl was yelling at me at my desk in front of everyone. I became angry with her and told her, "If you were educated you would know to call me into the office and talk to me in private. You can go to the community college and take a class in Human Relations for Business and you would learn how to be the supervisor you were promoted to." I said this loud and in front of everyone. She ran into her office and closed the door. I knew I was in trouble. I went to her boss and told him about the situation. He told me, "I will talk to her."

The next day Cheryl called me into her office and handed me an envelope with a big smile on her face and said, "This is your last check. There is no more money for the program you are working on and as of now you are laid off." I asked her, "Why can't I get one of the jobs posted on the board? Why do I have to be laid off?"

She told me, "No other department will hire you because of the letter I put in your employee file. Anyway, you should take the layoff because it would be a good opportunity for you." She then said, "If you hurry up, you can make it to the unemployment office" as she pointed to the clock on the wall. I asked her, "How the hell is unemployment a great opportunity for me?" She told

241

me, "It's your problem and you can leave now because we no longer need you."

I went to the Affirmative Action office within the company where I had been helped before. They worked at Litton to make sure minorities were treated fairly. I spoke to the manager. She was the only black manager they had in the company. Man or woman. They would hire a black in a manager position to interface with the government program so it would appear blacks and other minorities were being treated fairly. The manager told me because of the letter in my file about drinking milk at my desk she could not help me. I told her, "I have worked here four years and I have two excellent reviews." I then asked, "What if my supervisor had it out for me because she did not like me." She became angry with me and said, "I can't help you." I yelled aloud and said, "I will find someone bigger and better than you to help me."

My rent was $450. My landlord would let me pay $225 every two weeks. When I told my landlord, I had been laid off, she said, "I can't accept partial payments from you anymore." I told her, "There is no way I can pay you all of the rent at one time." She said, "I will have to start eviction procedures." In a week, I got a notice to pay my rent in three days or move. I could not produce all the money, after three days passed, I got a notice from the Los Angeles County Marshall's office to appear in court. I thought I would tell the judge I am willing to pay my rent. I need more time. I was looking for a job and I knew I would be back on schedule soon.

When I got to court, which was about two weeks after my notice was served, my landlord's attorney approached and asked, "Can you move out by the twelfth of the month?" I told him, "I need more time than two weeks. How about I stay until the end of the month?" The attorney said, "The judge is going to make it harder for you if you do not accept my offer." I did not believe him because all I wanted was more time. I intended to tell the judge I was planning to move but needed until the end of the month, and I would pay her through then. I was confident the judge would rule in my favor.

When I got in front of the judge, my landlord's attorney said, "Your Honor, she refused to sign this agreement." The judge was black, and I was the only black person in the courtroom to go before him. The courtroom was full. The judge asked me, "Why didn't you sign the agreement?" I told him, "It is very difficult for me to move by the date he suggested."

I told the judge, "I have a child" and I raised her hands so he could see Chelle standing next to me. "I was laid off and I am looking for a job. The end of the month would be enough time for me to move but to move before then would be a hardship." The judge asked me again, "Why didn't you sign the agreement?" I said, "Because I did not understand."

The judge yelled at me, "You don't seem to understand anything, do you?" "I do understand I want to stay there until the end of the month and not by the twelfth." He then said, "I don't think you can move in a month and I order you to move in five days." He then hit his gavel on the desk and asked for the next case. I was hurt and upset, and I started crying in the courtroom. The bailiff came to me and said, "You have to leave because your crying is disturbing the next case." I cannot believe the judge gave me fewer days to move than my landlord was willing to give me. I was so devastated because I had no place to go. Gia and Daren had broken up and she had someone new. Gia and her boyfriend were expecting a baby, and they were living with his mother. There was no room for Chelle and me. I had five days to decide what I was going to do.

I decided to chant a lot about the situation. I had nothing else to do. Chanting was my only hope. It finally came to my last day. I still had no place to go. While trying to figure things out, my phone rang, and it was Willis calling me from Oklahoma. He said, "Hey girl what's happening?" I told him, "Well I'm moving." He said, "Where are you moving to." I said, "I don't know. I got evicted and I have to leave today, so Chelle and I will have to sleep in my car tonight." He told me, "No. I'm paying the rent for my place in Santa Monica and Chelle and you can stay there as long as you need to." He did not charge me any rent.

Willis saved me again. He called me at the right time and at the right moment. Chelle and I moved into his place. It was a small place. We had hardly any room to move but it was a roof over our head. I was chanting more than ever, and I was having more problems than ever. I went on a lot of job interviews, but no one would hire me. Chelle was still giving me a hard time, and I was very lonely and miserable. Not to mention my car broke down and I had no money to have it repaired. I had to ride the bus to look for work.

I was in the middle of a bad winter storm, metaphorically speaking. I still had hope, however, because in Buddhism we are taught problems only make you stronger. I chanted every day. I was confident my situation would change soon. In his Gosho, Nichiren Daishonin wrote, "Winter Always Turns into Spring." I did not know when, but I knew I would be okay.

My sister, Willis and me

CHAPTER 33

VARIOUS JOBS BUT GOOD SKILLS

Chelle was more trouble than ever. She knew I was having difficult times, so one would think she would be a little more understanding. Instead she said horrible things to me. I could not understand why. All I could do was chant and hope the situation would change soon. She was in the tenth grade and starting to skip school. I wanted her to graduate from high school and go to college and have the opportunities I did not have.

I ran into Pierre in a restaurant. I had not seen him in two years. I gave him my telephone number, and he called. I told him, "I'm not working. I'm looking for a job and my car is in the shop and I can't get it out because I have no money." I got a phone call from the Datsun dealer. "You can come to get your car. A gentleman has paid the bill."

Pierre got my car out and it was $400. Of course, he wanted sex. I started feeling like a prostitute. However, considering my dad's friend made $200 a night with multiple tricks, I was not so bad getting $400 from one. We started seeing each other again from time to time. He was helpful to me. He had lots of money. The last time we were together, he had no money. He started working a part-time job in addition to his full-time job and he was making good money. Every time we were together, he would give me money.

Chelle was terrible. She threw a bottle of nail polish remover at me. The bottle missed me and hit my mirror which broke in a million little pieces. She thought I was the Wicked Witch of the West. She hated me, and I did not know why. The best thing happening to me in a long time was getting a ticket to see Smokey Robinson at the Beverly Theatre in Beverly Hills. I wrote Smokey a poem. It goes as follows:

A Tribute to Smokey

If I wake up tomorrow and find myself full of sorrow, I can put on a song you sing, and it makes me think about happy things.

No other song that anyone else sings can compare to the joy hearing your voice brings.

From a very young age when I first saw you singing on the stage.

I had no idea that there would be so many years of listening to all your sounds, and none of them has let me down.

So, this is the way in which I choose to say.

You are most definitely the best and please keep on singing about true love because you are better than the rest.

I sent it to his office, and I did not get a response. I thought he would send a letter and at least say thank you. I guess he had more important things to do than to answer one of my letters. The only way I could get to Smokey was to be a peer of his. Being a fan, I would never attract his attention.

I cannot sing. I started writing poetry. I thought my poems would make great songs. I would write Smokey and ask him if he was interested in song lyrics. I still never got a response. I even had one of my poems turned into a song and made into a record.

I sent him a copy, but I still never got a response. I wrote a book of poetry titled *Nedra's Sweet Moments of Intimacy.* Nedra spells Arden backwards.

Here is my favorite song I wrote:

I Can't Wait

I can't wait till we reach; that sweet moment of relief; whoo I can't wait - so let's set the date; We are both very mature and you know I want your loving' for sure; so, let's get it on because this feeling is strong. So deep inside of me I know it's going to be ecstasy – making love you and me.

OK another favorite goes:

My Favorite Songs

I'm going to party hardy all night long – Yea yea yea yea – Dancing and singing to my favorite songs – Yea yea yea yea. What you did to me was not right and to party is my only way to fight so I'm gonna dance till my feet hurt tonight. I'm gonna party hardy all- night long. It's been a long time since you've been gone.

OK another favorite is:

Baby When I Get You

Baby when I get you yea I'm gonna keep you right here by my side - Got to let you know that I love you so I'm gonna get you it's a matter of time – and I'm telling all the women around don't you touch that man cause he's mine.

I think they are great lyrics for a great singer. I wrote fifty-eight of them.

I was speaking to a woman in my algebra class. She asked me, "Do you have any children?" I said, "I have a sixteen year old daughter." She said, "You don't look old enough to have a child that age." I told her my past was hard for me to discuss with anyone. I shared both my parents were drug addicts and I had my child When I was fourteen years old. This woman encouraged me to write a book about my life. She said, "Writing a book would be great therapy for you because I can see how nervous you are talking about it plus you have a very interesting story to tell." I also told her I had written some poetry. She said, "No, you need to write a book." I never thought my life story would be interesting and encouraging to others.

I went home and started writing my life as a story. I thought with my poetry and my book, I should be able to meet Smokey with no problem. Also, I met a young man who was a disc jockey on a radio station, and he invited me to read my poetry on the radio. I knew I was on my way to meeting Smokey.

I had to pick up Chelle from school. When I got there, she was waving at me all crazy and pointing to a car. It was Smokey waiting at the stop light to make a turn. I got there as he was turning. Some of the children spotted him and got his autograph. Chelle got his autograph for me. Had I got there a second earlier, I would have met him myself.

It would have been the right time to meet him because the next day was his concert at the Beverly Theatre. In my purse, I had my ticket and the poem I wrote to him. I could have showed him all of this. However, he was pulling off when I got there. It was not the right time because he was still married. I did not want to have anything to do with a married man. At Halloween, we would take the kids trick or treating in Beverly Hills and went to Smokey's house. I never did see him, but a couple of times I saw his wife Claudette and she would come out of the house and give kids candy and comment on their costumes. She seemed like such a lovely person. I was mad because I had such an impossible dream to fulfill.

The next day at the concert, I brought him a yellow rose and

I wanted to find a way to give it to him. One of the guards told me, "Walk up to the stage and give it to him while he is singing." I saw the security was strict. One woman tried to get on the stage and his bodyguard came out and told her, "No." When it was my turn to give him the rose, I was not going to try to touch or try to kiss him. When I gave him the rose, he bent down from the stage and gave me the biggest kiss on my lips. On the outside I was cool, but inside I was shouting with excitement.

I had attached to the flower a copy of the poem with my address and telephone number. I knew he would write because I knew he received it. When I mailed it to him, I was not sure if he received it or not. This time, I gave it to him personally and I still got no response, but I was not going to stop trying.

Chelle and I had another big fight. This time she said, "I'm moving in with Mia," Mia lived in the building I had moved from. I was so upset. "You can't live with Mia, she just got married and you will be in their way. I don't think it's a good idea for you to move in with them." Chelle replied, "Mia said it's OK for me to move in." I cannot believe a grown ass woman would let a sixteen year old child come to live with her without discussing it with the parent. I let Chelle move in so she can see no one will take care of her like her mother.

I was so depressed because my child absolutely cared nothing about me. Also, I had not found a job. I was on my way to a Buddhist meeting one Friday night and I ran into one of my leaders. As we were entering the meeting, she asked me, "How are you doing Arden?" I broke down in tears and I told her, "I'm terrible. I really need a job and I want my own apartment and I'm more depressed about Chelle not living with me."

She said, "Let her go. Do not worry about her because when she is ready, she will come around. You need to do something special for yourself." She encouraged me and I felt better. I decided to go to Chicago and Michigan for a vacation. Barbara Lee knew I was worried. She said, "When you get back to Los Angeles Arden, you are going to find a job and an apartment." I said, "I am also determined to change my relationship with my daughter." She said, "You will."

Barbara Lee and I went out and partied the whole time I was there. I got a chance to see all my aunts and cousins and my grandmother. I stayed in Chicago for one week and then I went to Michigan and saw Pat and my brother and my sister Ava. It was so good to see everyone.

While I was in Michigan, I got a telephone call from Mia. She was complaining about Chelle. They had a fight and she saw Chelle for the way she really was; a spoiled brat. When I talked to Chelle, she said, "I'm angry with Mia because she bought her husband, her child and herself some food to eat and did not buy me anything."

I told Chelle, "You thought I was lying when I told you no one will take care of you but your mother and if you want to live with someone else, you better be able to take care of yourself." Chelle asked me, "When are you coming home?" I told her, "I'll be back in a week." She then asked me, "Can I come back home?" I was glad she was ready to come home. I could not wait to get back to Los Angeles to get my child back. I wanted so much for us to have a good relationship. I knew things would not change overnight but I was willing to work at it. When I returned home, Chelle moved back in.

I finally got a job. It took me eight months. I was so tired of living in Willis' apartment because I wanted my own place. All my furniture was scattered all around town. I wanted to be settled. I was saving money, but I had another minor setback. I got fired from my new job after two months of employment. The reason I was fired is because the woman I worked for did not like me. She yelled at me on my first day, and I kindly put her in her place and told her how she can and cannot talk to me. From then on, she never liked me.

Two weeks latest, I found another job. This was the most exciting job. I worked for a radio-syndicated company. Each week they interviewed a celebrity for a Gospel radio show. The first thing I noticed in the client files was Smokey's name. He had been there and was subject to come back. I then met Jayne Kennedy, Mary Wells, George Duke, Angela Bofill, New Edition, Bill Withers, Irene Cara, Larry Carroll, Don Cornelius and many more.

My boss and I had a good understanding. I told him my situation how I was looking for an apartment. I had $1000 saved and I was hoping it was enough. He told me, "If it is not enough, I will be happy to give you an advance or a loan." I was happy he was willing to help me.

Something else wonderful was happening. Chelle decided if she did not straighten up in school, she was not going to graduate with her class. She was in the eleventh grade and she had one year to make up three years of credits she had not earned.

Chelle was enrolled in evening classes as well as Saturday classes. She was starting to get good reports about her behavior. I started noticing a change in her. I chanted about the situation as my leaders encouraged me to. I have no doubt Chelle's change was due to my sincere prayer to the Gohonzon.

Chelle had gone out to a teen's dance club with some of her friends. When I picked her up, she said, "Some girls got into a fight." I asked, "Did you fight anyone?" She said, "No, I didn't have anything to do with it." She said, "By the time we rushed across the street to see what was happening, the fight was over. I never even saw who was fighting." About two months later, I got a call from the Los Angeles Police Department. "We have your daughter in custody because she participated in a gang fight." I had to leave work and get her out. They did not charge bail because she was a minor; however, we had to go to court about the incident.

I had gone to look at an apartment, and I fell in love with it. It was big and nice. It was mine. I claimed it. The rent was $550 a month, which was not bad. The woman who showed me the apartment said, "I really want you to have the apartment because you don't have small children. I already rented to a woman, but she has small kids." The apartment was on the second floor and she thought small children would disturb the man who lived in the apartment below.

She said, "Let me check your credit and if everything checks out, I will rent the apartment to you." I knew I would never get the apartment if she checked my credit because of my prior eviction. However, the next day she called me and told me, "Everything checked out and the apartment is yours. Bring the $1500 when you get off work and you can pick up the key."

I told her, "I will give you $1000 today and when I get paid later this week, I will bring the rest." She said, "Oh no, if you can't pay it all today, I will have to rent it to someone who has all the money." My boss had gone out of town for a business trip. In fact, he was on a plane. He had left my paycheck because he was not going to be back on payday. Because he said he would help me when it came to moving, I thought if I cashed my check a few days early he would understand.

I was doing him a favor because I was babysitting his ten-year-old daughter. Someone would drop her off in the office in the morning and I would drop her off at home when I got off. Also, I knew he had enough money to cover the check because I had balanced his checking account. I found a $10,000 addition error in his favor and he said, "Isn't it nice to be missing $10,000 and to not know it." I decided I would cash the check and call him in New York to explain why I cashed my check early.

I received my key and finally after eight long months, I had my own place again. I was the happiest person in the world. I called my boss in New York and told him what I had done. He said, "Oh we will discuss it when I return." I worried because I loved my job and I did not want to lose it. I thought since he said he was going to help me anyway, well this way he really did not have to because I used my own money. I knew he would understand. The only thing I did was cashed it early.

The next day at work, his assistant asked me at the end of the day, "Arden would you have time to take a package I'm sending to my mother to the Federal Express office?" I told him, "Sorry but when I leave here after I drop off Denise (my boss's daughter,) I have to rush to an appointment, and if I take your package, I will be late." He got angry with me and told me, "If you do not take my package, I'm going to tell Henry to fire you." I still could not take the package. A few days later, my boss called from New York to fire me because of my dishonesty.

I was hurt. Had I not told him I cashed my check; he would have never known. I was honest with him. I tried to talk to him about the situation, but he ignored me. Henry was a black business owner and had white people working for him. They stole his supplies and postage. They would mail personal packages and charge it to Henry's account. They were ripping him off. After I was fired, I could not grieve or feel bad because I needed to find a job and fast. I was finally getting myself on track.

It did not take me long and I found another job which was a disaster and then I found another job where I stayed for a year and a half. I saw myself getting better and knew it was a matter of time before I would sell my book and turn my poems into some hit songs for Smokey.

My beautiful daughter

My daughter and me

My friend

Friend from the Ida B. Wells Projects

Friends

My friend and her grandkids

My dog Kyoto

CHAPTER 34

MEETING MY DREAM – CAN I MAKE IT COME TRUE?

After a year of steadily working, I found it easier to survive. I was still seeing Pierre. Chelle was in her last year in high school and all was fine. Though I was paying my rent, paying my car note and surviving, I found myself lacking enough money for Chelle's graduation. She had done so well in school. The court case went on for over a year. Every week I had to take off work and go to Juvenile court with Chelle because of the gang fight they said she was a part of.

I knew Chelle was not involved. She only ran across the street to see who was fighting. The police considered it was taking part. She was never a fighter; only with me. Her court appointed attorney kept talking as if they were going to send her away for a long time. I would have thought someone had been killed or something, the way they were acting. When it finally came to the last court appearance, Chelle was either going to go to the juvenile home or go free. The judge asked me a few questions about Chelle's behavior. He then said, "I want a report from her school about her schoolwork, her grades and her behavior and this report will determine what I'm going to do with her." The report from her school was good. I was happy she had decided to straighten up because had it been a year earlier, she would have gotten a bad report and sent to a juvenile home for a long time.

I was so thrilled because now all I had to concentrate on is how to give Chelle the best graduation ever. She was taking medical classes and she was getting good grades. I wanted Chelle to go to her prom as well as have a nice graduation. She was receiving a special award at graduation for being an "A" student in medical terminology.

I was chanting for money like crazy. There seemed to be no extra money. Chelle had a good attitude and she knew she might not go to her prom or have a new dress for graduation. Her attitude was completely changed. After a long and sincere prayer to the Gohonzon about getting some money, I got a telephone call about my case with Litton because I had sued them. I had forgotten about it. My attorney called and said, "Get down here right now Litton's insurance company made an $11,000 settlement with us." I could not believe it. I then got a check in the mail for over $7000 after attorney's fees.

Getting the money was more actual proof - chanting works. Chelle had the prettiest prom and graduation dresses. Chelle's next problem was finding a date for the prom. She did not have a boyfriend. There was a young friend of hers who I was going to buy his ticket so he could escort her. However, a few weeks before the prom, Chelle met a nice guy who was also graduating from the same school. He already had his prom ticket and he needed a date also. They got together and went to the prom. I was happy because I did not have to buy another prom ticket.

She Graduated

Well, here is what I bought with the money I won on my suit. I bought new furniture, a new TV, a video cassette recorder, a washer and dryer, piano, new wardrobes for Chelle and myself, and I bought Chelle a car for her graduation gift. The car I bought Chelle was a 1975 Toyota Celica. I paid $400 for the car, and the car was in excellent condition. I was happy. The other wonderful incident in my life was I got a chance to see Smokey at the Universal Amphitheatre. Also, I read in Jet magazine Smokey and His wife of twenty-three years were divorced. I could not believe he was available.

I went alone and got a good single seat. If you buy one ticket as opposed to two, the seat choice is much better. The section I was sitting in was a VIP section. I saw Barry Gordy, and Claudette Robinson (Smokey's x-wife) sitting in the same section as me. I was so excited. I had an aisle seat. A guard was securing the row and he and I were partying together during the concert.

Before the concert was over, everyone sitting in my section got up and walked towards a side door. I asked the guard, "Where are they going?" He said, "Backstage to see Smokey. It's a party." I asked, "Can I go too?" He told me, "Without a pass or someone escorting you they will not let you back there." He then pointed to Leon Kennedy and said, "Ask him if he will escort you."

I approached Leon and asked him, "Will you take me backstage with you, so I can meet Smokey?" He told me, "I cannot." I walked away. I then went back to my seat and started chanting. I then went back to the backstage entrance and asked the guard, "Can you please let me backstage?" He told me, "No."

I stood around a few minutes. Then I felt stupid, so I decided to leave. As I was about to leave, I changed my mind and decided to try one more time. I then saw Leon again, and asked, "Will you please take me back. I'm only a single person all alone and I will not cause any problems."

He said again, "I cannot." I then saw Claudette Robinson walk up. I looked at her and asked her, "Would you take me backstage with you." She hunched her shoulders and said, "I don't see why not." She put her arm around my shoulder as if we were friends and started walking me backstage.

I got separated from her. There was only over seven hundred people trying to get backstage. As I was walking down the steps, a guard said for me to stop. I kept walking. Then I looked behind me and saw Leon again. The guard was asking me to leave. Leon then said to the guard, "Let her go, she's okay." I thought I was going to die. There I was backstage. I did not know anyone or what to expect. I saw a few people standing in line at the bar, so I decided to get something to drink. While I stood in line, I was talking to a young man.

He told me, "In a little while Smokey will come out and greet everyone." I asked, "Where is he now?" He said, "In his dressing room around the corner." And he pointed to where it was. I then went around the corner and saw a guard standing at the door. I asked the guard, "May I please go in?" He said, "There are too many people in the room, as soon as someone comes out then you can go in."

The door opened and about five people walked out. As the door opened, I saw Smokey standing up talking to someone. I walked into the room and Smokey looked at me as if he knew me and walked over and hugged me. I told him, "I am writing a book and I use your name several times and I would like for you to read it." He looked at me and said, "I want to read your book."

I then told him, "I have been sending you letters for years and I have never gotten a response." He hugged me very tightly and kissed me and told me "Thank you." He then grabbed me by my hand and walked me through the crowd a bit. He also told Earl Bryant to give me the address to write him. Earl was there to protect Smokey. He is also a good-looking brother.

I gave Smokey my phone number and said, "Please call me." I also asked him, "Will you marry me?" He laughed. I was serious though. There were so many people back there until it was impossible to talk about anything else with Smokey. I left with the biggest smile ever. I could not believe I had finally met Smokey. I went away hoping he would call me soon.

When I arrived home, it was one-thirty in the morning and I could not sleep. I called all my family and friends and shared my excitement of meeting Smokey. I wrote him a letter and reminded him he wanted to read my book. I said all I could say to help him remember me.

After about two months passed, I concluded Smokey was not going to call me nor was he going to answer my letter. I even wrote Earl a letter hoping he would pass it on to Smokey for me. Nothing happened. Of course, I went on with my life. I knew I would not give up. I was going to continue writing letters to him and I would keep my ears open for any of his upcoming concerts. The next time I meet him will be the right time.

I found a fantastic job working with an accounting firm. I felt so professional because I was the office manager and I had two people reporting to me. I was making more money than I had ever made before. Also, I was learning so much. My career was off to a great start. I also met another man, Jermaine, whom I cared about. Our relationship started out so well. He would call me every day and he would come over and cook great meals for Chelle and me. One day, however, after about a good three months, our relationship started declining. I was hurt. I finally found a man who could take the place of Smokey in my heart, but the relationship could not work.

Though Jermaine and I did not have a working relationship, I found it hard to deal with the situation the way it was. I gave Jermaine such a hard time because I tried to force the relationship to work when I ran him out of my life. I would go over to his place when he told me not to. I would call him, and he would hang up in my face and I would keep calling. I could not understand why I was taking our relationship so seriously.

I wanted our relationship to work. He was a good man, but he was so mean to me. Some days he treated me as if I did something wrong to him. He would tell me, "I don't want to be bothered with you or anyone else." I could not understand why he did not want me around. I thought I was a good friend to him. However, I do believe the relationship did not work because something better is in store for my life. None of my relationships seemed to work. I always found myself alone as I was when I was a young girl; Smokey dominates my dreams and desires. None of my relationships worked because I always compared the men in my life to Smokey. If he did not fit the mold, then eventually our relationship turned sour. Subconsciously, if I were to fall in love and get married before I met Smokey then I would have to give up my dream and live miserable for the rest of my life.

My sister was working for the advertising department at the Wherehouse Record Company. They would put on the halftime show at the Forum where the Los Angeles Lakers played. We were invited to many games and had floor seats. Once Smokey was appearing at one of the Wherehouse record stores promoting his new album *Double Good Everything*. Through my sister's job connection, I went to see Smokey there and he recognized me from backstage of his concert. I asked if I could take a picture with him. Mr. Earl Bryant, Smokey's bodyguard, recognized me from backstage too and gave his approval to take the picture. It was Earl who took the picture. The picture is beautiful. It looks as if we make a great couple. He is squeezing me so tightly.

Smokey and me

A few months after the Wherehouse promotion it was time to see Smokey's in concert again at the Universal Amphitheatre.

I got a good single seat as I did the year before. As I was about to leave for the concert, Jermaine called. I still found it hard to get Jermaine out of my system. I really enjoyed him sexually. He was so strong and gentle. It had been a while since I had seen him. He asked me, "What are you doing tonight?" I told him, "I'm on my way to see Smokey in concert." He asked, "Would you like to come by to see me on your way home?" I said, "Yes."

At the concert, I saw Leon Kennedy and Earl Bryant as I did the year before. It had not been long since I saw him at the Wherehouse promotion, so I was familiar. I did approach Leon Kennedy and asked him, "Like last year, can you take me backstage again?" He said, "Sure I will." I went backstage and I met Smokey again. He recognized me. I showed him the picture we took together, and again I gave him my phone number as I did the year before. I was disappointed because Smokey did not want to get to know me. I did not want to stay backstage long because I had a date with Jermaine. I stayed long enough to see Smokey and give him my phone number and could only pray for him to call.

I went to Jermaine's. We had a wonderful time. I was so happy to be with him again. We had not seen each other in almost a year. Jermaine was about to graduate from school. I was so proud of him. He moved into a house where he was taking care of people with disabilities. He had a room-and-board type of deal. We decided to renew our relationship.

I was still hoping Smokey would call me. However, he never did. I still wrote letters to him and he still never answered them. Also, it was not long before Jermaine started to be the same as he was before in our relationship. He took me in, acted as if I were the most special person and then dumped me and would be so cruel. I could not understand.

Another year passed, and Jermaine and I had not seen each other for a while. It was time for Smokey's concert at the Universal Amphitheatre. I got a good seat. I saw Leon again and I asked him to take me backstage and he did. When I got backstage, Leon and I started talking. He told me, "It's no coincidence I get you backstage every year." I told him, "You're right it is no coincidence because the only reason I am here is because I have been chanting Nam Myoho Renge Kyo for Smokey for fifteen years and chanting works. The power of chanting is the only reason I am here. In fact, the only reason Smokey is famous is because I have been chanting for him." Leon insisted, "Pray with me." I said, "Chant with me."

My organization was having a general meeting, and I was asked to give an experience at our auditorium located in Santa Monica, California. I was to give an experience about my life and how chanting changed it from a negative situation to a positive one. One of my favorite Buddhist Terms is "Hendoku Iyaku," which means "Changing Poison into Medicine." Which is what I did. I was to deliver my speech in front of two thousand people.

I invited Leon to the meeting to hear my speech. He said, "I may come." He then asked me to pray with him. I told him, "No. Not right here." The next thing I knew, he grabbed me by my hand and took me around a wall and started praying. He was praying loud and everyone could hear him. Even Smokey saw him praying with me. I saw him look at us as he was walking around greeting people. A beautiful woman was standing beside Leon and she was praying along with him but in a different language. Leon was saying, "God please come into Arden's life and show her the way..." He went on and on for about fifteen minutes. Then he started praying in a different language.

I never experienced such a situation. After he prayed to me, he and the women were acting as if they had an erection or something. He said, "Wonderful Arden. I got a good feeling from our prayer with you." He then wrote his telephone number down and told me, "If you want to hang out with me give me a call."

I did not want to call Leon. I wanted to call Smokey. I did get a chance to talk to Smokey. He hugged and kissed me. I invited Smokey to hear me speak at the general meeting. He said, "Sorry I will be out of town and can't make it." Then I took out a piece of paper and said, "Here's my number Smokey. I hope you call me." He took the number and put it in his pocket. When I left, I was confused and excited. I had Leon's phone number, and he and Smokey were close friends. Smokey called Leon his little brother. I thought I would call Leon and try to get him to set me up with Smokey.

I did call Leon about a week later because I wanted him to come to the meeting. However, he did not return my phone call. I could not understand why Leon would not call because I never did ask him for his phone number. He gave it to me. I would have never asked for his number because I did not want him to get the wrong impression. I was not interested in him. Although he is good looking.

Delivering my speech at the general meeting held in our Buddhist Auditorium was one of the greatest experiences of my life. The speech went as follows:

"Good evening. My name is Arden, and I have been practicing Buddhism for fifteen years. The year I was born is when my parents started using and selling drugs. By the time I was five years old, my father was one of the biggest drug dealers in Chicago, making ten-thousand dollars a day. We had the best of everything, but along with all our so-called wealth came one horror story after another.

"There was always chaos at our household. My parents were constantly fighting with each other. The police were always breaking our doors down, and the addicts would come into our home with guns and would steal everything. Several times my mother tried to commit suicide. Once, a woman even died from a drug overdose in our home.

"By the time I was twelve years old, my parents became their own biggest drug customers and eventually we lost everything. My father was in and out of jail and my mother became completely consumed with drugs and alcohol. I then met a man who I thought would be my friend, but instead, he was violent and abusive to me. I became pregnant by him and had a baby when I was only fourteen years old. He never acknowledged my daughter, and I was left to raise her completely alone.

"I dropped out of high school and moved into my own apartment, a rat- and roach-infested hotel was all I could afford. At night, I would feed the mice in fear of them eating my baby.

I got a job working in a cafeteria. I was so ashamed of my life. I was only fifteen years old.

"When I was eighteen years old, I was taking care of my daughter, my sister's baby, plus my drug addicted parents. My life was hell! I wanted to die. It was at this point I came to my first chanting meeting. I heard an experience there and it made me want to try chanting.

"I received my Gohonzon. Also, at the same meeting, a woman asked me, "Of all your problems what do you want to change the most?" I said, "I desperately want my sister to come home from prison."

"I didn't think it was possible because my sister was not getting out for another year. However, it did not take me long to see the wonderful power of the Gohonzon. The very same night I received my Gohonzon, my sister was released from prison. Already, I had the one thing I said I wanted the most.

"I began reading the Gosho, Letter to Nikki. The one quote I was encouraged by was, 'The journey from Kamakura to Kyoto takes twelve days. If you travel for eleven but stop on the twelfth, how can you admire the moon over the capital, (Kyoto?") I then decided to use the Gohonzon to build my life. I will never give up.

"I did lots of shakubuku, chanted a lot and started to improve my life. First, I finished high school and enrolled in a secretarial training program. Up until then, my jobs were working in cafeterias or being a cashier in a drug store. However, the more I chanted, my jobs started improving. Finally, I landed a great job working for the Federal Government.

"I transferred my job to Los Angeles where I began to have terrible problems with my teenage daughter. We fought all the time, even violent fistfights. We felt nothing but hate and resentment towards each other.

"I desperately sought guidance from my senior leader. She told me, "Understand your daughter is suffering and accept it is your own karma, and chant from the bottom of your heart for her happiness; then she can become truly happy." As I began chanting this way, I was able to deeply self-reflect. I could see

I was treating her as a burden. For the first time, I truly began to chant about her from my heart. At this point our relationship truly changed. She not only returned to school, but also received a special award at her graduation. She now has a wonderful job working for a doctor in Santa Monica and she is here today.

"As for my parents, at the age of fifty-eight, my father received his own Gohonzon and amazingly, after twenty-five years of drug usage, he totally lost his desire for drugs. He changed his life and before he died, he changed his destiny. My mother also chanted with me before she died, and I know because of my practice my parents are happy.

"I am happy now. I am currently working as an office manager in a beautiful Century City certified public accountant's office. I can comfortably support myself and have a beautiful apartment as well as a nice car.

"Thanks to the wonderful power of chanting to the Gohonzon, I have been able to change a violent drug abusing family and a teenage pregnancy into a happy daily life of creating value in society. I am so grateful to my leaders for their tremendous guidance and encouragement which has allowed me to not only change all my problems but also to make my dreams a reality. As a Women Division Group Leader, it is my determination to encourage my members with my own past experiences there are no problems and no sufferings they cannot overcome. And, in addition to overcoming problems, there are no dreams which cannot be fulfilled. Thank you so much."

Hundreds of people congratulated me. I felt so special. Pretty much like a star. I encouraged so many people to use the practice of chanting Nam Myoho Renge Kyo to change their lives and their problems. I still had a lot of chanting to do myself. My next big project was to find someone special to share my life with.

CHAPTER 35

HAPPINESS NOW AND FOREVER

Another year passed and I lost my job. My boss who was an accountant started treating me badly. I worked hard for him, and he had no cause to treat me the way he did. I did not get fired, I walked out one day and never went back. I had some temporary assignments for a while, and I took on a couple of permanent positions. None of them worked. I was desperately chanting to find the right career for myself. Because of my great typing and computer skills, I could get temporary positions making over $25 an hour in great Fortune Five-Hundred Companies. I had a great job in a well known movie studio as Assistant to the VP of Video Productions. My name is in movie credits My boss said, "I'm a racist. I'm talking KKK." I sued them and won. A good permanent position seemed impossible. A lot of jobs did not hire me permanently because I am black.

It was time again for Smokey to come to the Universal Amphitheatre. This time I called Leon and he returned my call. I asked him if he would be getting me backstage?" "Yes," he said. I could not wait because I was going to see Smokey again. I went to the concert, and I saw Leon and he got me backstage again as he said he would.

Smokey wrote a book, and I had a copy of it for him to autograph. When Earl saw the book in my hand he said, "You stand here because Smokey is going to sign your copy." When he got to me, I said, "Smokey, I wrote my book before you wrote yours and I'm still not published. Will you turn me on to your publisher?" He asked me, "What are the publishers saying?" I told him, "I did not submit it yet." He told me, "Submit it to a publisher."

I was so angry with myself because when he asked me what the publishers were saying, I froze. I could have said the publishers told me I needed an agent and an agent told me for them to represent me I had to be published already because I am not famous. He could have read my book and recommended it if he liked it. We could have talked about it further. But I said what I did, and I could not change it.

I handed Smokey my copy of his book and as he was signing it, I said, "You can put your telephone number there too." He laughed. There were a few people in the room who heard me ask for his number and they laughed. One woman said, "We can hear you." I said, "I don't care because I want the entire world to know." I left giving him my phone number and hoping he would call.

Pat got a promotion which brought her to California. She still worked for the Federal Government and she lived eleven miles from me. Friends together again. Once she said, "Let's go to Las Vegas for the weekend." I was so excited to go. As we were driving there, I saw a poster advertising Smokey Robinson was performing at the Desert Inn. When we got to the hotel room, I called the Desert Inn to see if they would connect me to Smokey's room. I left a message on a phone and a few minutes later Earl called me. "You called Smokey?" I told him, "Yes I'm coming to Smokey's show tonight and I was hoping my friend and I can get backstage." He said, "I can arrange it. Make sure you look for me." He didn't know me by name, but he knew my face.

I got backstage and took Pat with me and we both got to talk to Smokey. I asked him, "Why can't we get together?" He said he was with Ivy, a singer in his group. I said, "Is it going to last forever?" He looked at me as if he did not expect me to say what I did. I still had a good time. I even saw Smokey another time a year later in Las Vegas. I always get backstage. It is fun and it was clear Smokey did not find me attractive. I know chanting works so why doesn't Smokey find me interesting? This is the one chance I had to capture him. As I walked away, I felt so depressed because I realized I would now have to wait another year until I could see him again.

I desperately needed guidance. I spoke to a women's division leader. I said to her, "I'm so confused; since 1963 I have admired Smokey Robinson and since 1974, I have been chanting to be his wife. Since Smokey has been divorced, I have met him seven times. I also took a beautiful picture with him and we look to make a great couple. I do agree progress has taken place because I have met him - so why can't I capture Smokey and have the relationship I dream of?" I wanted to hear Smokey say to me as he says in one of his song the quote by Julius Caesar's - "You came, you saw, you conquered me."

The leader said, "The power of the Gohonzon is correct. You not getting with Smokey from the several times you have met him does not mean it is not possible. Never give up on your dream. If you have a dream and you are trying to fulfill it and at the same time you are practicing sincerely and correctly to the Gohonzon, then you will never be defeated. Trust it."

She also told me to concentrate on giving Smokey the truth. She said, "Since you feel chanting is the treasure of all treasures, don't you think giving Smokey the opportunity to know about True Buddhism would be a great gift to him, especially since he has helped you so much?" I told her, "He does not know he has helped me." She said, "It does not matter if he knows or not. You know what's important."

I said, "I don't understand how I am going to convince Smokey chanting is the tool to bring absolute happiness in his life because he is so religious and talks about God all the time." I knew, though, if he ever decided to chant, he would see the boundless joy chanting promises. She said, "You are not asking for results. Tell him about it and chant for his happiness. Occasionally, I would write to invite him to our introductory meetings.

She also said, "Your reason for wanting Smokey is selfish. You need to grow up because the part of you who wants Smokey is still a nine-year-old little girl." I said, "I want him to come into my life, fall in love with me, and then we can gallivant around the world." She said, "It may not be realistic. Maybe you two will meet and marry or not, but do not worry, as long as you chant. You should consider going on a pilgrimage to Japan to visit the original Gohonzon. The Dai Gohonzon. It could deepen your faith. Take your sincerest prayer and ask for it to come true."

I took the leader's advice and went to Japan on a group trip. The Dai Gohonzon is in Fujinomiya in the middle of nowhere hundreds of miles from Kyoto. I wanted to visit Kyoto too because of my book title. I ventured from the group and visited Kyoto.

Me in Kyoto, Japan

In Japan I prayed I would forget about Smokey and find someone special and real to share my life with. The day I got back from Japan my prayer was answered because I met Eddie O. He was my sister's neighbor for over ten years, and I was meeting him for the first time. After we dated a few times he asked, "Do you want a committed relationship with me?" I finally found some who loved me as I loved him.

My lover for fourteen years
R.I.P.

I have a lot to be grateful for., and many people have helped me. Sometimes when we are caught up in doubt or debate within ourselves it is easy to rationalize without commonsense. I am so fortunate to have my family and friends also my Buddhist family. We all care, and we are there to encourage each other when we need it.

Today Chelle is not only my daughter but she is my good friends, and I love her so much. She has three children. They are by far the most beautiful children and they bring me great joy and happiness. Now I know what true happiness is. It is not the car, the house, or the man. True happiness cannot be taken away. It will last an eternity. I have made such a spectacular mark in this world. Chelle and my three grandchildren are my contribution to society. They are my legacy. If nothing else happens in my life and I should die tomorrow, I absolutely have no regrets.

My legacy

People go crazy when I tell them Chelle is my daughter and I have three grandchildren and now a great grandson because they say I look too young. Chelle came to me and said, "I think I found my father living here in California. Will you take me there so I can see?" When Chelle was fifteen years old her father moved, and she lost contact with him. I took her and she found her father. She was able to establish a relationship with him until he died. She also got to know her sisters and she also had a brother who died. Chelle became close to him.

All of us

My family is doing wonderful. Ava my dear sister passed away. The world is not right without her. Asia her daughter is doing well and is a social worker with a beautiful family and two beautiful children. My heart goes out to Bear who is in prison and I hope he finds the right way soon. It is so ironic how Bear was born in prison and now serving a sentence of life without the possibility of parole, he may die in prison. Clayton went through some tough changes with drugs, but he has recently joined a drug program and is drug free from the awful drug crack cocaine. I am so proud of my brother. He has three beautiful children and six grandkids. I love them dearly.

Gia is a rising movie actor and has three wonderful and beautiful children and four grandkids. Gia has had major roles and worked on major films. She also teaches song and dance to children through Amazing Grace Conservatory in Los Angeles. I am sure soon the world over will know of my sister as an actor.

My nephews and my niece

I promise to chant each day, so my family continues to have good health and live long and happy fulfilled lives. I want them to know I am available whenever they should need me. I am dedicated to chanting twice a day for the rest of my life. I know 'No Matter What,' I will continue to practice this True Buddhism. I am determined to help my members grow and overcome any hardships through the practice of Nam Myoho Renge Kyo, and as we help each other and grow together, I hope we all prosper in our daily lives.

I found an ad in the newspaper, and I completed a training and had my own business for over ten years until I retired. I loved it. I am looking forward to successfully enjoying happiness throughout the rest of my life. I feel so wonderful about myself.

My nephew called me and asked, "Hey Auntie, you want to see Smokey at the Greek Theatre tonight? I have tickets and can't go." I asked Eddie if he wanted to go but he was preparing for some big fishing trip. I went alone and got backstage. I saw Smokey and learned he got married to a woman who went to school with Eddie's sister. It did not matter because I was building a special relationship with Eddie. I still love my Smokey Robinson songs and they are still my friends and if I'm ever depressed, they brighten up my spirit. Despite everything in my life, I am happy. For once I can say I am gorgeous, and I love, honor and respect myself.

I have many good friends whom I trust, and they know they can trust me. In addition to my blood relatives, I consider my good friends, Barbara Lee, Pat, Brenda, and Jolanda to be members of my family, and they can most definitely depend on me to be there if they need me. My good friend Willis died. I do miss him. Pierre moved to Louisiana prior to me meeting Eddie. I speak to him from time to time.

I never did get the opportunity to be with Smokey. However, life is full of new and exciting adventures. My dream now is for *The Moon Over Kyoto* to become a movie and I will accept the Academy Award.

THE END

THE BEGINNING

REFERENCES

The Chant- NAM MYOHO RENGE KYO – Pages 118, 119, 122, 123, 124, 128, 129, 140, 178, 194, 201, 209, 258, 262

Gohonzon, Buddhist Scroll – Page 269, 270, 273

GOSHO QUOTES BY NICHIREN DAISHONIN

Letter to Niike (Gosho) – Page 129, Written 1280; taken from Major Writings of Nichiren Daishonin; Vol 1, pp 1026

Lotus Sutra – Page 123, Meaning: It is the law to which Nichiren Daishonin was enlightened and which He practiced, as the True Buddha from the eternal past…Taken from The Doctrines and Practice of Nichiren Shoshu Page V

On Prayer (Gosho) – Page 177, Written 1272; Taken from Major Writing of Nichiren Daishonin; Vol 1, pp 336

Winter Always Turns into Spring (Gosho) – Page 200, 242, Written 1275; Taken from Major Writings of Nichiren Daishonin; Vol 1 pp 149

Happiness in This World (Gosho) – Suffer…Enjoy… – Page 215, Written 1276; Taken from Major Writings of Nichiren Daishonin; Vol 1 pp 681

How Those Initially Aspiring to the Way Can Attain Buddhahoo
d through the Lotus Sutra (Gosho) - ...saw the practice...P age 223,
Written 1277; Taken from Major Writings of Nichiren Vol 2 pp 872

Buddhist Term:

Hendoku Iyaku, Page 258, changing poison into medicine – Found
in a passage from Nagarjuna's Treatise on the Great Perfection of
Wisdom, which mentions "a great physician who can change
poison into medicine.

Printed in the United States
by Baker & Taylor Publisher Services